Dumpster Fire

Lela Markham

Published by Breakwater Harbor Books

Copyright 2020 Lela Markham

Thanks!

This book is dedicated to Fred Iles, a sometimes recovering addict who lost his battle to stay clean, but I believe will find redemption before the bema seat. Don't worry. God's got this.

No book is the work of a single individual. The author gets all the glory but standing behind every published writer is a host of support personnel. Peter, Ben and the rest of their friends are borrowed from many struggling young teens I knew over decades as an unchurched teenager, a church youth leader and a mom.

DISCLAIMER

For Christian readers – there is a small amount of swearing and referenced sex in this book because that is part of American society, especially among teens. If it bothers you, this may not be the book for you, but seriously, folks, get over yourselves. Non-Christians swear, fornicate, do drugs and drink. Christians don't do ourselves any favors by pretending they don't. 1Corinthians 5:9-13. I struggled whether to put it in and then I decided to be honest about the world we live in and utilize a light touch. I think I've struck a fair balance. You may not agree, but I believe I honor God in that endeavor.

Table of Contents

Avoidance	1
Dawn Powder	7
Unsatisfying	13
Close to the Chest	19
Confessions	27
Family Pancakes	35
Skyrim	45
Distracted Living	49
Lumberjack	57
Rinx	63
Self-Destructive Behavior	67
Tattoos are Forever	73
Reconnecting	77
Light in the Darkness	81
Beware the Bad Boy	89
Balancing Act	93
Mendings	113
Meeting	117
Recrimination & Temptation	123
Bad Boys Never Forget	129
Caught in the Revolving Door	133
Milestone	135
Failure	139
Wise Advice	143
Help Denied	149
Getting Out Some	155
What's Not Said	161
Ice Cream Social	167
Unexpected News	185
Disturbed	189
Missing My Best Friend	195

Secrets to Keep	199
Self-Analysis	207
Communication	213
American Bohemia	223
A Good Guy	237
Fateful Choice	251
Keeping More Secrets	259
Apology	265
Dad	271
Hot Licks	275
Art Talk	281
Photos	287
Guilt	293
Alien Possession	297
Hatred	303
Reinstatement	307
Blocking	311
Responsibility	313
Patterns	317
Best Friends	321
Party Central	329
Party Favors	339
Realizations	343
BJ's Way	347
Strategy	351
Party Planning	357
Turning A Corner	361
Briercliff	367
Uncertainty	371
A Party Worth Having	379
Grandpa Jack	387
Misdirections	393
Party of the Year	395
Is He or Isn't He?	399

Be Careful Where You Stand 405
A Change 411
Well-Laid Plans 419
Truth-Telling 421
Consequences 427
Interference 431
Detours 437
Falling by Degrees 447
Boredom 453
Impact 457
Steps 460
A Word from Lela Markham 461
A Taste of "Pocketful of Rocks" 463
Other Breakwater Harbor Books 465
Other Books by Lela Markham 467
About the Author 468

"You burn bright and you burn hard, like a fire in a dumpster, and nobody is so worried about you burning as they are worried about the fire spreading."
— Kris Kidd, Down for Whatever

Dumpster Fire

Book 2

What If...Wasn't

Avoidance

Peter

The coffee shop closes at ten o'clock. I've got enough caffeine in my system that I'm not going to want to sleep anytime soon. Even if I were tired, the last place I want to go is the dorm, so I start walking toward Old Town in the most roundabout way possible. Fortunately, most of the books for tonight's study reside on my tablet, so I'm not carrying a loaded backpack as I stroll through the darkness. It snowed a little this morning, but that mostly melted earlier, so I just need to watch for puddles and avoid the occasional slick of ice. Occasionally cars drive by in the road, but I'm not looking for a ride. That would get me back to the dorm earlier than I want to be. As it is, I get back before the party ends.

Where's the one place a recovering alcoholic doesn't want to be when he's thirsty?

You guessed it in one. A blowout end-of-the-semester party in an Ivy League college dorm definitely holds risks to the sobriety challenged. Booze flows like water and absolutely no one cards you. The whole point is to get as drunk as you can, and it all goes on Daddy's credit card.

Newly-recovering alcoholics need to avoid parties if they want to stay sober. At least I do. Parties trigger my cravings, but they're hard to avoid when you live in a Yale college. There's at least a small one every weekend. I can usually ignore those – hang out with my suitemates, concentrate on studying, go to the mirror room and dance until things settle down, or curl up with a book at the library. I'm getting better at ignoring it so long as it isn't in our suite.

This party is not avoidable. It's the biggest so far. It's not ignorable either. I need to get through it if I want to sleep tonight. The commons rooms are all filled with strobing darkness and writhing bodies as I make my way toward the stairs, my nose telling me every drink I pass. That one's weak, but I'd drink it. That one's strong. I *love* strong. When I drank, I didn't even like beer and wine, but they smell pretty good from where I'm standing now. I want them so-so much and yet I also know why I can't have them. My drinking was off the chain and I know what happens if I give into temptation now.

There's no sign this is winding down anytime soon. It's the end of the semester so my dormmates are partying to the wee hours of the morning. It's gotta be 1 am. Given that I have no brakes when I drink, I'd be under a table and passed out by now, but there's plenty of people dancing to the ear-busting music, cups held up to my nose height, forcing me to practice my refusal skills. People say "hi" along the way and I keep pushing. By now, they know I'm not unfriendly when we're all sober. This is just a circumstance where I can't afford to linger. I've made it four months and I want to make it another day, so I continue weaving through the crowd until I meet up with a blonde barely wearing clothes who doesn't get out of my way. I'm almost to the stairs, which is not free-and-clear, but is closer to my locked bedroom door and earplugs so I pretend this isn't a risky stop.

"Hey, Peter." She purrs into my ear as she drapes an arm around my neck that pulls me down to her level where I can smell the beer on her breath. Nice beer, very hoppy. I don't like beer, but we've already established I don't need to like alcohol to want to drink it.

"Hey." I don't know her name. She lives on the second floor. We've passed on the stairs a few times. She's pretty when she's not shit-faced, but we haven't really talked. I'm used to people knowing me even though we haven't really met. I'm over six feet, lean and athletic and my father makes me famous. I never really asked for any of that.

"I want to dance with you."

3

"I'm still wearing my coat," I tell her. It's a lame escape tactic. I know I don't really want to escape her. It's the alcohol I want to escape. She's moving her hips to the beat of the music and I feel my anatomy rising to the occasion. I'm weak on so many levels so I try to choose my safest weakness. Alcohol may be off the table, but safe sex isn't. I nod to the stairs. "C'mon."

She giggles and we make our way up to the third-floor suite I share with six other guys. She's already dragged me down into a tonsil-caressing kiss before I get through the open and unlocked suite door. I really want that beer she drank so many of, but I can scratch my itches without being stupid. I can hear someone having loud sex in Lee and Jan's room – probably Jan who is headed back to Sweden for the holidays and so wants to satisfy his girlfriend before he goes. I don't even know this chick's name, but I'm hard enough to cut diamonds, so I don't care. I fumble with the lock on my door while she tries to undress me in the common room. We fall back through the door and I kick it shut as we sprawl on my bed.

The beer on her breath drives me crazy. Every cell in my body starts screaming I need to get some of whatever she's drinking. I don't need it, but I do want it and I almost leave her in the bed to find a cooler. One beer would make the sex even better, and twelve would make my liver swell up like a balloon. She pulls me down on top of her and I forget about the cooler.

Dawn Powder

Ben

This is so a Pete-thing to do, standing at the top of the Papoose Run of Dartmouth Skiway as dawn edges over the horizon. The world is gray-white, and my breath fogs the air. I can't yet see well enough to launch myself down the mountain, but I know it's maybe five minutes away.

A couple of years ago, Pete and I drove up to Loon Mountain and he shocked me by waking me up before dawn to carve the powder of Accolades. We did the same thing I've done this morning, slogged through a backtrail to the top of the mountain to wait for dawn. We weren't alone that morning. There were a handful of others. Pete learned about it from the snow bums while making use of his fake ID in the bar after I turned in for the night. It never occurred to me to wonder if he'd even slept that night.

Just because the idea came from a problematic source doesn't mean it's a bad one. I've been thinking about doing it ever since the ski slopes opened last week. I'm waiting for a sublime moment when the sun turns the monochromatic flat world into color and depth. Wait for it! Pete's voice whispered that morning and now it whispers again. I miss him. I miss my best friend.

The sun peeks over the horizon, sending rays of bright light across the snow. That morning at Loon Mountain, we waited for the locals to start their runs, one by one dropping into the slot. Pete and I followed them down, acknowledging their primacy on the slopes. This morning, I'm the only one on the slope as I shove off. Fresh powder sprays up to either side of me as I carve the slope. Cold nips my cheeks and nose and blood surges through my arms and legs. The McLane Lodge's green-and-white Craftsman structure grows closer and I start slowing down. A lone skier carves another section of slope about halfway up. I step out of my bindings, grab my board and go into the lodge. I knew I only had time for one run before I need to eat some breakfast and get on the road. I'll swing by the dorm to grab my bag and drop off my board.

The ski lodge is pretty empty while I retrieve my street shoes from a locker and sit down to swap them for my snowboarding boots. I can hear workers chatting. I order the pancake sandwich at the café and sit down at a window table to eat and watch a few other early risers carve the slope.

"Ben?"

Janelle is in my English class. She's a slightly pudgy girl with light brown hair and small brown eyes.

"Hey. What are you up to?"

"My brother just had to hit the slopes one last time before we head for Connecticut."

"Me, too." I jerk my thumb toward my board.

She sniffs.

"Skiing is an act of privilege. Do you realize how many people can't afford to make use of facilities like this? And have you ever seen a black person here except as a staff member?"

My roommate Travis is black. He and I came snowboarding last weekend, despite the mostly-fake snow. He's from Colorado and talks about snowboarding the back mountains there. He'd contemplated delaying his flight home to join me this morning, but he couldn't get another flight out until tomorrow, so would miss a friend's party. Apparently, someone forgot to tell him he's not allowed to use the facilities. Odd, the staff didn't stop him at the door.

Janelle continues to spout on about social justice and the "reality" of the refined world we live in. She's not wrong about Dartmouth being expensive. God, I'm going to be so broke by the time I get my degree. Travis got a partial scholarship too, but his sister decided to forego college, so he got all the college savings his parents set aside. He's studying to be a computer engineer and has a side gig of building websites, which has got to be more lucrative than waiting tables at Pine. He'll graduate with less debt than me. He'll probably make more money than me because...computers...but I prefer mechanical engineering, so maybe I'll be happier...after I pay off my loans.

She's babbling about how all white people are racist and I need to examine my white privilege. Yeah, I'll get on that. She has no idea about true "white" privilege. I grew up middle-class in a Gold Coast town. My best friend's father is the governor of New York. Our neighbors – well, used-to-be neighbors – the Carsons were black. He owned a construction company – had built it up from a handyman firm and sold it for a couple of million to fund their retirement. He used to hire my dad as an accountant, suggesting he made more money than my dad. Not that I ever felt deprived, but there were people way richer than us all around us.

"I'm not a racist," I finally mutter.

"Of course, you are. All white people are. We can't help it because we benefit from it."

"My roommate is black. When I think of Travis, I think of hanging out with him, playing video games. I hardly think about him being black unless I need to describe his physical characteristics for some reason." Why am I wasting my time? It's an argument you can't win.

"And you think that makes you 'not racist'. Seriously, people are so stupid. The fact that you're denying your racism proves you're a racist." She sneers. "You have a black friend."

"Maybe I should ask Travis what he thinks."

"Why should he help you fix yourself? That's racist too."

I've heard all the Social Justice Warrior crap before. Travis says they're mentally ill. He wishes they'd stop trying to rescue him from the evil white people who are offering him website jobs. Social Justice is whacked. I'm a racist, I can't change that. If I deny it, I'm a racist. If I admit it, I'm a racist. If I try to do something to change myself, I'm still a racist. Who can win in an irredeemable scenario?

The guy who comes up behind Janelle is a little older. They look a bit alike. I'm going to guess he's her brother. If he joins her, I'm done eating breakfast.

"Hey, Janelle, we need to head out. Jason." He holds a hand out to me.

"Ben." We shake and he mouths "Sorry." I smile and nod.

"Enjoy your breakfast." He moves her firmly toward the exit.

They leave me and I finish my breakfast. Outside, the slopes fill with weaving bodies enjoying the powder. I need to head south so I can get home before rush hour. I grab my board and head back to the dorm. Travis will have left for the airport by now. I wait for my car to warm up and text him, describing Janelle's meltdown. He sends me a Snoopy emoji where Snoopy looks like he's going to bust a gut. It's followed by a GIF of rolling eyes. I like Travis. His humor reminds me of Trevor's, who can say more with a GIF that most people can say with a novel.

I drop my board in the dorm room, grab my bag and pull my lunch out of the mini-fridge. My phone vibrates in my pocket.

> TRAVIS – I forgot to water my plant. Can you do that? Jilly's swinging by next week to water it.

I text back that I will, and I do. Jilly's his girlfriend who is a barista at his favorite coffee shop. She lives in town. She'll have to work while we're goofing. Yeah, almost four whole weeks just sleeping and reading next semester's books. It'll be great. I turn off the lights and pull the door closed behind me.

Unsatisfying

Peter

Morning dawns gray through my window. My arm's asleep under her and it hurts to drag it free. Rubbing pins and needles, I pad naked into the bathroom and find Jim, Rick's roommate, passed out on the floor, half under the toilet. I remember how good the cold porcelain feels when you hug it while fighting off nausea. Most people don't start shivering with the cold chills of withdrawal. That's a new one for me this year. Then the porcelain becomes your enemy. I don't like other people to see me naked, so I go back to my room to pull on sleeping shorts before nudging him with my toe. The toilet smells like a fermented yak paddy and Jim doesn't smell much better. He groans and sits up, head in hand.

"Grab a shower, man. You smell like shit." He does what he's told, and I flush the toilet twice before using it. God, we're going to have to clean the bathroom before we go home. Rick comes to the open bathroom door just as I finish.

"I couldn't find you." He's got *that look* on his face. As my sponsor, his job is to worry about my choices, but I'm sober so he's got another concern. I'm beginning to realize that sobriety starts a long way back from taking the first sip of bourbon, but it's hard to analyze where I'm about to screw myself up.

"I stayed at the coffee shop until they closed and then – well --." We laugh together, but then he sobers.

"You shouldn't use sex as a substitute, man. It's just stuffing stuff down and someday, it might not be available."

"You telling me you've never done stuff to distract yourself?"

"Of course, I have and still do. But you notice I distract myself with cleaning the bathroom or going for a run. I don't rely on another person to give me an endorphin boost. Girls feel good, but they don't really solve anything – especially not the way you're doing it. Do you even know her name?"

I shake my head. College has changed my view of sexual mores. I spent most of high school three sheets to the wind and hyper-moral toward girls and now I don't drink and I'm admittedly a slut. I think this is my twelfth hookup in four months. Not bad for a guy who was a virgin until two weeks before he got here and doesn't even remember his first time. Or maybe it is bad. In the cold light of dawn, it feels like it isn't good.

"Enough said on that topic." Jim starts to move in the shower, so Rick beckons me to his room. His side is neat, his bag packed, the bed slept in but easily smoothed. Jim's going to have fun cleaning his side up while nursing a hangover. We'll be back in January. We can leave our stuff, but the administration asks us to neaten up so the cleaning crew can do its job. I plan to neaten my room after the blonde leaves. It's not that much. I got my laundry back yesterday, so I need to put that away...and make my bed. "So, really, how are you doing?"

"Parties are hard, but I'm still sober." I'm also in the best shape I've been in since boarding school in the 10th grade. Every time I get a craving and can't find Rick or a girl to hook up with, I go to the gym. It started trying to get my shoulder back in shape after a dislocation in the fall, but it's become a way to disrupt the addiction process.

"Good. Wasn't really worried about that." I cock an eyebrow. It's been a rough four months and I'm surprised I made it all the way to this morning sober after passing through the crowd last night. "You're up at 5:00 am, so ...." He's got a point, so I grin. I drank too much coffee last night, so I needed to pee. "You sure you're ready for home? The folks wouldn't mind a tagalong for the holidays."

"I really need to spend some time with my sister. And the way I left things in August ...."

"That's Step 8. How about you work on getting through Step 4?"

Every time I write something on my inventory, I want to reach out to that person and say something or do something, but Rick keeps pulling me back, telling me to concentrate on Step 4 and not get ahead of myself. He doesn't think I'm being "searching or thorough" enough. He knows I'm avoiding shit I'd rather not deal with. And then the last week ....

"I'll work on it. I got a little obsessed with finals."

"And, that's fine, but you need to finish your inventory – at least get enough down so you can confess it."

"You know the main thing." That one hurts.

"I don't think that's the only thing bugging you. I mean, if you'd prefer to tell a counselor instead of me, that's fine, but you *need* to talk about it. You were drinking a long time before that wreck. Your friends are pissed off at a pattern, not an incident. The accident was a result, not a cause."

I nod. Jim comes into the room naked, gingerly rubbing his hair with a towel. I hate looking at other guys' junk. There's no privacy in this dorm. I turn for the bathroom and my room beyond.

"Remember, you can call any time."

"I will. And, I already looked up meeting times. See you in January, man."

I go back to my room where the blonde is awake, looking adorable with bedhead despite the horror show mascara.

"What time is it?" She makes her hair even bigger by scratching fingers through it. I find my phone in my jacket pocket on the floor.

"Five-thirty."

"Crap!" She scrambles for the few clothes she wore at the party. "My dad's going to be here in two hours and I'm nowhere near ready. God, my head. You got any Alka Seltzer." I shake my head, not missing the hangovers. I find my bottle of Tylenol in the drawer and give her two, pouring water into her empty Solo cup from last night. "Sorry."

"For?" I can't think of one thing about last night that I regret except that I had sex with a girl whose name I still don't know.

"You know."

"It was fun." I always enjoy the deed. It's the aftermath when I start to second-guess myself.

"I didn't pass out on you?"

"Nope."

"We did it then?" Oh, no! My heart sinks into my toes.

"Yes. With a condom. You telling me you don't remember?"

She shakes her head, wincing. I sigh. She clearly wanted it. She undressed me and pinned me to the bed. I could easily mount an argument that *she* seduced *me*, though I participated fully and willingly. She didn't even want to wait on the condom. Thank God I insisted. Well, truthfully, thank you, Mom and Dad, for getting pregnant with me when still in college and passing that cautionary tale to me. I'm not making a baby with a girl whose name I don't even know. It's still uncomfortable to know she doesn't remember. I'm pretty sure I have at least one time I don't remember too, and I hate the blank spots and fear what might crawl out of them.

"Thanks for that," she tells me and then, now sort of dressed, walks out of my life. I still don't know her name and I wonder if I'll ever see her again. There is something highly unsatisfying about hookups and now my bed smells of beer and cum.

Close to the Chest

Ben

After taking the New York City route home on Thanksgiving, I decided to take the Long Island Ferry for Christmas and save myself several hours of driving. It's worth the money just to be able to eat lunch while I'm traveling. It saves wear and tear on my Jeep too. I didn't use the ferry when I drove to Dartmouth in the fall because I towed a U-Haul and I hadn't gotten my act together to arrange it, but it's not that expensive. It would cost me the same amount in gas and then my time has a value too.

I'm in Bridgeport getting ready to load when it occurs to me, I could have swung by Yale to pickup Pete...if I were talking to him. The snowboarding this morning got me thinking about him and now I can't stop. He's been a friend for so long and I did promise to give him a chance to redeem himself. I don't really know that he hasn't been doing that. He doesn't have a driver's license, so getting around has to be a pain. On the other hand, I'm not talking to him and I'm not backtracking to New Haven to get someone I'm not talking to. For all I know, he's already in Port Mal organizing a Christmas party for all our friends.

As soon as my car is secure, I head up the observation deck, but I've never taken the ferry in the winter before and quickly learn It's too cold up on the observation deck to enjoy the ride, so I got to the cantina for a burger and fries. There's lots of people here, a fair number of college students. I wouldn't be surprised if Pete were onboard. Since he hasn't got a car, he'd have to take the train or the ferry. Would Vic drive all the way to Yale to get him? I guess he's paid to do that. But Pete has never been one to rely on the perks of his father's wealth. The ferry would be his speed and then he'd have Vic pick him up at the dock.

Some college-age guys across the way play a travel board game. Pete could be highly entertaining on a trip like this—bold enough to use his fake ID to grab some beers from the lounge, observant of human behavior even if he didn't always understand it, able to see the humor in the world around him. He doesn't need to be the center of attention like Trevor so he's not nearly so exhausting. But I'm not talking to him and he last texted me at Thanksgiving. He sounded kind of fed-up with me that day, deciding to go to his roommate's house for the holiday because he didn't feel welcome in his own hometown. I would have replied to him except

I let Pam read it and she said he sounded whiny. I agreed after she pointed it out. She almost talked me into blocking him, but I've thought about it since and I want to keep my promise that he can redeem himself. I just don't know how to do that and keep him at an arm's length until he's proven to me that he's changed. Maybe I'll analyze his next text and tell him what he's getting right, because before Thanksgiving, he did sound like he'd been thinking about it.

After I finish eating and bus my tray, I sit down by a window to watch the water. It's cloudy out today, so the water is gray, but I don't mind that so much. I imagine sailing. It's too cold right now for my two-man with your butt inches above the water, but on a warmer day it would be lovely. I'm kind of daydreaming when someone sits down across from me and bumps my knee. I look up to see Andy Harmon grinning at me.

"Hey," I say.

"Deep thoughts?"

"Not really. Just glad to be able to think about something that isn't school work. How was Burlington?"

"Pre-med's kicking my butt, but not so bad I want to switch to basket-weaving. You?"

"Engineering is doing the same. Plus I'm working 30 hours a week, so...."

"Yeah. I'm glad my grandparents are footing the bill. How's Pam?"

"Dating someone with a trust fund, but we're still friends."

"Well, that sucks. At least she didn't decide she's both a girl and a guy at the same time."

My neck feels hot. It's a topic I never know how to respond to. Andy laughs at my expression.

"Biologically, it's not possible, so is therefore a delusion. There's going to be a whole lot of people when they're our parents' age wishing they'd never posted that insanity on the internet where their kids can find it."

"My grandfather says it's the equivalent of the naked bathtub photos of his day." Andy nods. The college-aged guys have closed their board game and are now headed toward the companionway at the end of the cantina. Andy's eyes follow the fittest of them. I don't have any actual proof, but I suspect he's gay. I do know Andy started the rumors that Pete is gay. Pete isn't. He's just a year younger than the rest of the class, so he caught onto girls slower, perplexing the ones who wanted his attention. They didn't understand why this gorgeous boy wasn't horn-dogging them. I still doubt the relaxed mores of the current era makes it all that much easier to come out without it changing relationships. Hence why Andy hasn't done it. Maybe if his rumors about

Pete had been true, he'd feel more comfortable doing so since he wouldn't be alone.

"How's Regina?"

"Great, I think. She's graduating a semester early so she can take a gap year without taking the actual time. She's headed to Australia for the winter."

"Nice!"

"How's Peter?"

I get the creep vibe again. Is it possible Andy started that rumor because he fancies Pete? Homosexual men follow Pete like bees after honey. He's the ultimate snacc. Andy always wanted to be his best friend and Pete's always been politely standoffish. He's been hit on so often that I think he's been onto Andy for a long time. And, like I said, Pete's not gay. He's got a whole other set of problems with sex, but there's no question he's aroused by females and not by men. He and I have been in enough locker rooms together for me to know that for sure.

"Not really sure. He seemed okay the last time he texted me, but things are still awkward over the whole Cheyenne thing."

"That was twisted. What happened to him, anyway?"

"What do you mean?" I expect him to ask about Pete's injuries from the accident.

"Something flipped with him last spring. That party he hosted for graduation went south like Trevor was running it."

Barely a week after his uncle's funeral, but I don't say that because I don't think most people know it and it's not my place to spill Pete's personal business. I've seen Pete really drunk on a number of occasions, but he always stayed mostly in control, even if he didn't remember it the next day. That party however – Pete drank Finn Conover under the table, which never happens. Even the captain of the football team, a real results-oriented individual, couldn't drink Finn under the table. And, then Pete passed out and I panicked and called Tilly because he wasn't breathing right. Thank God I circled back as the designed driver to make sure I hadn't missed anyone.

"Yeah, maybe. He admitted he was drunk the whole time in Europe. Some people can't handle their liquor."

"It's just too bad. Anyway, I'm going to head down to my car. Know if any of us are getting together?"

"No. I figured Pete might have planned something and just didn't invite me since we're still awkward."

Truthfully, we're not talking at all, but I sense Pete would prefer if I not tell his gay stalker that.

Allegedly gay. Awkward sounds like we're still friends, but not hanging out a lot right now.

"Nope. He's done a few thumbs-up on people's FB posts, but he's flown real low under the radar this semester. And with Trevor out of town that leaves – naw, Finn's in Oregon or something."

"We could do board games at my house, but my parents aren't down with underage drinking."

"Yeah – my folks too. Maybe Hil Cavanaugh will get bored."

"I thought he took the yacht to the Outer Banks."

"Right! Yeah. Anyway...gotta go. Probably see you around. By the way, have you heard from Trevor beyond the homoerotic dance photos he posts?"

Trevor's not gay either. I think that's just the essence of modern dance. I realize I'm quoting Pete on that.

"Um, not since—maybe October. He's in a traveling company so he's constantly on the move. I've texted him a few times and his responses have been brief. And you know Trevor—total ADD."

"Right." Andy laughs and there's something—I just don't know. "See ya."

I settle back into my seat to watch the water some more and daydream until the overhead announces that we should go to our cars to get ready for disembarkation.

Lela Markham

My little brother Wes texts me while I'm waiting
in the car.

> BEN – Home soon – like less than 45 minutes. You
> out of school?

> WES – Short day. Vacation tomorrow. Mom
> wants to know how you feel about fried chicken.

> BEN – Sounds great.

More than anything, this time home will be
about reconnecting with family, but I know I need to
think about what to do about Pete. Pam and I aren't
really dating any longer and he has been my best
friend since kindergarten. Yes, he did a wrong thing,
but I can't just write him off without knowing if he's
irredeemable.

Confessions

Peter

I meet Alan for dinner at Portofino, taking a cab to get there. I'm amazed I'm glad to see him. Last year at this time, I needed a drink to get through a dinner with him. Tonight, I feel no more anxious than I normally do, which is to say my cravings are loudly asserting themselves. When Alan orders a scotch and soda, I immediately want to order one for myself, but of course, Dad knows I'm not even 18 yet and I can't very well use fake ID in front of him. I think his guards might have law enforcement powers. It takes effort to say "water." It's been four months and it feels like four minutes.

"So, how are you doing, son?" Alan asks, spreading a napkin on his lap.

Lies are easier than truth and I excel at lying, but I don't want to. Rick anticipated this question and so I go with his suggestion.

"Better. I mean, I'm all healed up. Shoulder still aches when it's wet and cold out, but that's going away." I imagine gay guys feel this way when they think about coming out of the closet. There's a huge sense of moment and for a second, I almost talk myself out of it. "But, uh, yeah, it's been 118 days."

Alan stares at me, forehead creasing.

"Since the accident?"

"No. That was a few days before." I take a deep breath and say what needs to be said. "Since I've had a drink."

Alan frowns, making me profoundly nervous.

"Given that you're 17, you shouldn't be drinking at all."

"Yeah, but it's the longest I've gone since I was, like, 15."

Right then, the waiter sets Alan's drink down on a coaster and then serves my water. I drag my gaze off the bubbly caramel elixir, forcing myself to meet Dad's gaze.

"This isn't news to you, Dad. Right?"

"I knew you liked to party. I thought it was an occasional thing."

"It wasn't, isn't. That's why I ditched you for Thanksgiving, by the way. I wasn't ready to face Port Mallory, so I chose to go to my roommate's instead."

"And you're feeling stronger now?"

"It comes and goes. I really want *that* drink right now, but I know I don't need it."

"And, you're ready to go back to Port Mallory?"

28

Uh, no, probably not, but ditching Dad for Thanksgiving also meant ditching Alyse. I can't do that for Christmas.

"You're not going to be there. And, I get it, you've got commitments. Alyse shouldn't spend the holidays alone and I owe both of you amends, so --. Besides, I probably should let Ben know that I've been dealing with it."

"Ben knew?"

"I think pretty much all my friends knew and if they didn't, they sure knew after Cheyenne."

I don't know that definitively. Although I'm in text- and Facebook-contact with most of my high school friends, I haven't told any of them about getting sober. I'm not sure how any of them will take it. Rick suggested Ben might stop being so angry if I tell him, but I think he'll just feel sorry for me and that's not the same thing as not being angry.

Alan grunts in assent. Does he feel guilty that my admission is his first clue? Does he know about all the parties? I have more immediate concerns and Rick would say I have no right to take my father's inventory when I can't even face my own.

"You've been protecting me from that, and I guess I should know what's going on."

"My accountants and lawyers are on it. She's getting excellent care and your indiscretion will not affect the rest of her life." Alan never pretended the accident could be wholly blamed on bad brakes. I'm grateful for that and at the same time, terrified of it.

"That's good." It is and it isn't. I feel like I'm supposed to do more. "Thank you. The restraining order limits what I can do directly."

"That's probably for the best. Getting yourself together is probably the best amends you can make right now."

That doesn't feel right, but I can make the offer in August when the restraining order expires. I drain half my water glass. Alan frowns at his high ball.

"This wasn't a very good idea, was it?"

I stare at the sparkling caramel liquid. I don't like bubbles in my booze, but it sure looks like nectar from here.

"You didn't know. It's one of those things I'm going to have to learn to deal with."

The waiter comes to refill my water glass and Alan asks him to take the barely touched cocktail and bring him a club soda. Now I feel guilty, like I manipulated him. I didn't intend that.

"You didn't have to do that."

"I did. For tonight anyway. Thank you for sharing it with me."

I nod. It's already easier to breathe, even as my cravings silently scream for the waiter to bring the glass *back*. I'm relieved, thirsty *and* surprised that he's taking it so well.

"How did finals go?"

"Great. I had a good semester. I might get a B in calculus. I think I got a couple of calculations on the final wrong."

He smiles at me. His standards for me are high, but I'm the one who used to put the perfection burden on myself. He never required higher than a B from me. It's been a long time since I made straight-As, but it's also been a long time since I got Cs.

"You've always been a good student. Except for that semester in boarding school. That C average worried me."

Okay, he's reading my mind.

"Lot of drinking at Greenvale, Dad." Alan's eyebrows shoot up. "Before, I binged on weekends if my friends were bingeing, but drinking wasn't every day. During and after, I couldn't go more than a day or two without drinking – so, yeah."

"Oh, my god. I should have taken Joel Barnes' advice to home-school you."

Joel Barnes is my lawyer. Rick finally forced me to consider there's something wrong with a 17-year-old with a criminal-defense lawyer on speed-dial. Barnes seems like a nice guy. He's certainly a good lawyer.

"Or sent me to rehab." It is a softball pitch to see how he will react.

"I just didn't want to believe …. I'm sorry."

That easy? I expected lectures, so now I scramble to keep up. What do you say to that? *Dad, I'm doing okay right now, but maybe I ought to go to rehab instead of spend Christmas in my hometown where nobody is talking to me.* Yeah, I don't say that.

"It's not your fault. Those were my choices. So, here's my possible courses for next semester. My advisor says I'm supposed to run them by you, and I don't know that we'll see each other again before January."

Alan glances at the print-out and puts it in his breast pocket. Alyse called him this fall about handing our personal information off to staff and he's adapted to her insistence that he deal with his children directly. I expect to get an email in a few days telling me why I can't take Beginning Architecture and need to take the business-oriented course instead. I'll keep the architecture course and add the business course on for way too many credits. Rick will scold me for overloading myself, but damn it, I want to be an architect, not join my father in the family business or politics. Alan will only pay for my education if I'm majoring in what Alan wants, so a double major is the only way around it. Alan thinks he'll change my mind – and I do have a history of not sticking with things – but I'm going to at least give it a try.

"I will try to make it to Port Mal on Christmas. There's just lots of duties surrounding being the governor." Alan is the governor of New York State. I'm lucky he came to Hartford to talk to the governor of Connecticut about Round 700 on the Long Island Sound Bridge. Dad doesn't want to build it, but a lot of other people do, and now the dock workers are threatening to strike.

"I watch the news. Tilly and I will surround Alyse with love and festivities and it'll be great. Maybe you could Skype us." I'm surprised that doesn't come out sounding petty. It sounds like a legitimate suggestion, offered in a semi-joking tone. Alan even takes it that way.

We spend the rest of the meal in pleasant conversation and then Alan and his driver drop me in Bridgeport before heading back to Albany. To avoid the bar, I go up to the observation deck to watch the water. I really do need to leave my fake ID at home now that I'm going there. It will be less tempting. The observation deck is cold and blustery, made worst because I hate where I'm going. I wish things were different, that I looked forward to going home. Ben laid down a challenge in August – don't text him until I understood what I'd done wrong. Well, I do understand now. I admitted it to Rick and sort of to my dad, but the thought of admitting it to Ben – scary. Yet I know I need to. I need Ben back

33

in my life. I mean to find a way to reconcile with him.

Family Pancakes

Ben

Pete's text arrived last night and it's the first thing that pops into my mind when I wake up.

PETER - Headed home for Christmas. I'll be there tomorrow. I was hoping we could talk. Please, Ben. Can we just talk? I promise I'm better.

I'm too sleepy to care at 7:30 am on my first day off since Thanksgiving. I amble into the shower and stand under the stream for a while before my mind starts running over the text.

Pete texted me off and on through the semester. He tried to apologize several times. A few times he even sounded like he might be getting it. He tried to share interesting events in his life. He asked me how Cheyenne was doing. I didn't reply to any of them and the texts became less frequent. The last one arrived after Thanksgiving, apologizing for sounding whiny in the text before Thanksgiving, but then saying he really didn't know what I want from him. I'm saving them, waiting for him to say something worthwhile. I don't know if I'll recognize it if it ever comes. Pam says I should just block his number, but Pete was my best friend since kindergarten and Pam's dating someone at Brown.

Did I let a chick get between me and my best friend? Maybe, but Pete also got in his own way. He had lots of opportunities to turn away from that wreck with Cheyenne and he kept heading toward the alcohol cabinet.

I noticed he sent a couple of his texts where he mentioned dorm parties and then took me on video tours of the campus, hinting at party avoidance. Is he trying to tell me something? Or has he just found a new way to lie? Since I'm not talking to Pam so much, I'm starting to weaken toward Pete. I did say I'd let him redeem himself if he'd think about what went wrong. Am I not giving him that chance by insisting I won't relent until he's perfect at it?

When I get back to my room, there's another text, this one from Pam. She'll be in town for Christmas. Do I want to go ice skating at The Rinx on Christmas Eve? Sure. It's not like I have a girlfriend who might get jealous and I enjoy hanging out with Pam when we can do physical things like ice skating. We bonded over tennis, but Pam really prefers social activities like sitting at the coffee shop and talking. I miss Pete for his willingness to do physical things like mountain biking and surfing.

Am I really comparing them? Neither Pete nor I are gay. Really! It's just that Pam made me see something in Pete that I'd been ignoring for so long. He's selfish, egotistical and careless with the people around him. She never liked him, though he liked her for about three seconds at some point in high school. Then when we were at Splish Splash, she made me see that he'd been drinking to enhance his good time and ruined everyone else's. I increasingly saw his misbehavior before he ran into that tree, but that made me stop denying it. Once the rose-colored glasses were removed, I couldn't see Pete's better qualities at all.

During this time apart, I've begun to remember Pete isn't a one-dimensional character and Pam really doesn't know him. In high school, he cared about people. He struggled to understand what they wanted, but once he figured it out, he'd bend over backwards to give you what you said you wanted from him. Still, I can't forget how Pete smiled when he was lying in that hospital bed, as if what he'd done to Cheyenne didn't matter to him. Yeah, Trevor pointed out Pete might have been loopy from the concussion and painkillers. The smile still galls me.

Before Thanksgiving, Pete texted me to ask if we could talk when we were both home. I'd almost replied, but Pam and I were still dating then, and she talked me out of it. Before I could second-guess myself, Pete took the decision out of my hands.

> PETE – I'm bailing on Thanksgiving. I'm not ready to sit at home and wait for you to call me, knowing you won't. So, I'm going to my roommate's for Thanksgiving. It's kind of ironic. I'm going to be at his grandmother's in Nashua. Maybe we'll pass you on the expressway. Ben, I'm really working on what went wrong and I'm sorry if I'm not giving you what you want, but I don't understand. You said you'd give me a chance. Why won't you reply to me, so I know if I'm getting it right?

For half a moment, I hated myself for the pain I sensed in his text. And then I felt manipulated. Cheyenne was going through hell and Pete still cared more about himself.

My father points out Pete might be going through stuff and not sharing because he doesn't know how to word it. Pete isn't good with talking about feelings and texting and social media don't really convey emotions. Maybe if we sat down across from each other and just talked, I'd find out Pete has figured it out, but then I'd also be open to his charm.

I head out to the kitchen to get some food. Mom and Dad are making breakfast. Wes is still asleep, though he's sitting at the table.

"Hope you brought your appetite. Your father went nuts with making pancakes."

"We can freeze what they don't eat." Dad wears pajamas covered in Santas. The stove is covered with drips of batter. Mom at least got dressed. She hands me a cup of coffee.

"And notice that he got up so early." She smiles fondly over her shoulder at my dad. I'm lucky and I know it. My parents love each other. They fight sometimes, but it never lasts long. Neither of them has my slow-burn, last-for-months anger. They're more like Pete – quick and over it. Theirs are more irritation with each other rather than a real argument.

"What's your plan for the day?"

I'm yawning into my coffee cup. Plans? Sleeping in? Oh, I already blew that. I'm not a napper. Even groggy, if I go back to bed, I'll not sleep.

"I did most of my shopping online, so I'm thinking of taking my mountain bike out to Mt. Calamity."

"By yourself?"

"Probably. Most everybody is still coming home."

"Maybe you should call Peter up, See if he's home yet."

"He's not." She cocks her head at me. "He texted me. I think he got home late last night."

"I thought you weren't talking to him." Dad has pulled the foil out and is transferring pancakes to it.

"I'm not, but he's still reaching out."

"What are you going to do about that?" Mom pours herself more coffee and tops off my cup.

"I don't know. I'm torn. What should I do about it?"

"Maybe stand still and listen to him for a few minutes." She's reading my expression. "He's still reaching out after months. Clearly your friendship is important to him. Maybe if you listen, you'll find out he's better."

"You said you wanted that when you started this." Dad's making a tent over the pancakes.

"I know. And I do feel torn. He pushed to talk with me before Thanksgiving and he did ask about Cheyenne and then he generally apologized for being a drunken idiot. So, he's been thinking about it. It's just – maybe I'm tired of worrying about him. Maybe I want friendships that don't involve drunken idiots."

"I can imagine how much fun you were in the dorms this semester."

"Yeah, pretty judgmental. Everybody looks a lot like Pete right now."

"So, maybe, for your own sake, you need to talk to him so you can move on." Mom smiles at me. Dad slides the pancake packet onto a platter.

"Can you take this next door to the Wexlers? I've clearly lost my mind with pancakes and they shouldn't go to waste."

Through the side door, I can see their kitchen light is on.

"I haven't met them yet."

"This will be a perfect time then."

I sigh and grab my coat off the hook. It's been a dry winter in New Hampshire, but Long Island is cold and chilly this morning.

Tapping on the neighbor's door feels odd. The Carsons lived there my entire life. This new family are strangers to me, and I can't help feeling that the young girl coming to the door is an intruder.

"Hey." Her gaze shifted from my face to the house behind me and then to the platter in my hands. "Good morning."

"Happy Saturday. My father asked me to bring you some pancakes."

"Oh, great! I was about to make some. Good timing. Lily, BTDubs." I haven't heard that phrase in a while. It's cute coming from her.

"Ben. I live next door."

"I figured that. You look a little like your dad."

My dad is darker than me and taller. I don't think I'm going to beat him on height. I'd have to grow another half-inch. Unlikely. It must be eyes or nose or something. I don't really see a resemblance.

Lily's early high-school-age, right on the cusp of being pretty, with shining hair, currently caught up in an inadequate ponytail.

"Enjoy."

"Thank you. We're still moving in, so this saves me having to dig in a box for the big frying pans."

"Wow. Right at Christmas?"

"Yeah. My dad wanted to get the house ready so Mom can stop living at the hospital."

Right. Her brother is ill. I don't remember with what and I hesitate to ask.

"Well, it was nice meeting you. I'll be around into January. I'm willing to do any heavy lifting."

"Good to know. I'll tell my dad. Although your parents already offered your strong back."

"Yeah, that sounds like them. Well, I'll get going. You have a good day."

I go back into our house where Wes has awakened enough to dig into a big stack of pancakes. I slide into my seat.

"How's Lyle?" Dad refills my coffee cup before sitting down.

"I didn't see Mr. Wexler. Lily answered the door. She says thank you."

I eat some bacon and pancake.

"What's wrong with their son?" I jerk my thumb over my shoulder, so they'll know what I mean.

"He's at Cedar Sinai. Some sort of brain injury."

"I met Madalyn a few days ago. She said he had a stroke." Mom eats some fruit. "It reminded me of Julianne."

Julianne is my sister. She died of leukemia when I was little, which is why there's such a gap between me and Wes. I don't really remember her well enough to mourn her, but my parents still get sad on her birthday. Pam thinks their attachment to Pete is tied to that loss. I've tried to see that in my parents, but I don't really. I think they like Pete for the same reasons I like him – he had positive traits before he just descended into darkness. Could he get back there if he tried?

"Have you considered talking to your grandfather?" Dad's question cuts right through my reverie.

"About?"

"Peter." I stare at him, confused. What does Grandpa Jack have to do with Pete? "Maybe talking to someone who is a recovering alcoholic will help you to see Pete in a different light."

"That still won't change his behavior."

"No, but it might help you to see his point of view. It's just a suggestion."

Dad bumps Wes' shoulder. The kid startles awake. He's eaten a remarkable number of pancakes for someone who is unconscious. The look on his face is so priceless, we all three laugh and Wes frowns in confusion, which makes us laugh again. It's good to be home.

Skyrim

Alyse

Ben stops by the house Peter's first full day back. His timing sucks because Peter went to the gym about an hour ago. I'm so glad to see him, I give him a big hug and draw him into the foyer.

"Is Pete around?" he asks, shoving his gloves into his pockets.

"Sorry. He went to the gym."

"The gym?" Peter surprised me too by getting up so early and leaving the house.

"He's still working on his shoulder and he's back to dancing."

"Seriously?"

"Well, not performing, but he took a class at Yale."

"Wow." Ben looks impressed. "How is he?"

"I don't know. He got in late last night and then he headed out first thing this morning. He planned to work out and do some Christmas shopping. Vic drove him."

"Oh, right. He lost his license. How's he doing with that?"

They must still not be talking and that makes me sad. My brother has a lot of friends, but he's not really close with any of them like he is with Ben.

"He says he deserves it." I'm not lying. Peter has said he earned the suspension and if he gets frustrated with the lack of independence, that's normal, I guess. I can't drive yet, so I wouldn't know.

"Does he text you at all?"

"Of course, silly. We talk all the time."

That's sort of true. I call him and he replies. He doesn't reach out to me much except to ask about Cheyenne. Like I know about her. I'm not her friend. Some of her friends at dance tell me things when I ask, but I must remember to ask.

"Really, how's he doing?"

"He's Peter. He doesn't share a lot with me."

"Do you think he's drinking?"

"Not since he's been home, but I've only seen him for about fifteen minutes."

"Does he ask about Cheyenne?"

"He does. You know there's a restraining order. He's not allowed to call her family. The only way he knows what's going on is if I've heard something at dance."

"And how's he taking that?"

"I don't know. He doesn't share that. How is she?" That's the right thing, I'm sure.

"Between surgeries. So, I'll call him. Thanks." He reaches for the door.

"He misses you."

"I miss him, but – I couldn't let him get away with what he did."

Why not? That's what I want to ask. Peter got hurt too and he's clearly sad about what happened to Cheyenne. Why did that have to end his friendship with Ben?

I don't ask and Ben doesn't read my mind. He heads to his car and I go back to watching Karen make Christmas cookies. There's definitely art involved. Peter comes home about two hours later, putting gift-wrapped boxes under the tree in the living room before coming to my door.

"I've missed you," I tell him. "Dad was hardly home, and Tilly is such a grump."

"I'm here now. You want to play Elder Scrolls?"

We relocate to his room where he boots up the game. He and I played it a little last summer, but it's been about a year since we've visited Skyrim.

"Ben stopped by."

Peter flinches.

"To see me?"

"Yes, silly!" He frowns at the screen. "He still cares about you. You just need to let him know you're not angry."

47

"I'm not angry. He's angry at me."

"Because of Cheyenne?"

He nods. For just a moment, he looks so sad and then he drags in a deep breath and forces a smile on his face. Ballet face. He looks at the screen.

"Where to?"

Really? Since when does he let me choose our destination? I usually solve the puzzles while he kills the monsters. I'm not sure if he's serious, but I love playing this game with him, so if he gives me a little more autonomy, I'll probably have even more fun. And I'll do whatever I have to do to keep him from being sad. Sad Peter scares me and so I need to keep him engaged in whatever makes him not sad.

Distracted Living

Peter

Lucy stops by late afternoon as snow begins to fall. Maybe we're going to have a white Christmas. That's not a given thing on Long Island because we stick out into the Atlantic like a sore thumb and get the moderating effects of the Atlantic current.

"You look good." She sets her bag down on the foyer floor. Lucy is very casual. Yeah, I call my grandmother by her first name because everybody, including her three children, call her Lucy. There's no use arguing about her name.

"I'm healed." My shoulder aches today because of the cool and damp weather, but I know I'm healing. I think the last time she saw me I was covered in bruises and suffering from hepatitis.

"We were worried about you." She's searching my face with her gaze. She's slender with long red-gray hair pulled back in a Celtic clasp.

"We?"

49

"Mike and me. Do you think Tilly would lose her mind if I brought Bosco in?"

"Tilly won't freak out. Aly might." Aly's afraid of dogs. "And Dad's not here, so he won't say anything."

"Alan likes dogs."

You wouldn't know that. I've wanted a dog since 2nd grade and we still don't have one. She brings Bosco in, his claws tapping against the slate. I pet his head and the chocolate Lab smiles at me, then starts sniffing around in the corners. We generally don't leave food lying around on the floor, but Labs are optimists.

"You really sure you're okay? Mike really worried about you last fall." She shrugs out of her green wool coat and slips off her Uggs, sitting briefly on the entry way bench to don socks – not that anyone in this household cares. I'm barefoot, for example.

Granddad Mike's called me almost weekly since I went to school. Lucy texted me and I texted her back, but Mike seemed really worried about me – enough to get over his reservations about calling me on my cell phone. Until the other night in New Haven, they were the only family I told about getting sober. They've been surprisingly supportive.

"Yeah. I, uh, had an ultrasound and liver function blood test a couple of weeks ago and I'm okay. Everything's back to normal. You want some coffee?"

"Sounds good." We go down the hallway to the kitchen and I pour her a cup. I'm still in my lounge pants and bare feet. I might finish my Christmas shopping this afternoon. I still need something for my grandparents.

"Did your dad or Alyse tell you that Collin is getting married in June?"

"Wow. Who is she?" My cousin Collin and I spent half of last summer together in Europe. If Collin had a lady love then, he cheated on her at least twenty times.

"He met her in Boston. She's a bartender."

Of course, she is. Collin is a student at Harvard, and I think his major might be Drinks of Europe.

"Should we be worried about him?"

Snitches get stitches, although Rick would say an active drug addict has no right to expect anonymity.

"We drank a lot last summer. And he did some other stuff. I wasn't really keeping track and I don't know how he is when he's not on vacation. You check out his Facebook page?"

I haven't. Collin and I spent a month together and I don't like him. Lucy looks like this is an idea she hasn't had before. She's a Baby Boomer, but not uncomfortable with technology. I bet she can find Collin's Facebook page without my help. She can ask if she needs it.

"So, tell me about school."

51

We spend some time talking about Yale, New Haven and my courses. She and Granddad Mike lived there when he was at Yale. She worked at a five-and-dime that no longer exists. She says I ought to go for the architecture course.

"If you don't want to go into business or politics, you don't have to."

I didn't mention my aversion to politics at all, but I guess she knows me. I ask her what she's been up to. She's still running a non-profit and doing some property management. She talks enthusiastically about a yoga-adjacent exercise program she's trying.

"It's a great stress reliever without all the navel-gazing of yoga. If you'd like to join me, you'd be welcome."

"Yeah, I don't know. I'm lifting weights again. My shoulder's getting stronger."

"That's good. Are you sleeping?"

I'm still waking up in the middle of the night thirsty and then I can't go back to sleep. Rick says it takes time. Last night, I woke up and knew the bar downstairs was unlocked. I didn't go check it out and I've managed not to test the theory this morning, so I'm better.

"Mostly. When you first quit drinking, you kind of have trouble sleeping, but I'm settling out." Most nights that's true. It's better here at home because the bed is long enough for me. At school, I must sleep at a slight diagonal because I'm so tall.

"Good. And I guess you're doing meetings?"

"At school, I was. I've been hanging out with Alyse since I got home. I guess I should go to one. I did look them up last night." That's what I did when I woke up with the bar whispering in my ear. Meetings can be a substitute for getting drunk. That's why they work. I just hate that I must keep doing it even on vacation.

Tilly comes in the back door, her cheeks rosy from the outside temperatures. She's carrying groceries. Bosco runs up to her to say "hello." He's met her before, and it wouldn't matter because he loves everyone.

"Oh, hi, uh --."

"Bosco." I figure forgetting the dog's name is fine. Lucy smiles at Tilly as Tilly sets the bags on the counter to give Bosco an enthusiastic rub. He licks her fingers and offers to bathe her face. She straightens to avoid that and he's well-mannered enough not to jump up on her.

"Hi, Mrs. Wyngate."

"Lucy. Everybody calls me Lucy. How are you doing, Tilly?" Lucy tells her that every time and Tilly always goes through the formality.

"Very good. I love Christmas."

"So, do I. It's my favorite holiday. I saw the tree. Amazing. Did you do that yourself?"

"Alyse helped. With just Alyse here now, it seemed like a good thing for us girls to do."

Alyse didn't mention Tilly helping her, though I figured Tilly did the work and Alyse dabbled. Alyse sticking with anything but dance for long enough to decorate an 12-foot tree, let alone put the artificial tree together, were never very high odds. I do believe Alyse did some of it. She's got a more artistic eye than Tilly. She's probably responsible for the champagne-and-gilt ribbons cascading for the crown to the floor. Those are new this year and very artsy. I always used to help Tilly with the tree and she left the star for me this year.

"I hope you'll join Peter and Alyse on Christmas." Tilly's come to Christmas brunch in Old Field several times because Lucy insisted, and Dad doesn't seem to mind. Lucy wasn't raised rich and she treats Tilly like she's a family member rather than a servant. I try to emulate her. Tilly seems to enjoy herself, but she mostly just sits back and watches. It's gotta be weird to be part of a family but not really. I wonder about her family. Doesn't she have one?

"Someone's going to have to drive." We might as well get that out of the way. I still can't drive, so Tilly must.

"I will come. I think Alan will be in Albany still. That strike is a major issue."

I sip coffee to hide my expression. Tilly starts unpacking the groceries. She never quits moving. Lucy and I retire to the big harvest table. She tells me she's trying to get Alyse to take a second driving course.

"I don't think that's going to help."

She laughs at me.

"Maybe artistic people shouldn't drive."

"Mrs. Sims and Miss Rebecca both drive. I drive – well, yeah." I shake my head in self-mockery. "You drive. Heck, my mother drives." I'm not sure that's a great idea. I have a vague memory of being terrified at my mother's driving when she was distracted by something that wasn't really there. How old was I? Alyse isn't in the memory. Could that be my earliest memory?

"Have you eaten?" Tilly asks.

"I toasted a bagel and ate some grapes."

"So, you're not hungry?"

"Not yet. Lunch would be good though."

Lucy's smiling at me like I've done something smart. I don't know what she means by that.

"Well, I'll be headed on my way." Lucy rises to put her empty coffee cup in the dishwasher. "After Christmas, you and your grandfather need to go play racquetball or something."

"Right. I'll talk with him about it on Christmas. It does feel weird that I didn't go 'duck hunting' with him this fall." Mike doesn't take me to shoot ducks with a gun. That's him and Bosco alone. When he takes me along, he uses a camera instead. He's got some excellent shots. I did some watercolors from a few of them. He's got them displayed on the wall of his private retreat by the pond like they're fine art. It would be embarrassing if it wasn't also ego boosting. Now that I know he might do that, I'll pay closer attention to what I'm creating. I'm not fully happy with either of my paintings.

I walk Lucy to the door. She tells Bosco to heel and he drops to his butt at her left knee like a soldier. She hugs me.

"I'm glad to see you're better."

"Me too." I mean that. I'm starting to like being sober. I'm still tempted, but I never again want to feel like I did after Cheyenne's accident and if sobriety is what it takes to avoid that, then I don't need to drink.

Her gaze wavers across my face. She's worried about me. I wish I hadn't given her reason to, but I can't change that. She hugs me again.

"See you Christmas morning." She heads for her car, Bosco following like a shadow.

Lumberjack

Ben

Finn's a big guy, as tall as Pete and beefier. He played football in high school before a bike accident tore up his knee. He still likes to do active things, which is why I ran into him out at Mt. Calamity. The weather turned chilly and drove us both off the mountain bike trail. We met in the parking lot, so we adjourned to the Speakeasy for lunch. It's this underground eatery with upholstered leather booths and décor from the 1920s. There's always jazz playing over the speakers and the waitresses dress like flappers.

"You liked school, huh?"

"I do. What about you?"

"Naw. My dad wants me to be a lawyer. I don't want to be a lawyer." He takes a swallow of his beer. Someone here on the Gold Coast makes fantastic money making amazing fake IDs. I'm not willing to spend that sort of money so I'm drinking a soda.

"So, you're just hanging out?"

"Taking a gap year. I hitchhiked to California and back – on different routes. Got a gig doing photographs for this Route 66 retrospective. Now I'm home for a while. I'm thinking of heading to the Caribbean for a while."

"Where you staying?"

"At my mom's. Ross is being all friendly. Not sure what that's about."

His stepfather Ross is friends with my dad, but I don't know him very well. He always seems nice. Finn has never liked him. I've noticed that's a thing with my friends from blended families. Pete's the only one who gets along with his stepparent, maybe because she's hired help.

"He wants me to attend this adult camp thing out west."

"Why?"

"Beats me, man. He says I might find 'clarity' there. I'm out of here right after New Year's. My dad's headed to Trinidad, so I'm going to tagalong and then maybe stay a while. White Mountains getting any good snow?"

"Mostly fake, but we got a snowstorm right before I left, so I got to carve some powder."

"I would have loved to stay long enough in the Rockies for snowboarding, but I caught that photography job in Denver, so …. I saw Pete shopping yesterday."

"Yeah? How's he doing?"

"You guys still aren't talking?"

"I'm still not ready to forgive him for Cheyenne and he's not showed me he gets it yet."

"I don't think he meant to hurt her. He asked me if I knew anything about her."

"Right. Ross is Rotary too, right?" He nods.

"We had lunch too. He was – I don't know – weird."

"What do you mean?"

"Well, we ate at a pub and he didn't drinking. That's weird. Even when I ordered one, he still had soda. And then he asked if I'd talked to you recently. Isn't that what you want, for him to clean up his act?"

"If he's not drinking that's a good sign, yeah."

"Well, I never thought to ask Ross about Cheyenne, so I couldn't tell him anything. I still don't know why you're still so angry with him."

"Yeah. He didn't need to drive that night. There were designated drivers for a reason and he still did it."

"And now he can't drive for a year and he's feeling guilty about something he doesn't even remember doing."

"Is that what he told you?"

"Well, it makes sense. He was .18 BAC and he got a concussion. Both will mess with your memory."

"Right." Finn waves the waitress over and asks for another beer. It's his third. Why does everyone around me drink like lumberjacks?

"I'm just saying, you ought to talk with him, see what he's thinking and cut him a little slack for not remembering."

"Maybe. I tried to drop by to see him the other day and he texted me to say he got the message. But he hasn't come over or anything."

"He has to arrange rides, Ben, so maybe you need to go to him."

"Maybe. It's been really nice catching up, but I'm supposed to pick my little brother up from the Port Club, so I better get going."

"Nice talking with you, man. I got the check."

"Not necessary."

"You can catch the tip. My dad is still giving me a generous allowance and I got paid really well for those photographs. You can catch it next time ... or not. Ain't no thing."

I toss down a ten and wish him a good afternoon, but then I hesitate.

"Three beers in an hour. You shouldn't probably be driving."

"I'm not. I'm going to hit a couple of shops around here before I head home. I'm probably not over the legal limit even now, but I sure won't be when I get behind the wheel of a car."

I guess Pete did teach a few people some things when he ran into that tree. I'm going to need to talk to him to see if *he* learned anything from it.

Rinx

Peter

Yeah, what happened with Ben? It looked good, right? He stopped by to see me. What do you think happened with Ben?

I text him to say I'll come by to see him, but that takes a couple of days because Alyse is so needy when I get there. She's been stuck in that house with Tilly, our housekeeper, for months and she just isn't the same person since I last saw her. She's always been kind of sharp, bossy and spoiled, but she's downright mean and grabby with me when I arrive. For the next two days, we play board games and Skyrim and she starts to act like herself again. It's been a long time since I felt like I could be that relaxed with her and I don't want it to end. I even escort her to the after-party for *Babes in Toyland*, of which she danced a lead role. I think it's the first one I've done sober in two years. It is as bad as you might imagine, but I survive it and I'm glad to do it for her.

I text Ben before *Babes*, asking if I can drop by and talk sometime. He doesn't reply. He hasn't replied to either text despite dropping by the other day. He hasn't texted me since August and I mostly gave up in September at Rick's insistence. I texted to wish him a Happy Thanksgiving, but that's been all. Maybe he thought I'd given up. Rick says to leave it alone until I get to Step 8, but I feel like I'm amputating a limb, letting go of my best friend forever.

Christmas Eve, Alyse talks me into going to the Rinx at Village Center with her. Although I still don't see a lot of signs that she's made great friends with anyone in her class, she is popular at the rink because she is so good at skating and there's a little cadre of dancers all trying to outdo one another. It's been a while since I ice skated and my ankles and knees aren't up to it, so I take a break with a hot chocolate and watch Ben across the way. I don't want to ignore him because it feels like sulking and I'm not sulking. I know I deserve what happened last fall. I'm hoping I've earned a little redemption now.

"Hey," I say.

Ben's talking with Pamela, who scowls when she sees me. He looks over his shoulder, sighs and turns to face me.

"Hi." He doesn't sound angry. More like reserved. We've never been awkward with one another before. It feels weird and my cravings try to tell me it would be easier if I did this with something on board.

"How are you?" I can't meet his gaze. I stare at my toe trying to rub a hole in the floor.

"Okay. You?"

"Embarrassed."

"Yeah, well that will happen when you have public meltdowns." That's from Pamela, muttering behind him.

I don't recall any meltdowns. I drove into a tree. I'm not sure what she's talking about.

"I just – can we talk about the accident?"

Ben tilts his head sideways.

"I told you. I'm not interested in talking to you until you know what you did wrong."

"I do. The accident...it was --."

"Go away! Before I forget that we've been friends since kindergarten, and I want what's best for you – just go away."

Why is this sliding sideways?

"Can you let me apologize? I'm sorry --."

"No, you don't get to cheapen what you did by saying you're sorry for the ten millionth time."

I had this carefully thought-out speech, but I always pictured it at his home, not in a public place where I already feel eyes on me, and I screw it up. When I open my mouth to ask if we could talk later, he walks away without a word and I just feel empty.

My best friend is gone. He isn't even going to give me the chance to repair things like he promised back in August, and I don't know how to deal with it.

I text Vic, wave Alyse down and say we're going. She doesn't understand what upset me and I don't want to talk about it. I slam into the house and go up to my room. What happened after that? I honestly don't remember.

Self-Destructive Behavior

Alyse

I'm smelling all kinds of delicious fatty foods being baked in the kitchen and wondering if Peter has calmed down enough to talk to me yet. My phone rings. I look at my screen and answer the call.

"Hey, Ben. How are you?"

"Merry Christmas. I saw you skating at the Rinx. You make it look like dancing."

"Well, I am a dancer. Peter's home, you know?"

"I saw him tonight."

"He's doing better. Or he was. Something upset him tonight."

"Yeah, we talked. He tried to lay his bull-crap apology on me and – well, I'm not proud of how I acted. I didn't really give him a chance to speak, but he needs to quit calling it an accident because it wasn't."

"You could text him."

"I tried that. He's ignoring me. I guess I can't blame him since I've ignored him since August."

"He'll get over it. Peter's temper never lasts long."

"Yeah, unlike mine. Slow to anger and keep it going for months. You said he's been doing better? How?"

"I marked all the bottles before he got home and if he's drinking, he's not doing it from the bar."

"Really? Imagine that." Ben actually sounds like he's contemplating it.

"And he's been – I don't know – less self-absorbed. He's wanted to do what I want to do. He even sat through my entire performance last night and then went to the afterparty with me. It was painful for him, I could see, but he didn't complain. And he went ice skating with me today. It felt like having my brother back."

"Until he ran into me. Sorry about that."

I know Peter will forgive Ben for tonight's tiff and Ben is important to me too. He's been like a second big brother for years. So even though I think he should ease off Peter, I say what's expected of me.

"It's fine. He's asked about you all fall."

"Has he asked about Cheyenne?"

"Yes. I don't know a lot because we're not friends, but every time I've asked about her has been because he's asked."

"Oh, Aly, you have got to stop lying for him."

68

"I'm not." Peter's asked twice, then stopped when he realized I didn't know anything. Anytime I've heard anything, though, I told him. He was kind of standoffish when I texted him at school, but I'd use Cheyenne as an excuse to call and he'd listen and talk with me for a while. "Maybe you two should talk. I can ask him to call you, tell him you're sorry for losing it at the rink."

Ben hesitates for a long moment and then says, "I don't think you should get in the middle, Aly. I'll text what I have to say to him, and he can either respond or not."

"I hate that you two aren't friends anymore."

"Yeah, well, sometimes you can't fix things that are broken that badly. If he is legitimately straightening out, though ... I don't know. I'm sorry you're caught in the middle."

Ben wishes me a good night and then we hang up. I uncurl from the daybed and open a wooden box where a blunt of sativa awaits my evening relaxation.

I swirl around the room, caught up in the music. The song ends and I look at the door. Peter has sulked enough. His door is locked.

"Hey, open up!" I knock. No answer. "Peter, open the door." Silence. I bang harder, yell louder. Tilly comes up the backstairs. She's been our housekeeper for years and always seems to have her finger on Peter's pulse. I only just realized that she's only about seven years older than Peter. She seems so much older than us, but she's not. She wears a striped robe and slippers now.

"Alyse, stop with that racket. Your brother is probably sleeping. It's 11 o'clock at night."

"He's not answering, Tilly. Something's wrong."

Tilly gives me an annoyed look and starts to turn away, then frowns. She knocks, listens at the door. She digs into her pocket for a simple key ring. I know it's the master key to every door in the house.

"Peter, if you don't answer this door, I'm coming in." She waits about ten seconds and then inserts the key in the lock. "Peter, if you don't want me to invade your privacy, you need to answer me." I don't hear anything from the other side of the door. She turns the key.

Peter lays on his sofa, arm trailing to the floor, fingers loosely wrapped around a fifth of whiskey. Tilly shakes him and he doesn't react at all, but the bottle falls free of his lax grip. No liquid dribbles out of the bottle.

"Alyse, where's your phone?" Tilly sounds on the edge of frantic.

"My room."

"Then use Peter's." She thrusts it at me. "Call an ambulance and then call Vic and tell him I need him up here. He's barely breathing. We need to get him on his feet until an ambulance gets here. Tell the dispatcher it's alcohol poisoning." I stare at Peter's limp body as Tilly tries to tug him upright. "Alyse, do it now or your brother dies."

Tattoos Are Forever

Peter

Fine Line Body Artistry looks like an old barber shop except for the photos of tattoos all over the walls. The gal waiting on us has this incredible full arm sleeve and enough studs in her ears to set off an airport metal detector. I'm leaning on Amy because there's a possibility I'm a bit drunk. Well, yeah – a lot drunk.

Hey, a guy's got to celebrate taking midterms and passing them, especially when his grades haven't been spectacular this semester. Too much hanging out with girls like Amy who provide way too much beer on top of the bottle of bourbon I drank earlier in the day.

You remember Amy. I finally learned her name. She thinks I ought to get a tattoo to match hers. She's got a butterfly on her ass – something I probably would have noticed had she allowed me to take any initiative that night we tumbled in my bed. It's tasteful and she's taut, so it looks lovely. I finally saw it this afternoon when we screwed and got drunk in her room.

"I'm not getting' a buttafly." I'm slurring and having trouble focusing my eyes on the sample photos in the books. "Thah's pretty girlie."

"You sure you want to do this tonight?" The tattoo artist working on a grimacing football player in one of the three chairs looks over his client and fixes me with a bright blue gaze. "You seem pretty drunk and tattoos are forever."

I wipe a hand down my face. I know I'm not even going to remember this tomorrow. It's like a trip to Margaritaville.

"This one's nice." Amy points to a picture in the book – a wave and surfer. I like surfing. "Or you could put my name on something."

"Don't get awkward." She knows we're just hooking up. I like the phoenix. It reminds me of something, not sure what. Oh, yeah, Christmas Eve. "That one."

The woman behind the counter looks at it and nods, tells me how much the down will cost and about how long it will take to do.

"I need to suspense the charge with your card before he starts."

I hand over my card and my identification, making sure to grab the one that says I'm over 18. Heat starts to wash up my back and the room takes on a glow. I burp beer. I don't really like beer, though Amy buys the good stuff. Her dad's a big shot corporate lawyer and her allowance is as generous as mine. The cashier's still talking, something about risk of infection and keloids because I tan well. She frowns at the credit card machine.

I'm not even sure I want to do this. An hour ago, it seemed like a good idea at the college, but now that I've sobered up a little, I'm starting to get cold feet. Tattoos *are* forever and that buzzing sound from the barber's chair and the grimace of the guy being tattooed isn't inspiring my confidence. I'm not really afraid of pain, but I don't know that I want to volunteer for it either. As a dancer, I've experienced a lot of discomfort, but discomfort for art doesn't feel useless. I try to remember what the phoenix represents. I almost died, but I didn't. Is that a good enough reason to endure the pain? Maybe I'm smarter than the football player and I *should* be sober for this.

"Card's declined. Twice." I focus on the cashier, confused. "We can do it for cash."

"That's not possible." Amy sounds amused. "Do you know who his father is?"

I know how my father is, even if the casher doesn't.

"Stop." I gesture for the card and my ID. "My dad didn't want me to go to Mexico, so he maybe limited my card. It's fine. Bet if I check my email there's a train ticket home. I didn't really want to do this anyway. You were kind of taking advantage of my being drunk. Let's go."

Amy grimaces, but she's not down for long. If she can't mark me permanently, she can still have mind-blowing sex with me. Yeah, I'm drunk, but I'll be sober enough by the time we get back to her room to rock her world. My legs aren't working so good but I'm not falling down yet. We head back to the college. I'm starting to feel nauseous, alternatively hot and cold. There's a party going on in the main hall, so I grab a couple of cold beers for her room and she grabs one for herself. The fizzy golden elixir quenches my thirst and turns my legs into noodles. I'm standing at the top of the landing, confused because the walls are bulging and rippling, and people sound like they're behind a glass wall. I drain the beer bottle, let it fall to the floor.

"There you are." Amy comes under my arm. "You overshot my floor. Come on."

She starts to turn me toward the stairs and the whole floor tilts wildly to the left and that's the last thing I remember of that night.

Reconnecting

Ben

I'm negotiating LIE traffic at rush hour on the first Friday of Spring Break when my phone dings. The road in front of me is a parking lot. I should have taken the ferry, but I wanted to stop in Manhattan to pick up something for my dad. Since nobody is moving, I answer the call.

"Hey, hey, hey." Trevor chuckles into the phone.

"Hey, yourself. Long time no hear."

"Been busy. Sorry. You dance all day, perform all night, and forget to call people when they're awake. I'm home for a while. Figured I'd check in with everyone. Peter didn't answer back. You talking to him yet?"

"Not really."

"Why not?"

"My fault mostly. He's tried and I've resisted. You hear from him?"

"Ships in the night. He texts me when I'm asleep. I text him when he's in class. Sounds like he's trying to clean up his act."

"Yeah, that's what he says to me too, but the last text I got from him he sounded weird – like maybe he was drunk."

"Freshmen at Yale. Isn't that a requirement?"

"He shouldn't, Trevor. Not after Cheyenne. Anyway, what's up with you? How's Joffrey?"

There's a long pause. Traffic creeps forward infinitesimally. I creep forward too.

"Not working out. They had other plans and so I'm home for a while and then I'm trying out for this off-Broadway troupe."

"Cool, I guess. I thought you were really excited about Joffrey."

"I was, but you know, they misrepresented themselves."

The hairs on my forearms tingle as my bullshit meter maxes out. Trevor and Pete share some similarities, drunkenness and carelessness with people, but Trevor remembers his stupidity, so his apologies are real. This feels like a lie and while Trevor will lie to himself all day long, he doesn't usually lie to others. Maybe I'm wrong. Maybe I'm just bruised from my association with Pete.

"I guess the dance studio is glad to have you back."

"Sure. And I'm glad to be back for now. I'm exhausted. I think I got four hours of sleep a night since August. So, how are you and Pam?"

"She met some guy at Brown and so – yeah. You hear anything through your dad about how Cheyenne is doing? Mom says she's stringing words into sentences and they make sense now. She's reading, writing, walking again."

Governor Wyngate asked Mel Grey to coordinate his giving to Cheyenne's family and Trevor has mad spy skills.

"Dad says she has got some real rage issues."

"Wouldn't you?"

There's that long pause again.

"Yeah. I think I'd curl up and want to die if I couldn't dance. Not so much professionally, but just – yeah."

"So maybe you understand why I'm still angry at Pete?"

"I don't think he meant to do it, Ben." There's a sound in the background like someone is talking to him. "I'm supposed to be driving one of my sisters somewhere, so I should go."

"Yeah. I'll give you a call when I get to Port Mal. We should go do something."

"Yeah. Mountain biking – you, me and Pete – BJ's Way."

"Not sure about Pete, Trev. I'm sorry, but I just --. You don't have to take sides."

"Keeping you apart feels like taking sides. I get why you were so pissed last fall. He wasn't getting it at first. But he had a concussion, in a lot of pain,

79

and on painkillers, so maybe he needed some time to sort it out. He's been different since. I mean, maybe if you gave him a chance, you'd see that."

I sigh. Traffic's starting to clear ahead.

"Maybe. I gotta drive now and so do you, so – I'll call you tomorrow."

"Sounds good."

We hang up. That last text from Pete – maybe it didn't make sense because he's flailing, no longer certain of what I want from him. I'm not sure I know anymore myself. I join a stream of vehicles headed east and resolve to think about it later.

Light in the Darkness

Peter

I should be lounging on a beach in Mexico with a hot girl and some Dos Equis, hold the lime, but instead, I'm here in chilly Lake Ronkonkoma waiting for my ride from the train. Not having a driver's license sucks. My whole life sucks.

I sip black coffee from a paper cup, shielding my eyes from the weak spring sun behind my darkest Oakleys. Two days since my recommitment to sobriety and I really want a drink and I'm not talking coffee, but the fact is Rick is right – I'm pissing my life away and I want to stop. I do!

If I'd gone to Mexico this week, I'd probably end up in an Acapulco hospital. I have a lot of tolerance for drinking, but since Christmas I've been forgetting to stop and that's a problem that interferes with breathing. I've forced Rick to put his finger down my throat twice, the last time three days ago. He stayed up all night worrying I'd die.

Coming home might not be the best choice, but the dorms closed this morning and my credit card

81

stopped working three days ago. Maybe it's drying out too. I'm kind of glad it did because Amy, that hot blonde from the second floor, talked me into a lot of beer and a tattoo. Fortunately for me, my card declined. Unfortunately, I still had beer.

I see the bronze Mercedes SUV pass by in the street, but I hope to talk to Alyse without any prying ears, so I lean back and wait, mildly nauseous and with a headache working into something massive behind my right eye.

Alyse comes in the door, her black braid stark against her ivory sweater dress over black leggings. She turns every head in the room and makes every man in the room except me horny as dogs. If she weren't my sister, I'd probably feel that adoration too, she is that gorgeous. I hope someday to meet a girl that hits all the buttons like she does.

So far, things haven't worked out with my girlfriends. There's something about relationships I don't get. I blame it on our mom, who cheated on our father and left us here in chilly Long Island the year I turned 12. That first opposite sex relationship not working out for me set the mood going forward, I guess.

Alyse sees me and turns up the heat on her smile – before a crease of concern mars that perfect forehead. I'm a mess, I know, and she knows me oh-so-well.

She orders coffee without coming to see me and I contemplate the tabletop until she sits down across from me.

"You look like crap." Those are literally the first words she says to me since I went back to school in January. I pissed her off by scaring the hell out of her and ruining Christmas. She's replied to my texts, but my personal battles so absorbed me the last two months, I haven't texted that often.

"You don't, little sis. Winter agrees with you." She doesn't hold her tan like I do, but our mother's Greek coloring makes it look like she sees some sun even if she hasn't for months.

"Are you drunk?"

"Not even close. Want to smell my breath?"

"Would that do me any good?"

I laugh because of how close she got to the truth. I taste aldehydes on my tongue. I'm still detoxing, so she probably wouldn't be able to tell.

"Probably not, but really, I've not had a drink for two days."

"So, what's with the sunglasses?"

"Headache."

"How come you're here? I thought you were going to Mexico."

"Dad suspended my card. Besides, I think I need a break."

"From what?"

"Partying. Your coffee's ready."

The barista waves her to the counter, and she comes back with three cups. She sets one in front of me. It's my favorite – white chocolate breve – but my stomach isn't ready for it yet. I try to figure out if the third cup is for the driver. I'm the one who usually treats the staff like humans. Alyse – not so much.

"How's school?" she asks.

"I got straight As last semester."

"Dad mentioned. How's it going now?"

"That's why I need a break from partying."

She sighs.

"Does Dad know yet?"

"No, and I did okay with my midterms, so I shouldn't actually be flunking any classes. He doesn't need to know if I get my grades up from Ds by studying."

She gives me this dismissive look and my heart hurts. She's been the one person left who believes in me and that has just been lacking since Christmas.

"What's different from last semester?"

I sigh. How to explain it to her? I've never admitted to her that I can't control my drinking. I've only ever admitted it in 12 Step and not all that recently. I haven't even told Rick this time. I rub my forehead rather than answer.

"He's going to ask."

"He's up in Albany and we're here."

"You never know when he might drop in. You're going to have to work your charms on Tilly, so she doesn't tell on you."

I've got Tilly wrapped around my pinkie, so even feeling crappy, I don't worry that I couldn't do it. I lean my head back against the seat and watch as a girl enters the cafe. She has brown hair loose around her shoulders and legs starting at her chin. I'd say she's attractive, but not Alyse quality, until she looks our direction and her face lights up. Her full lips curve perfectly, and light shines from her hazel eyes.

Alyse shifts to the left to give her the space on the outside.

"Lily Wexler, meet my brother Peter."

"Hi," she greets, sitting down. Fortunate I wore sunglasses because I can keep my admiration laidback. "Nice to meet you." Something silent passes between them and Lily wraps her hand around the third cup of coffee. I used to treat my friends all the time too, until I realized it makes less-wealthy people feel like crap. Seriously, they aren't grateful. They feel obligated.

"You too. School friends?" She's way too young for me and I'm way too sick to do anything about it, but my anatomy knows this is a pretty girl I'd like to spend time with if she were a year or two older and I felt less like roadkill.

"We're in English together." Alyse answers so Lily can sip coffee. Alyse gets this weird look in her eyes. My head hurts too much to analyze it.

"So, Lily Wexler, how haven't I met you before?" Our mother never taught us how to socialize, so Alyse needs to be reminded, gently, that I'm talking to Lily, not her. Lily shoots a glance sideways. She's used to Alyse monopolizing a conversation. Then she smiles at me slightly. We're on the same wavelength.

"We're kind of new friends." Alyse's a sophomore, but I gauge Lily to be a freshman. They couldn't be any further apart since our high school isn't combined with a middle school. "I'm new in town. Just moved in this semester."

"Where you from before?"

"Manchester, New Hampshire." I remember a flash of an iconic scene from the movie *Peyton Place*, which I watched with Rick one night after I asked about his hometown. It was a soap opera. I don't think I know anything more about Manchester than I did before. Beautiful scenery, though.

"What brings your family to Port Mallory?"

"My brother is at Cedar Sinai so my father took a transfer here so we can stay near."

She looks sad, but it's rude to ask medical questions, right? So, I don't. She sips her coffee, so I sip mine and my stomach turns ominously. I spend the next couple of minutes trying unsuccessfully to follow what they're saying. Fortunately, Alyse knows me oh-so-well.

"Your headache getting worse?"

"Yeah. And, I should probably take a nap so I can hit the books tonight."

"We're dropping Lily at her house."

I leave the coffee and climb into the front seat with Vic the driver, so I don't have to listen to their chatter. My head pulses by then and I just want to sit quietly with my eyes closed. Vic asks me if I'm going to be sick and I assure him I won't. Vic has picked me up drunk before, so his skepticism doesn't surprise.

I kind of doze off until the car pulls to a stop and I open my eyes to watch Alyse and Lily saying goodbye. Surprise, Lily lives right next door to Ben's house. I get out to get in the back.

"Nice meeting you, Lily. Maybe I'll see you again sometime."

I look past her shoulder and see Ben getting into his car. I'm so tempted to go talk to him, but I don't want to be humiliated in front of a pretty girl, so I don't. We aren't back in the car longer than a breath and Alyse turns toward me.

"What do you think?"

"Think?" I'm not doing a lot of that right now. My head hurts. "About?"

"She's great, right? I saw that stunned look when you first saw her. Even hungover, you saw it."

"I'm not hungover." I'm not, but she doesn't believe me. "She's pretty. Young."

"It's not quite three years."

"I gotta get my grades up before I do anything else — girls included. Besides, I'm only here a week. Let's go home."

I just want some peace and quiet and a chance to get my feet under me. Alyse may think ignoring my problems will work out for me, but I'm kind of tired of that and I really want my life back, so I'm done ignoring them.

Beware the Bad Boy

Lily

I look up from my homework assignment when the doorbell rings. My parents are visiting Bram at the hospital, so I answer the door. Ben Anderson stands on the porch, hand on the back of his neck.

"Hey," I greet. "Who comes home for Spring Break?"

"Broke college students with papers due next week. Can I come in?"

"My folks aren't home. Can we sit out here?"

It isn't warm but keeping my promise to my parents feels important. Ben nods. I grab a jacket from the hooks by the doors and join him on the porch swing.

"Remember when I told you about my friend having surgery?"

"Yeah. Susan, right?"

"Cheyenne. She had a car accident because of a drunk driver. She was having her third surgery that day and she's getting ready for her fourth surgery now. That should fix all the bones in her face and then she'll start the scar corrections."

"That's too bad."

"It's been a sucky seven months for her, and she's probably got another year of pain and people looking at her like she's a freak."

"Are you wanting me to visit her in the hospital or --?"

"No. She wouldn't be your cup of tea. She's not in the best mood these days. I'm warning you. You're friends with Alyse Wyngate, yeah?"

"We have English together and she's been so nice to the new girl."

"Alyse collects admirers, but she's not dangerous. Her brother is."

"Peter?"

"Pete was the idiot driving the car when Cheyenne was hurt."

I remember my cousin Jon hungover once and now I recognize the symptoms from Peter's behavior earlier in the day.

"I guess that explains why we were picking him up at the train station. He wasn't driving."

"Yeah, he lost his license for drunk driving. But he's telling everyone the brakes failed, so he has absolutely no clue about what he did wrong. Obviously, I can't tell you what to do, but I hope you'll keep that in mind if Alyse and you stay friends."

"Why wouldn't we stay friends?"

"She's kind of fickle. She can be a great friend when she's happy with you, but she can turn on a dime."

"You sound like you think you're an expert."

"Pete and I were best friends since kindergarten. I grew up with him and Alyse. He used to be a really good friend. Last couple of years, though --. I tried to stick in, but after Cheyenne – I wish I knew what to do to get my friend back, but I don't want to lose any other friends because he can't handle his booze."

I trust Ben and it occurs to me that Peter is too old for me anyway. I can hear Dad telling me that I should date boys my own age – not that Peter showed any signs of wanting to ask me out or anything. He was politely hungover.

Ben asks me how Bram is doing, and I explain that he's coming home for a visit this week. He suggests his brother Wes might make a good friend.

"That might be complicated. He's paralyzed on one side and he can't talk. They say he's still kind of comatose."

"He'll heal." I want to believe Ben's assurance, but it's been nearly a year and a lot of setbacks along the way. Ben pulls his phone out of his pocket. "I gotta go. Enjoy the rest of your day."

Balancing Act

Peter

My dad keeps an open bar and algebra goes down better with a back of bourbon. But I'm not drinking. I promised myself and I'm on Day 4. My handwriting looks wavering, but no more headache and I actually want breakfast when I wake up at eleven o'clock.

My bedroom just seems too small, close, like there's no air, so I take my book down to the comfy couch in the den. I make good progress for a while, but then I get thirsty. You know ... THIRSTY! I get into the minifridge for a club soda, but then end up staring at the beautiful caramel of the Four Roses, my tongue getting drier and drier. I leave my book on the end table and take my bottle of club soda out to the patio.

It's too early for roses, so all that's out here is thorns, which feels like a metaphor for my life. I drop the empty bottle at the portico in front of the house and just start walking. There's a slight breeze off the sea with a hint of cold to it, but the sun battles it back enough that my hands aren't hurting.

I choose east because – yeah. I don't know. Maybe I know I'm headed toward Ben's house. Maybe it's just a random choice. I hate walking, but I need to burn nervous energy. That's what Rick would tell me, and his advice got me through four months of not drinking.

Ben's house is on a dead-end road and my dad owns property across the road and at the end. I know as I walk that sooner or later, I won't be able to pretend I'm just walking by. And, it is dumber than dumb because I'm four days sober and I couldn't handle Ben's anger when I'd had four months. I have my head down, thinking about calling Rick when I sense movement ahead of me and look up just in time to avoid being run over by a bicycle. I turn sideways and step back to the right side of the path while the girl on the bike, clearly surprised to see me, slams on the brakes immediately, sliding on sand off the far edge of the path and ditching in the dirt beyond.

"Are you okay?" I lift the bike off her.

"I think so." She's uncertain. "I'm so sorry. I didn't see you."

"I'm fine. Little worried about you. Nothing broken?"

She has a scrape on one elbow and then she rolls up her yoga pants to find a rapidly forming

94

bruise on the side of her knee. She starts shaking then, stripping off her helmet and putting her head on her knees.

"I could have hurt both of us." Tears brim in her hazel eyes.

Yeah, I could have and all because I was walking in the middle of the path, but she doesn't need to feel guilty.

"But you didn't. Soon as you stop shaking, I'll walk you home, Lily."

She looks at me, surprised.

"Right. Peter. Alyse's brother."

"I am." There's a small first aid kit and tire repair kit strapped to her drop frame, so I unzip it and find an alcohol wipe and a Band Aid to treat her elbow. I then lend her my arm so she can stand up.

"I'll walk you home," I offer. She limps and I push the bike.

"I've just never seen anyone on this bike path. Once it goes into the woods, everybody follows the street."

"You aren't worried about muggers?"

"You were walking here. Are you a mugger?"

I laugh nervously.

"Apparently I'm an obstacle in the way of bicyclists."

"You were in the middle of the path. I was in the middle of the path. Maybe if we'd both been to the right --."

"Like driving. Good idea."

She winces, but not because of her knee and I figure she knows. Cheyenne made me infamous in a way I wasn't infamous before and there's nothing I can do about it. But I don't want to ruin the mood, so I don't let on that I know she knows. We emerge from the woods with just a few blocks more to her house.

"You're in college, right?" she asks.

"Freshman at Yale."

"You like it?"

"I wanted to go to Columbia, but my dad's a Yale alum and I'm not 18, so I didn't get a veto."

"What's at Columbia that isn't at Yale?"

"I don't know." It's true and I laugh. "I didn't get to go."

"Will you when you turn 18?"

"I doubt it. I recognize I'm getting a good education and I've made some friends, so insisting upon Columbia would just be sulking."

And, there's that nagging concern that I might not even pass this semester, but that's another thing I'm not going to mention to her.

"So, now that I've mugged you in the woods, I guess we know each other well enough for me to ask – why's your brother in the hospital so long that your father can arrange a transfer and buy a house?"

She smiles at the "mugging" joke, but now gives me a long sideways glance.

"You and Alyse are a lot alike."

"We were both raised by our parents." Alyse and I aren't that alike. I doubt she's ever asked about her friend's brother. She feigns compassion for me occasionally.

"Curiosity killed the cat, but he died satisfied." That's one of my favorite sayings – courtesy of Granddad Mike – and I guess Alyse has adopted it. So, Lily is worthy of feigning too? Interesting.

"That too." She smiles now, then sighs. "Bram had a stroke last summer."

Whoa! I think I expected a car accident or cancer.

"Wow. How old is he?"

"He was ten. And, it can happen at any age."

"But usually when you're old."

"Yeah, usually, but not always."

I try to imagine if that happened to Alyse, how would I feel, but I just can't.

"That's sucks. Is he going to be okay?"

"He's coming out of the coma and starting to take a few steps. He can't talk or use his right arm and – well, they don't know." Now I really can't imagine Alyse in that condition. "Or aren't telling me."

"Parents like to protect their kids, I guess." My dad tried to do that with us when he and Mom were

97

divorcing, but I'd already known a lot because I'd walked in on her and Sam.

We walk most of a block without talking. I'm freaked out by awkward silences, but I can't think of anything to say at first and then something pops into my head.

"You must really miss him, the way he was before."

She stops walking and stares at me.

"Nobody has brought that up. That's – insightful."

Yeah, I'm all over insightful when I'm sober and I've gotten past the worst part of being stupid. I wait for her to continue onto her house, considering whether I should ask her to switch arms because my shoulder is starting to complain. It's no longer injured, but it doesn't like to be held in the same position for too long. But since she's turned, it's had a chance to stretch and now when we continue forward, it doesn't complain anymore.

"Do you know who Alyse is dating?" I figure Alyse's friend will know and might not keep it a secret. Alyse has been cagey about it.

"Yeah. Um – gosh. I haven't met him, but she's said his name a few times. He's your age, I think. Thomas – no, Travis --."

I know a couple of Tom/Thomases and no Travis from Port Mallory. The Tom is seriously dating from forever ago and both Thomases are gone to distant colleges. Then I think of someone with a similar name.

"Trevor?"

"Yeah, that's it."

Trevor's a dancer too. A friend since elementary school, he went off to dance with Joffrey Ballet, but he stopped posting photos about that a couple of months ago. Now I need to have a safe sex conversation with my little sister. It kind of bothers me that she might be getting laid. While I wish Trevor has learned new respect for his women, I think I might need to settle for hoping he just uses a condom.

"You okay? You just went somewhere for a moment." Lily's frowning at me.

"Sorry, just thinking of some big brother duties. When you haven't got a mother and your father is never around, you sometimes have to have conversations outside the norm."

Her forehead creases. I've perplexed her. Maybe Alyse isn't baring all her secrets. Or maybe Lily's worried she'll never get a chance to have such conversations with her brother. We reach the end of her driveway. Before we get more than two steps off the sidewalk, Ben pops up in my peripheral vision.

"What happened?"

"She tanked off her bike. I'm just helping her ho--."

"And you made her walk? What's hurt, Lily?"

"Just a bruise on my knee. Really, he was being a gentleman."

"Yeah, I'll bet. Let's get you into the house."

"Peter, thank you for helping me." Lily's compliment trails over Ben's shoulder as he scoops her up in his arms to carry her into the house, leaving me standing there with the bike. Apparently, he knows the way around her house so well that he knows the side door will be unlocked. I follow, stopping at the door to stare into the garage. They've already gone into what is probably the kitchen. I lean the bike in the back corner where I figure it will be out of the way if a car pulls in.

Recognizing I've been forgotten, I consider just walking home, but Helen, Ben's mother, waves at me from their porch.

"Is she okay?" She joins me on the sidewalk.

"Big bruise on her knee from tanking off her bike, but she'll be okay. Ben's kind of acting like I might hurt her."

"Ben's upset with you, Peter, and you should know why."

"I do. I screwed up. He's right to be mad. I just hope he gets over it."

"It's going to take time."

Rick pointed out before that I lack patience. I want things and I want them now and I'm willing to lie and cheat to get them right now. It's a problem.

"So, I should head home."

"Where's your car?" Helen seems perplexed.

"I lost my license coz of Cheyenne." She frowns. Rick would say pay attention to what people are telling you. "I said that wrong. I lost my license for DUI. I don't get it back until August."

"That's better, Peter." She touches my cheekbone. "You not sleeping?"

"I wasn't feeling well for a few days. Like I said, I need to get back home. There's this stack of textbooks calling my name."

As I walk away, I think about bourbon. Why go through this if there's no reward? Surely life isn't meant to be this hard. I'm on the bike path in the woods when I decide to dial Rick's number.

"Hey." I'm a little afraid he might be mad at me too. He yelled at me when he dragged me out of bed the other day to make it to my last midterm. I've done a lot of things hungover in my life, but a chemistry test ranks as one of the harder accomplishments. Getting a C on the test totally shocked me.

Rick sort of talked to me that night he put a finger down my throat after I got wasted with Amy. He told me I scared him, and I scared myself enough to reconsider sobriety.

"Hey yourself. This isn't a drunk dial, is it?"

"Nope. Four days." That's not quite the longest I've been sober since Christmas, but it's an accomplishment and Rick understands that.

"Good for you. So how bad is that open bar at your dad's tempting you?"

"Like I have a hard-on for a naked babe."

"Suggestion. Ask that housekeeper of yours to lock it up."

"Yeah?" It never occurred to me before that I could do that. "Yeah, probably a good idea."

"Nothing wrong with putting temptation a little further away at this stage. What else are you doing to help yourself?"

"I'm on a really long walk."

It's starting to get cold as clouds pile up. I pull the sleeve of my sweatshirt over the hand that's not holding my phone.

"Good. What have you eaten today?"

"Breakfast."

"No lunch?"

"I got up at 11, so no. But I'll eat dinner. I actually want to eat today. I've had a three-day-long hangover."

"Yeah, that's withdrawal just like in January and probably in August, but you were too bruised to recognize it."

Withdrawal is tough with a hepatic liver. The ultrasound I had in early December showed no swelling, but after my Christmas stupidity the hepatitis returned. I haven't really given it time to recover. Of course, I didn't stop drinking after my Boxing Day release from the hospital. I got wasted with Finn on New Year's Eve, spent a week drawing down Dad's bourbon supply, and got wasted again at the dorm's welcome-back party. I then tried to quit and puked for two days. According to the internet that is a sign of alcohol dependency and that doesn't bode well for my future.

"You sleeping?"

"Not great, but yeah." I hear music in the background. "Where are you?"

"Florida Keys. I'm kicked back on a beach near one of those outdoor bars that serves umbrella drinks."

My tongue sticks to the roof of my mouth. I couldn't possibly be there and not drink. Rick isn't really an alcoholic, though I know he's drinking virgins because he's so serious about never touching heroin again that he doesn't even drink caffeine. I kind of resent that he can be that close to temptation and just blow it off. Rick's also psychic.

"Last year, we came down here too and my brother had to sit on me for half a day because I really wanted to screw myself up." I probably look stupid with my mouth hanging open, but his mind reading skills always surprise me. "I don't usually crave alcohol. It made zip sense, but there you have it. I felt fine when I woke up the next day and we had a great vacation after that."

"Why were you doing Spring Break when you weren't in school?"

"My parents thought I'd keep my brother from being stupid. My parents might not always be that smart in understanding my issues. They mean well, though."

I liked his parents at Thanksgiving. As holidays go, theirs was fairly stress-free.

"You got anyone who is really mad at you?"

"I did. My sister. But we're good now. She doesn't really wholly trust me yet, but she talks to me now."

That must be the sister who got stranded by tornados in Minneapolis.

"So, what are you drinking?" He laughs, knowing how my mind works.

"Iced tea with fruit juice in it. And I got a good book. Getting a great tan while little bro sleeps off his hangover. We went dancing last night. That was a lot of fun. Met a couple of fun babes."

"I thought you didn't approve of hookups."

"Did I say it ended up in bed? I don't approve of anything that numbs me out and I did try to warn you that the sex was going to walk you into a relapse."

"That's not what happened."

"It is. Instead of working on what you needed to so you could fix your damaged relationships, you were scratching itches with pussy and that was bound to screw you up."

I sigh. He's right. I know it. I even knew it then, but I just wanted to feel better. I switch the phone to my other ear and cover my free hand. I feel droplets of rain as I walk, but I'm turning toward home.

"I know I can't control my drinking."

"Good. So, are there any meetings where you are?"

"I don't --." That's not entirely true. I looked them up when I came for Christmas. The closest is Setauket. The information is still in my phone. "I can go tonight. And, I'll have Tilly lock up the bar."

"Good choices."

We talk a few minutes and then I tell Rick to go back to his book. I walk into the den to find my books exactly where I left them. The house feels empty, so I'm not surprised to discover Tilly and Alyse aren't home.

My mouth dries out immediately and every nerve fiber demands I go back to the bar and have a drink, just one drink. I have four hours to a meeting and nobody to stop me from drinking from an open bar. This morning, I filled a water bottle and I half-drain it now. It helps, but not enough. I open my algebra book and try to concentrate on one of the problems. I'm going to flunk the semester if I don't concentrate on schoolwork and that means staying away from the bar. I draw a blank on how to work the problem. It's about balance. Equations are always about balance. My head starts to ache.

I open my phone screen and text Vic.

> PETER - I need a ride at about 7:30 tonight.

A = 5. Now solve B.

> VIC - Your father says you should be home from 8 to 8.

Fatherliness. My father absolutely sucks at being a parent. He couldn't figure out timing if my life depended on it. And tonight, it probably does. I'm working the Steps and he stymies me with his stupid rules. I want an excuse, but fuck, he doesn't have to give me one.

I open my contacts to text Tilly.

> PETER - Vic is refusing to give me a ride somewhere tonight. Can you help me?

B = 7

> TILLY - To where?

C = -35

I don't want to tell her, but I'm not getting to Setauket without a ride.

> PETER - I want to make an AA meeting. Dad would be okay with that.

I do two more problems before she replies to me.

TILLY - Vic will drive you there and drive you
back.

That's what I asked for, but now it feels like
slavery.

PETER - Yeah.

My headache resolves and I'm suddenly able to
concentrate on algebra again ... for the next hour
until I'm hit by an even bigger craving. I head
toward the den and am stunned to discover Tilly
locked the bar without my asking. Of course, that's
the last thing I want right now, even as I know it's
what's best for me. A locked bar doesn't take the
craving away, but it keeps the craving from winning
and gets me to the meeting that night which gets
me through the night. One day at a time? Fuck, I'm
like two hours at a time.

Royal Treatment

Lily

I love going to the Wyngate house. I feel like royalty when I'm there. The couches are down-upholstered, and the carpets are real wool Orientals. Alyse treats me like an honored guest. We eat off bone china and drink from crystal glasses. Peter wasn't here when I arrived last night, and he went right to his room when he got home. Now we're eating croissants with actual coffee when he comes down to breakfast, barefoot, dressed in flannel lounge pants and a t-shirt with an off-color joke of a type my parents would never let me or my brothers wear.

"How goes the schoolwork war?" I ask.

"It's going. You two sounded like you had a lot of fun last night."

"You can't hear us from your bedroom," Alyse counters.

"I can when I'm in the hall. I got a little restless last night, so I passed by a few times."

"English is exhilarating?" I suggest.

"No, but chemistry is boring, and I needed to stretch my legs. Who's that new band you were listening to?" He hums a few bars. He has a good voice, a great sense of rhythm. Their mother is a pianist. Alyse dances but claims she doesn't really sing. Maybe Peter got the talent. Alyse provides the name of the band and he searches on his phone. "Cool. Too bad I can't download anything right now."

"Dad's really locked you out?"

"Yeah. Can't really blame him. I burned through my allowance this month. I just wasn't paying attention and he wants me to act like a grownup, so --. It'll be fine. I'll do better next month." He sighs. "Nice seeing you again, Lily. When you take her home, I'd like to catch a ride with."

"Sure. It'll be about 2 o'clock."

Bram's coming home for an overnight. My parents expect me home about three. Peter leaves us, taking his coffee, croissant and fruit with him. We paint each other's nails and then it's time to go.

"How come your brother can't drive us?" I believe Ben, but since hanging out last night, I'm starting to doubt.

"Dad took his car away," Alyse answers.

"Why?"

"Peter did something stupid and our father believes in discipline."

"Obviously. Is he okay?"

"Peter? Yeah. He's fine."

Peter comes around the corner, dressed in jeans, a t-shirt and light jacket. I start guiltily and he laughs.

"Caught you talking about how fine I am, huh?"

He is fine – like a Greek statue, intense green eyes, high cheekbones and a full mouth. I wonder why he wants to go with us. He tells jokes on the ride over. When we get there, he tells Vic the driver he will walk back and heads up the Andersons' driveway.

"Is he going to visit Ben?" Alyse nods. "Ben's still really angry at him."

"Peter's stubborn that way," Alyse explains. Her forehead creases as she watches him walk. She is one of the prettiest girls I've ever met – black hair, blue eyes, porcelain skin and a great body. "If hanging out with your brother gets too boring, give me a call. We can go to a movie or something."

"Sounds good." Truthfully, I want to spend time with Bram. He can't carry on a conversation or do much for himself, but he's home and that means he's getting better. I know Alyse wouldn't understand, so I don't argue with her. I promise I'll call her and go into the house to prepare for Bram's homecoming.

Mendings

Peter

Helen Anderson opens the door with a sigh. "You are a glutton for punishment."

"Can I talk to him, please?"

"I can get him for you, but he doesn't want to see you and you can't make him listen." Since Christmas, I've tried texting Ben a few times, but he never answers. According to my phone history, none of them were drunk texts, so I'm hoping if I apologize, he'll listen.

"Please. Helen, I'm just trying to salvage something out of this year. I know I screwed up and I just – Ben said he'd listen if I knew what I did wrong. And I think I do. Please."

She gestures for me to come into the house and I anxiously stand in the living room waiting for Ben to come out. I feel like I might vibrate right through the wall, I'm so nervous. Ben comes into the living room frowning. That about represents my life right now.

"Hey, Pete. You here to tell me more lies?"

"Don't be like that, Ben, please. Just listen for a minute. I promise I'm trying."

Ben sighs and rolls his eyes. He's changed a lot since last summer, gotten a little taller, filled out across the shoulders. He's clearly not spent the last two months drunk or hungover.

"Go on. Tell me the latest bullshit."

It isn't a great way to start the conversation and I know the Andersons keep a small stash of whiskeys in a cabinet by the fridge. I imagine I can smell them and that distracts me.

"I know I screwed up. Yeah, the car had a mechanical problem, but I was drinking and so – she got hurt because of me. And, I'm trying, Ben. I am."

He hesitates. I don't know what to say beyond what I just did – the carefully crafted, if inelegantly performed speech that I had planned to give him on Christmas Break. In the short silence that follows, he tries to look into my soul.

"How are you trying, Pete?"

I could tell him about AA and Rick and how hard it is to go five days without a drink. Would that make a difference or just make me look weak? I don't know, so I don't do it. Maybe I'm still a little ashamed that I can't stay sober without a crutch and I sure think Ben will scoff.

"I was hoping that maybe you'd tell her that I'm sorry. They won't let me call her, but you could. I just need --."

"—to realize that she doesn't want to hear from you. Until you can stop making excuses, I don't want to hear it."

What? I'm not making excuses. I'm trying to make amends.

"I'm trying, Ben. I am."

"From my perspective, Pete, you're just trying to get out of the trouble you put yourself in."

"I don't understand, Ben. What am I missing?"

"Seriously. You're still an Olympic liar."

I don't know what he means. I'm working on being sober and I'm trying to be honest. Why can't he give me a little credit for trying?

"Just go." He shakes his head like I'm the dumbest thing he's ever encountered, but then his face softens a little. "Next time, when you think you've got it figured out, just text me. Or email me. Because this way – even if you're serious – you end up getting hurt and I don't want to have to do this every time you think you've got it figured out."

"I just – why can't you give me a little bit of a break?"

"Has anyone showed you photos of Cheyenne's face?"

No, of course not.

"I'm not allowed to see her." Even to me, it sounds like an excuse.

"Why don't you ask your father to show you some pictures? Just stop hiding from it, Pete. Maybe we can talk after. Now go away."

I sigh because I know there isn't anything I can say. I walk out the side door, thinking my life's over. My eyes fall on Lily getting mail at the street and I get an idea.

Meeting

Lily

I smile at Peter as he moves to meet me on the walkway.

"Visiting Ben?"

"Trying. So, your brother's home?"

"My parents are getting him settled. You really going to walk home?"

"Yeah. How do you like living here?"

"I miss winter."

"Winter? We have winter."

"No. You have freeze, thaw, rain, freeze, thaw."

"That's winter."

"Not like New Hampshire. We get snow."

"We get snow. White stuff on the ground and everything. It just doesn't last."

"Not a skier, I guess."

"I've gone skiing in the White Mountains. It's beautiful ... and cold ... and ... yeah. So, you miss that?" He makes a face like he doesn't know what to make of that. We laugh.

"You want to come in?"

"And – meet your parents?" He looks toward Ben's house and then shrugs. "Sure."

We enter by the side door, chatting as we go, taking our time. When we walk up into the kitchen, my mother turns from the stove. She's a natural redhead who has started to gray at the temples.

"Who is your friend, Lily?"

"Peter, Alyse's brother."

"Nice to meet you."

"Nice to meet you too, Mrs. Wexler."

There's a banging noise behind us, and Peter turns to where Bram struggles to wheel himself through the door from the living room. His hair's long enough now that it almost covers the massive scar on the left side of his head. His right arm curls up against his stomach. He can push the chair with his feet – mostly his left one – and his left hand. His steering sucks so he has hung up on the door frame.

Wes blinks at us, lips drawing tight. I freeze, not knowing what to say or do. Peter flashes a distressed look at me, but then he smiles and looks right at Bram.

"Is this Bram?" I nod. Peter holds out his left hand to Bram. "I'm Peter." Bram blinks a few times before shaking hands with Peter. Then a ghost of a half-smile plucks at the left side of his mouth.

"Lily, can you get him to go back to the living room?" Mom asks. "Dinner will be about half an hour, but I don't know how to explain that to him."

I move behind the wheelchair to grab the handles, but Bram grunts as if in protest and grabs the wheel rim.

"Whoa, careful there," Peter advises. "No need for broken fingers. Bram, you want to show me the rest of the house?" He pantomimes.

"He doesn't really understand," Mom warns as Bram backs the wheelchair up. Peter smiles over his shoulder at her and follows me into the living room.

"So, is he home permanently?"

"Not yet, but he's moving that direction. Maybe another month."

"So, this is what — like a vacation?"

"Kind of. When he's come before, there's been a therapist watching to see what his difficulties are, so they can work on it in rehab."

"Wow. That sucks." Peter sits down on the ottoman so he's on Bram's level. "Bet you're tired of hospitals."

Bram half-smiles again.

"He seems to understand you." Bram seriously stares at Peter's face like he's trying to catch meaning. "The doctors say he doesn't understand anyone."

"Maybe he understands some of it."

Bram passes his hand over the side of his head. "What's that scar from?"

"He had surgery."

"For what?"

119

"When you have a stroke, your brain swells. If the bone is still there, it causes more damage, so they removed it for a while and then put it back when the swelling went down."

"Wow, that's a lot to go through." Bram strains as if to read Peter's expressions while we talk some more. Peter gets a few more non-verbal responses from Bram.

"What do they tell you about communicating with him?"

"Gestures, facial expressions, speak slowly, use simple vocabulary." Pretty much what Peter is doing naturally.

Mom comes from the kitchen just as Dad enters the front door.

"Oh, good, you have great timing. Dinner's almost ready. Would you like to join us, Peter?"

Peter straightens, his gaze flickering from Mom to Bram.

"No, I think I should start heading home. I've got somewhere to be at eight and it's a long walk." He looks right at Bram. "It was nice to meet you, Bram. Can I come to visit again?"

Bram stares at his face, blinking, then he half-smiles again. I follow Peter into the kitchen.

"You really are welcome to stay for dinner," Mom says.

"No, I do have to go and ... If I were Bram, I wouldn't want someone I barely knew watching me eat when half my face is paralyzed."

Mom freezes for a moment and then favors him with a widening smile.

"You're very observant."

"I have my moments."

I walk him through the garage, thinking how Ben has misjudged this guy.

"You going back to school on Monday?"

"I am, but you'll probably see me again."

He strides toward the bike path.

Recrimination & Temptation

Peter

Right about where Lily and I crashed into one another, I round the corner and find Ben and Pamela Torneau talking. According to Facebook, they aren't dating anymore, but they look like they're in passionate discussion. Unfortunately, I can't avoid them.

"Peter Wyngate."

"Hey, Pam. Ben."

"What are you still doing here?" Ben demands.

"Walking. I'm feeling nervous. Walking helps. Gotta go."

"Hey, Peter," Pamela says. "Tell me about the *accident.*"

I cut a glance at Ben, uncertain.

"Can't tell you much. I don't remember it."

"That'll happen when you're drunk off your ass." Pamela didn't like me even before I hurt Cheyenne, so I'm not surprised when she bites.

"And, when you hit your head on the steering wheel."

"You may not remember, but Cheyenne told me you aimed right at that tree."

What?

"Why would I do that?"

"You tell me."

"I – don't know. I – the lawyer said there was something wrong with the car. I – I didn't do it deliberately."

"Then why'd you lose your license?" Ben asks.

"I was drinking underage. It's DUI even if I wasn't over the limit." My BAC was over, but it wouldn't have mattered.

"And you still don't know what caused the *accident*?" Pamela prompts.

I'm confused and *so thirsty*.

"I'm trying, Ben. I am. Can you just give me a little more time?"

"Why? So, you can keep lying?" The words come from Pamela, but Ben doesn't correct her.

I can't take anymore today, so I turn toward home because I don't know where else to go. I text Vic as I walk, asking for a ride to the eight o'clock meeting. Vic agrees and I keep walking. I jitter my way through the meeting, having trouble concentrating, though some of the stress eases in my shoulders as I listen to the stories. Just as the meeting ends, I get a text from Vic saying he'll be fifteen minutes late. The sound of people chatting, and metal chairs being stacked rattles my nerves, so I walk out into the parking lot, leaning back against a bollard. Across the way, a handful of young men stand between two vehicles, giggling. I smell the booze they're passing around – some cheap rotgut I'd hate the taste of, but I really *want* right now.

"You want some, man?" one of them calls. "This is our reward for coming here. You want some?"

I lick parched lips, so wanting just a sip. The guy holds out the bottle and I smell the contents. Cheap, some kind of rye. My stomach doesn't play up as quick with rye as with scotch, but I don't like the taste. I move toward the bottle, hand starting to come up, and then someone toots a horn and I look over my shoulder to see Vic pulling into the parking lot.

"Gotta go." I run for safety.

After I take a shower, I restlessly pace my room, every fiber of my being insisting I need a drink. I need a distraction, so I knock on Alyse's door. I smell the lingering odor of ganga when she opens the door.

"If Dad smells that, he's going to be pissed."

"Dad's not here. You want some?"

"No. It doesn't give me what I need."

"You always say that, but you never explain what you mean."

"Pot makes me feel – thick – slow --."

"It makes me imagine cloud kingdoms. Indica."
She points at me. "Sativa." She points at herself.

"Yeah, I tried that the second time." A European
café offered dozens of varieties and even blends.
"It's the only time I've ever understood what Mom's
bipolar must feel like and I didn't like it."

"I know what you like." She giggles, skipping
into her dressing room and coming back with a small
brown bottle. My throat tightens.

"How'd you get that?"

"I have my ways. You want some?"

I shake my head.

"I can't study drunk."

"Is there enough there for you to get drunk?"

"Don't tempt me. I'm going to head back.
There's an English paper that needs to be written.
Gotta go."

I flee temptation. When even AA and home
aren't safe, how am I supposed to stay sober this
week? My eyes cross by the time I draft the paper,
so I shut down my laptop and roll into bed.
Withdrawal messes with your sleep patterns, so I
sleep about an hour and then wake up to the sound
of wind whipping by the eaves. It's coming in from
the ocean. I roll over, staring at the pattern of
shadows on the window and the wall. The house is
well-built, and the roof is shingled, so I can't hear
the rain on the roof. I roll onto my back and cover
my eyes with my forearm.

I must have dozed off because I don't hear
Alyse enter the room. I blink in confusion as she
slips in between the covers. A roll of thunder growls
over the roof and wind whines around the corner of
my room like a giant is gnawing on the siding.

"Hey," I mumble. "What are you doing?"

"Scared." She snuggles into my side. She
shivers. When we were little, she'd crawl into my
bed during storms. I kind of like them when they're
not keeping me awake. Dad put an end to her
crawling into bed with me after he found out about
Mom. I don't want my sister that way, but it
sometimes feels like she might have other ideas.
She tries to put her arm across my stomach, but I
roll onto my side away from her.

"You can stay but keep your hands to yourself."

"Pot makes me impulsive." She's referring to
kissing me last summer.

"Yeah, no shit. Just – I need to sleep. Go to
sleep."

The house quivers slightly in a gust of wind. Her
breath quickens. I concentrate on slowing my own
breathing. I slip into a pleasant daydream where
Ben stands still long enough to hear me confess that
I'm an alcoholic and a jerk and I want to ...
something I can't think about because I'm falling
over a cliff into sleep.

Bad Boys Never Forget

Peter

It's been two weeks. Fifteen days, seven hours and some minutes. It doesn't get easier as time passes, though having Rick just next door gets me through the first few days back at Yale. Of course, the problem with college is everybody thinks they're adults now and they want to drink. I'm not even 18 for another few weeks and I'm an alcoholic. I know I can't join the party going on right outside my door, so I'm studying, which is basically what I've done all this week. Rick drags me to meetings, and I try to listen, but I'm distractible. We discussed Step 4 tonight and I'm trying to work on my inventory, but I have so much schoolwork to do. The music down the hall is enough of a siren's call without someone banging on the suite door, screaming "party".

I try to ignore it, but the party moves into the sitting area outside of my room and it becomes really hard to ignore. I'm really trying to be good when my bedroom door opens.

"It's you." This chick I barely know laughs at something on her phone. She lives on the floor above me and is one of those girls who is pretty as long as she wears makeup – dark hair, big features.

"I am me. What does that have to do with anything?"

"You've got major balls."

"They are impressive at times. What are we talking about?"

She turns her phone so I can see the video she's watching. That stupid fountain video. Last summer, I got really stupid drunk in London, and I peed in a fountain on camera. I can't run away from that, no matter what. There's me with a stream of urine aimed at a statue. I hate that guy!

"That really turns me on." She shimmies right up to me and lays a big wet, beery kiss on my mouth, in celebration of the most embarrassing moment of my life.

I'm weak. If I'm not being weak with alcohol, I'm weak with sex. I can distract myself from one by indulging in the other, even though Rick's warnings against numbing myself out echo in my head. We start moving to the music, which is heavy on the beat. I like dancing. It's not sex, but it is sexy and I'm not planning to drink anything. I just want to dance with her. I'm not even planning to tap her. Rick's admonitions about meaningless sex really did sink into my dense head. But as the dancing continues, I think about the booty I could get and then she puts a beer in my hand.

Damn! I didn't see that coming. It's hard to say no when it's across the room, but when it's in my hand infusing the air with its hoppy scent -- can't say no to that. Bottoms up!

Caught in the Revolving Door

Peter

I'm kind of an expert at hangovers and I normally prepare better for them – drinking lots of water before I pass out and sometimes even popping some Tylenol. My head's thundering a drumline when Rick offers me coffee. I wash down the Tylenol I should have taken last night with a swallow of coffee and lean back against the headboard. It's decaf, but he buys good beans and the heat of it relaxes my neck a little.

"You mad?" I ask. Rick's sitting at the end of my bed, bare feet practically in my lap.

"Frustrated." He sips coffee, then sits staring into space with his hands wrapped around the steaming mug. My stomach turns ominously. "Sobriety comes in cycles for a lot of people. I went through a few. But, Peter." He scratches his beard with one hand. "You maybe need to try rehab because you're clearly struggling to even get to where you can work on sobriety."

He's right. Dry two weeks before last night, I've had zero attention span for the Steps, and I lasted maybe five minutes in the presence of temptation.

"Where were you last night?"

He stares over the rim at me.

"The library. I meant to come back, but the study group ran long. And, that doesn't excuse you getting drunk. You could have left, right? You could have called me."

I feel like crap – scraped off a bum's shoe and peed on by a dog. I set the coffee aside and stumble into the bathroom to dump whatever is left in my stomach into the toilet. When I'm done, I brush my teeth. He's still sitting on the end of my bed.

"You're right." I sink onto my desk chair. "I'm, uh, drifting. I don't want to. I want to do better."

"Until you decide it's the last time, it won't be."

"I want it to be."

"I believe that, Peter. I'm not the one you have to convince."

Yeah. *I'm* the one who needs to decide. And, I want to. There's just this niggling uncertainty that I can't do it.

"I'll talk to my dad about it."

Rick nods. Neither of us really believes me on that topic anymore, but I want to try. And, I will.

Milestone

Alyse

Trevor doesn't get it. Guys don't. It's so easy for them to lose weight. Drink a 6-pack of beer and you can't see it on them. Carbs make me bloat. I've gained two pounds since starting to date Trevor mainly because he keeps offering me beer. Men! Idiots!

I really wanted Trevor to come back into the dance troupe. After being a lead in *Babes in Toyland*, I got another lead role in the Spring Revue. I'm the Spring Fairy. Trevor got back just in time to snag the male lead. Some of the younger boys are unhappy, but Trevor can actually lift girls. But not if we get fat. It's really something he needs to understand.

"I don't want it." I push the beer back at him. We're sitting in the pool house at his dad's place. The snow outside makes the pool look weird because it's landing on the cover.

"You're too skinny."

I am not. I weigh 102 pounds. That's two pounds too much. I don't argue with him, but I don't take the beer either.

Trevor's giving me a ride home from dance – the roundabout way. He's rubbing one of my feet because pointe is hard on the metatarsals. He's got this goofy look on his face. I'm not sure what he's thinking. I wonder if I should make use of that old trope – a penny for your thoughts. Before I can decide, he moves in close, laying a kiss on me.

"Hey." He's a good kisser. I'd never been kissed before he came back into town – well, yeah, I kissed Peter last summer, but that doesn't count. He's my brother. I just wanted to know what it felt like and Peter wasn't very cooperative.

"Hey, yourself." He kisses me again, then leans back. Gently, he grabs my ankle and pulls me along the couch. Since I'm leaning back, I sprawl flat. He leans over me, kissing my mouth, then my cheek and caressing my ear with his lips. A shivering thrill runs down my torso. He moves downward along my neck, my collar bone, my arm. My body flushes with heat as he starts unbuttoning my shirt with one hand and easing my warmups down with the other.

"If you're not ready, say so." He whispers this to my bellybutton. I squirm instead. He pulls up, smiling at me, reaches into a drawer, mutters a swearword. The condom box there is empty. He digs further back in the drawer and finds one. He lays more kisses on me before donning his jacket.

"You're sure?" I nod, my fingers twining in his frosted hair. He smiles. "First time's not always great, so talk to me. Don't let me hurt you."

He's so experienced and I couldn't ask for a better guy to lose my virginity to. When he's on top of me, for just a moment, I wish his hair were darker and his eyes were green. Yeah, that's not going to happen and, truthfully, Trevor is less complicated. A girl could get used to this.

Failure

Peter

I'm packing for home, knowing I've flunked at least two of my finals. How do I know that? Well, my head pounded with the hangover from hell when I took them and then I got really drunk last night to *celebrate* flunking them. My head's pounding. I've puked twice. I'm an idiot and I know it and I hate myself for it.

Rick comes to the bathroom door. I sit down on my stripped bed, waiting for the lecture.

"How big of an ass was I last night?"

"The room couldn't contain your ass-ness." Rick closes the door. It's not like it's a secret that we're keeping from our suitemates. My ass-ness knows no bounds. But Rick does try to respect my privacy even as I have no expectation of anonymity.

"You need to go to rehab. Revolving door sobriety is not working for you."

I breathe in deeply and let it out slowly. He's not telling me anything new.

"You can still call me, but if you're not going to be serious about staying sober, I can't help you. I don't want to be mean, but someone has to just say this. You need more help than I can give you until you want it and that's just the way it is."

I nod. Nobody wants to waste their time and I understand.

"I'll call him."

He knows I'm lying. I know it too. I mean to call, but even when I get Alan on the phone, I don't ask. And technically, I'm an adult. I could just check myself in. He'd probably pay for it. What choice would he have if I just did that?

Rick gives me a friendly hug.

"Decide to save yourself, man." And then he's gone. Vic is coming soon. Dad's going to be so pissed. He wouldn't have applauded the Cs, but I passed both of those classes until I bombed the tests. Damn! I'm such an idiot! And, now I have to face the music.

Or not. I pull up Laren on my phone.

"Hey, Mom."

I try to remember when I talked to her last. I made tentative plans to visit her and take my brother's trick-r-treating for Halloween, but I'd been pretty shaky in that brief period of sobriety, so I'd stayed at Yale rather than risk interacting with Laren. She'd given me frostbite when I called to explain and hadn't really thawed since. Mom holds a grudge longer than Ben.

"Peter. How are you?" Her voice sounds too bright, just a little too loud. I already know this call is a bad idea. Mom's manias are too much for me. Always have been.

"Just finished my finals and wondered if I could come down to see you and the boys."

"Oh, no, you can't. I'm off to visit Aunt Athena in Atlanta this week and then the boys are headed to camp. Or no, Sam's taking them camping. Why ever would they want to sit in a bug-infested forest, but there you have it. Are you doing well?"

I swallow tears, remembering pleasant times camping with the Andersons. Maybe if I spent some time in a forest, I'd get myself clean. I'm not doing well, and I wish I had Rick's mother who knows her son so well, even if her detection software for pitfalls is sometimes offline. At least she gives a shit.

"Mom, I just – I really need to get away for a while. Could I just --?" Sam keeps a drug-free home and Mom's medications don't tempt me at all. I could hang out there alone and – no, alone sounds scary.

"Sorry, darling. Now I must run. You have a good time."

She hangs up, leaving me alone. My phone vibrates. Maybe she didn't hang up. Maybe she accidentally disconnected. But no, it's a text.

CHEYENNE You fuck asshole.

Last summer, right before I came to Yale, I drove drunk with Cheyenne's car and we wrecked. I took an airbag to the face, so I don't remember what happened, but I know from the lawyer that Cheyenne hit the windshield and shattered bones in her face. For a while, I planned to make it up to her by staying sober, but then I got drunk at Christmas and now I don't know what to text in reply. I make several attempts before the one I send.

PETER: I know. I'm sorry for what I did to you.

I want to ask her what amends I can make, but I'm scared she'll ask for something I can't give, so I don't.

That she doesn't text back seems like a victory, but not one that feels good.

Wise Advice

Ben

It's pouring down rain and I'm soaked through just getting from the car to the garage. I should probably acquire an umbrella sometime, but I've survived several years without one, so I know I probably won't work very hard to make that happen. I'll unpack in the morning, when I can see, and hopefully not drown. The rain thunders on the roof. Maisy Callahan walks by in a bright yellow anorak and hot pink muck boots, thoroughly enjoying herself. She's an odd character, old enough to marry my granddad, who waits in the kitchen with my mom.

"Hey, Grandpa Jack. How you doing?" He seems a little shorter and his hair has gone quite grey.

"Drier than you. You and I never did get together at Spring Break and when you texted your mom, I thought I'd just hang around and say 'hi'. You remember what you wanted to talk about?"

I sigh. I don't know that I want to talk about Pete. I hardly heard from him since Spring Break –

once I think, and although I still miss my friend, I don't miss the complications that come with him. Still, when we get up to my room, I tell my grandfather my thoughts.

Jack leans back in my desk chair, scratching his mustache.

"Took you long enough."

"For?"

"To realize he has a drinking problem. I knew that – I don't know. You guys were still in high school."

"Why didn't you say something?"

He sighs.

"Because he'd just come back from boarding school and I figured that was a lot like the Army. A lot of guys who drink like fish in the Army don't become alcoholics later. And, he's tricky. I never saw evidence of it after that. You did because you were around him all the time."

"So, what should I do about it?"

"Depends. Do you think *not* being his friend has made him drink less?"

"I don't know. Alyse tells me he drank himself into a stupor after I was mean to him on Christmas Eve, so I guess probably not."

"Do you still care about him?"

"Yeah – maybe. Not sure."

"Okay. That's fair. That's kind of where your grandmother left me all those years ago. I wore out my welcome and I felt like everything I wanted might slide over a cliff on my next night out. That's rock bottom, but recovery wasn't a straight line. I know I had at least one lapse like what happened with Pete at Christmas. So, maybe you just want to stand still sometime and let him talk for a few minutes. He might surprise you. Or not. Caring about someone who is self-destructing can be tough, so I'm not going to try and talk you into it, but – my friend Roger Callahan – Maisy's husband – he was about the only non-AA friend I had left when I first got sober. He stuck in. Sometimes, when I just didn't want to talk about drinking and recovering, I'd go hang out with him. We'd go bowling or fishing and it would help. I hope it helped Roger too."

I chuckle because he does. I'm not used to talking about such serious topics with Grandpa Jack. He's usually the fun grandparent.

"Now, let's talk about why you're so angry at Pete."

"He hurt Cheyenne."

"He did, but I doubt he meant to run into that tree."

"Cheyenne says he did."

"Cheyenne had a head injury and was in a coma for a couple of weeks, right? Do you think she's trustworthy?"

Well, no. Her memory is dodgy for a lot of things these days.

"Were you and Cheyenne friends before the accident?"

He calls it an accident too, but it really wasn't.

"No, not really. We knew each other from classes and then Pete started dating her."

"But you became friends after?"

"Kind of. I don't know."

"So, let me suggest something. You were the designated driver at that party, right?"

"One of them."

"Do you maybe feel guilty that Pete drove that night?"

"It's not my fault."

"I didn't say it was. It's nobody's fault but Pete's, though maybe Cheyenne had a hand in it by asking him to drive her car. Can't really figure out how he'd be driving it unless she gave him the keys. But, let's not blame the victim here. You feel guilty – maybe thinking you should have circled back or any number of other scenarios. And, so you're mad at Pete for not texting you and saying he needed your help."

I stare at Grandpa Jack because his guess feels accurate. Maybe I'm not so angry with Pete as I am angry with myself.

"Think about it. If you need to talk about it, call me. Now, I'd better get home before Anabel's cat decides to eat the dog."

My grandmother died my senior year of high school and her cat and Jack's dog are in competition for the single human in their house now. He built this house when my dad was little. A retired contractor, he does custom woodworking out of his garage now and sells it through a furniture consignment store. I used to love going to his workshop and just smelling the wood shavings. A lot of those memories involve Pete.

I walk him to the garage door. Mom asks if he wants to stay for dinner, but he reiterates that the cat and dog need his referee skills and then dons his slicker and heads out to his truck through the pounding rain.

Help Denied

Peter

I'm hanging my head over the toilet, considering puking when I hear the knock on my door. I've been home less than a day and I'm not ready to talk to Tilly, so I reach over and turn on the shower as cover. When the knocking stops, I pull the trigger and feel so much better. The shower sort of awakens me and I dress casually, trying to decide if I should risk breakfast or just spend the day napping.

The knock comes again, and I know it's not Tilly or Alyse. There's only one person in the family who knocks like that – short, even blows, always three spaced evenly. Dad. I sigh and get up to unlock the door. He came all the way from Albany, which means he's got some sort of tracker on my grades. Damn!

"Hey," I greet, in case I'm wrong.

"Rough night?"

"Yeah." My hangovers last days ever since I had hepatitis last year. "Just go on and say it."

"How could you go from the Dean's List to flunking in one semester." He's dressed casually in jeans and a sweatshirt, far more relaxed than I've seen him in over a year. Apparently, yelling at me is the equivalent of a few holes of golf.

I swallow bile, which is exactly the wrong thing to do. I leave him yelling in the bedroom to go puke in the toilet. He follows me.

"What the hell is wrong with you?" he demands while I wash yak out of my mouth.

"I'm an alcoholic who is off the wagon. And I'm sorry about school but expecting me to go back after what happened at Christmas – I probably need to go to rehab, Dad."

Turns out I'm not a lying coward after all. Shivering, I grip the vanity, waiting for him to say he'll take care of it, but that's not my life. There's a reason why I lie and deny reality.

"Peter, you didn't drink for four months. You don't need to have your hand held. You just need to choose not to be stupid. You can make up the courses this summer and Yale says they'll let you back in in the fall if you're in good standing. You're grounded until you get your grades up."

I'm 18, so I don't think he can ground me. A thousand conversations with Rick remind me that honesty needs to be firm sometimes.

"I'm telling you what I need, Dad. Why aren't you listening?"

"Because I'm sick of hearing excuses."

He leaves me in my room. I'm blind with tears as I sit down on the edge of my bed. It feels like I'm on a desert island and the boats that float by are ignoring my signal fire. When I wake up later, sweaty from sleeping in jeans, the house is quiet. I look down at the garage from my bedroom windows and it looks like Dad's already gone back to Albany. Alyse doesn't answer my knock on her door. Did she mention a dance intensive? My memory stinks when I'm in withdrawal. Tilly's not around either.

I stand outside the library thinking about the bar. *I* don't want to drink, but my cravings sure do. I go to the kitchen, eat an apple and that helps, but it just takes the edge off. *Bourbon,* **bourbon,** **BOURBON.** I'm in the bar before I even realize my body is moving.

I pour my first glass of Four Roses since my December binge. Mostly I've been getting plenty drunk on party supplies and what Jan would pick up for me for a delivery fee. Without a driver's license, it's been hard to go to a liquor store. I sit down on the leather couch like a grownup and savor my first sip. Heaven! I roll it around in my mouth, letting it caress my teeth. It doesn't burn when I swallow. The maelstrom in my chest quiets, my head stops pounding and my stomach stops heaving. My shoulders relax. It's been a while since having a drink felt like a deliberate choice conducted for pleasure. It's nice to not feel like my skin is peeling off.

I stand to pour myself another drink.

I'm sitting in the den about three-quarters of the bottle down when I hear the growl of Trevor's Fiat in the driveway. He whispers too loudly as they come in the front door and she giggles. I leave my drink on the coffee table and open the door to the foyer. They're locked in a lip clasp, playing tonsil hockey and I stare in shock because Alyse's braid is gone, replaced by a pixie cut since I saw her at Spring Break. Trevor sees me and pushes her away.

"Hey." He wipes his mouth like the guilty man he is.

"She's fifteen." I don't feel drunk, but I'm slurring. "It's so a felony what you're doing."

"Peter, stop it." Alyse looks older with her hair gone. "You've got no idea how grownup I am."

"And you're drunk." Trevor would know. "You might want to have--."

I grab Trevor by the shirt and propel him backward into the wall.

"Leave her alone!"

I smack the wall beside his ear with the flat of my hand.

"Stop it!" Alyse pummels my shoulder. I push her off. Trevor has both hands wrapped around the wrist of the hand I'm holding him against the wall with, but now he shoves me.

"Don't you hurt her!"

I've got reach on him, but the world slants to the left side a little and I suddenly need to puke. By the time I stop puking, Trevor leaves. Cold sweat runs down my back as I come out of the bathroom off the library. Alyse sits on the couch, my drink in her hand. Terror washes over me.

"You don't want to get hooked on that, little sis."

"But it's okay for you to be hooked on it?"

I snort, which makes my nose run. It's not okay for me, but I'm shitfaced, so I can't really argue either way. I try to walk to my room, but it's not really a straight line. Alyse grabs my arm and helps me up the stairs. I collapse on my bed, which feels like a raft in a rough sea.

"You're scaring me." Alyse sounds like a little girl.

I roll onto my side, grip the edge of the mattress and hang on. Nothing's going to feel good right now.

"I'm scaring me too."

I'm not sure what happens after that. She cries for a while and then I doze off and dream I'm shipwrecked on a raft and dying of thirst. At one point I'm in the car after we hit the tree with the paramedics asking questions I didn't understand. It's the only part of the accident I remember – the red-and-white flashing lights and the agony of trying to inhale. Then I'm back on the raft with a desert in my mouth.

Getting Out Some

Lily

The sundress is orange with blue and yellow flowers and I'm not sure how I feel about it, but Alyse insists it will look "smashing" on me. She can't wear yellow, I realize. Her skin has a slightly olive tone that looks sallow against yellow. She looks good in white and black while I look – well, you can't even see me when I wear either color. Or they're tones, I think, not colors.

I take the dress, two pairs of shorts, a swimsuit and a couple of t-shirts. My breasts are getting bigger, so I suspect I'll need a whole new wardrobe come fall.

"What's your favorite coffee?"

I honestly don't know. I never really drank coffee before we moved here. I still prefer hot chocolate. I say mint chocolate, but it's probably not.

She buys me one. She's always treating. I felt special at first, but now I'm starting to feel like a mooch and I don't know what to do about it. True, my parents struggle to make ends meet until Mom sells her bookstore back in Manchester, especially since she isn't working here, but insurance covers Bram's medical costs. Daddy's lucky to work with such a great company. They halved my spring clothing budget, but that's okay. We're not poor. It's just they don't like to put a lot on their credit cards and they're a little nervous about what happens if Mom can never go back to work because someone must stay with Bram. Right now, he can't be alone for even a minute, although he is getting more physically able to do things.

Alyse looks at her phone, muttering.

"Trevor! I guess I was wise not to call off Tilly."

"Something wrong?"

"Trevor's not answering my texts, so I texted his step-sister Bethany because she's visiting right now. He got tied up."

Trevor seems to get tied up a lot. I haven't met him yet because he always seems to get tied up. I imagine him bound to a chair by ropes. We go outside the shopping center and sit on a bench in the warm summer afternoon while we wait for Tilly to arrive. Alyse opens her phone and shows me her tutu for the dance performance she's doing next week. Is that what they call the long flowing skirt? It is. I got it right. It's beautiful, whatever it's called. It's a mix of silver and purple and ends below her knees but above her ankles.

"You should take an adult ballet class this summer."

"Oh, I don't know. I'm not sure I'd be any good at it."

"It would take a while to go on pointe, but if you're committed, you'll build strength pretty fast."

"I'm not sure I want to do that. And this summer – I'm going to be needed at home and my mom can't drive me all the time. I don't know. I'll think about it."

"Why isn't your brother in, like, a nursing home?" I blink at her. Um, I – yeah. My parents want him home. I want him home. Why wouldn't we bring him home? But, yeah, he's a lot of work and there's some question whether he'll ever get better.

"He doesn't really need to be in a nursing home. That's for people who need nurses, and my parents and I can take care of whatever he can't right now, so--. And, he's getting stronger."

"I'm sorry. That was insensitive. I just feel so sorry for you, cooped up at home all summer. Forget I said anything. Open mouth insert foot."

I smile and nod. This isn't the first time Alyse has said something that kind of hurt my feelings, but she always makes quick work of smoothing it over. She lives in a different wealth class than I do. She really doesn't understand middle-class people.

Peter gets out of the car when it pulls up and holds the door for us. He looks sick. There are dark circles under his eyes and his lean cheeks look hollow. He's not wearing sunglasses like when we picked him up at the train, so maybe he's not hungover. He mimics a chauffeur in handing me into the car.

"Why, thank you." Unlike a chauffeur, he slides in beside me.

"So, what are you ladies up to?" A smile transforms his face. So maybe he's just tired and a little down. Alyse said their father grounded him.

"We bought some great clothes." Alyse sounds so enthusiastic. "Look at these shoes."

"Wow! Don't you have three pair that look just like that?"

"No!" Peter mugs a face and she bursts out laughing, almost admitting that she has three just like that. I don't pull clothes out to show him, but in the end, Alyse does show him my dress.

"I like that color on you. Makes your eyes sparkle."

When we get to my house, I invite them in. It occurs to me that Tilly might have somewhere to go, but Peter asks her if it's okay and she grants permission. Alyse announces she's tired and we ought to do this by ourselves. She does look like maybe she's a little sick to her stomach. Peter carries some of my bags.

Mom's encouraging Bram to eat. Coordinating movements to get a spoon from a bowl to his mouth are still hard for him even with his left hand. He can do it now, but he'll lose interest if he's not cajoled. We explain Peter's just helping me with my purchases and he doesn't go any further than the bottom of the stairs. When I come back down after my second trip upstairs, he's gone to the kitchen to talk with Bram.

Most people treat Bram like he's not there or they talk to my mother about Bram as if he's a piece of furniture. Peter talks *to* Bram as if he might respond.

"Strawberry yoghurt. Mmmm." He's got a very expressive voice and he controls the pace so well. He talks like he expects Bram to understand and maybe he does, at least some of it. His mouth twitches up into a half-smile. Mom laughs.

"Thank you for stopping to talk with him."

"Sure, Mrs. Wexler. It's got to be hard to not be able to talk."

"It's hard for us trying to figure out what he wants and needs and then to try to explain stuff to him. And you can call me Madalyn."

"Cool." Peter sees me in the door. "I should get going. Lily, hope to see you around sometime. I'll see you later, Bram." He waves to assure Bram understands. My phone vibrates.

ALYSE - Is Peter staying or coming?

"Alyse?" Peter asks. I nod. "That girl!" He rolls his eyes. "Anyway, I'll see you sometime."

I walk with him through the garage. His gaze flickers toward Ben's house. I think Ben is at work. Does Peter want to run into him? Or does he fear the confrontation? I think a little of both. We walk to the car.

"Come on," Alyse cries. "Just because you're allowed a prison break now and then shouldn't mean I have to wait for you while you visit *my* friend." She licks her lips like she's trying not to barf.

Peter rolls his eyes at me again and then flashes me a smile before getting into the car. Tilly wishes me a good day through the open window, and I thank her for the ride before going back inside to help my mom with Bram's physical therapy. I so appreciate Alyse getting me out of the house occasionally.

What's Not Said

Ben

I'm getting Captain Russell's *Mimi* ready for the season, painting the cabin exterior, and Trevor is sitting on the railing watching me. It's the role Pete used to play before I exiled him from my life. Trevor likes to talk more than Pete does, so it's entertaining just listening to his unintentional monologue. I kind of feel like he's trying to tell me something but doesn't know how to say it. A couple of his comments pique my interest.

"So, you're dating Alyse?"

"Yeah." His eyes twitch side to side. Something's amiss.

"Pete know about that?"

"We're not talking at the moment."

"Pete got mad and he's stayed mad for longer than five minutes? That's different."

"Naw, I'm not sure he's still mad. He hasn't called me. I texted him a few times and he's texted back saying he'll get back to me."

"He's pretty protective of Alyse and I kind of want to kick your ass myself. You are *way* too old for her."

"Yeah, maybe." He pauses as if contemplating, then sighs. "She's pretty mature, though."

"What does that mean?"

"She handles stuff better than a girl her age usually does. That's all."

I turn from painting to frown at him. He's looking off across the marina, dark blue eyes misty. Something in his expression reads sad. Sad? Trevor doesn't do sad.

"You okay?"

"Yeah, just – thinking about something somebody told me." He breathes out in a long exhale. "I at least care about her. Isn't it better if she's dating someone who cares about her?"

Now there's a question. Ordinarily, I'd agree, but in some ways, Trevor is a worse mess than Pete. Trevor kept a harem of girlfriends in high school and while most of us laughed watching him try to keep them apart, Pete pointed out Trevor's antics amounted to lies to a half-dozen girls at a time.

"Trevor is following in his parents' footsteps and ought to come with a warning label – might give you a STD but will definitely break your heart."

A watershed observation from an inveterate liar, I haven't really gotten over it. Trevor is a serial cheater and he's dating a 15-year-old girl who is my best friend's sister. Although Alyse annoys me, *I* actually care about what happens to her. I fear Trevor is lying to himself.

"You thinking about other girls yet?"

He casts me a distressed and annoyed look.

"No! It's not like that."

"Uh-huh."

He rubs a hand through his silvered hair.

"Only when I masturbate." He watches my expression. "I wouldn't think you'd want me fantasizing about her."

"I don't, but I also don't want Alyse to get her heart broken and we both know you don't sustain relationships well."

"You mean because of my string of ladies back when. I don't do that anymore."

"Since when?"

"Since I think that's why I lost Macaria. I think that 'not exclusive' thing actually bothered her and that's why when I came back into town, she told me to screw off."

I ran into Macaria at a store a few days after I got home. She looked healthy and *sober* for the first time in years. I doubt exclusivity was her reason for dumping Trevor. You can't stay sober around him, especially when dating.

"Just don't hurt her, man. I will definitely take Pete's side if it comes to kicking your ass."

"Yeah, I hear you. I think she understands that when I go to the city, we won't still be dating, but for now I'll keep her as my one chick."

I turn back to painting. I'm almost done and that'll pay my slip fees for the summer. I'll crew for Russell for several of his cruises too, but he'll pay me wages for those. I step back to stand near the railing and inspect the whole wall.

"Looks good." Trevor points to the middle window. "Just to the left there. Is that an imperfection or something you missed?"

I go closer to inspect, touch up the blemish, walk the length of the wall to assure I didn't miss anymore spots, then walked all the way around the cabin as a final inspection, touching up in one or two spots.

Trevor's dropped off the railing and his stretching out a leg along it. He's an amazing athlete.

"You ready to go?"

"Soon as I put away the tools and wash up. Where we headed?"

"Skateboarding?"

"Sure. I've got mine in the Jeep. It'll be about half an hour – or faster if you help."

"I'll go buy us some coffees. Should take about half an hour."

We both laugh because that's so totally Trevor. Not for the first time, I wish Pete and I were talking because he is far less predictable. Sometimes, he might help just to do it. But then again, I could use a coffee after working hard in the hot sun all day. I tell him what I want and collect my tools to take to the boat shop while Trevor dashes off up the pier, all nervous energy and Adderall.

Ice Cream Social

Peter

I close my laptop with a sigh. Yeah, maybe it's easier to do the work when you've already done some of the work. I'm already a quarter of the way through the two courses I need to salvage, and my self-score is 95%. Not bad for the first week home and restless as a spring squirrel.

I pick up my phone to look at my calendar. It's Day 8 and I'm starting to feel okay. I ventured out with Tilly about Day 3, but I've been doing a lot of sleeping, trying to eat healthy and drinking so much water It's surprising there are no streams running down my face. I don't even particularly want to drink alcohol. I've been lucky the bar's been locked since the night I got drunk, but I'll take getting detoxed anyway I can. I promised myself if I made a week, I'd call and apologize to Trevor for whatever the heck happened the last time I got drunk. He texted me the day after and I said I'd get back with him.

"Hey." I don't need to lose anymore friends, but I know I can't hang out with Trevor until I've had a whole bunch more dry time. So why am I calling him? Oh, yeah, because I value his friendship. After Cheyenne, only Trevor still talked to me, although other people began to reply to me after a few weeks.

"I'm really sorry for the other night."

"No problem. I've been idiotic far more often than you have, and you never even ask for an apology."

"Did I punch you?"

There's a long silence as Trevor remembers that I'm a black-out alcoholic. He drinks as much as I do, but he almost always remembers what happened. I don't, which may be a reason why I struggle to believe I'm such an idiot.

"No. You held me against the wall, and I thought you might clock me, but you didn't. Look, I know you're pissed that I'm dating her. It just sort of happened."

"She is too young for you."

"It's true, but—I'm treating her good. I am. And we hooked up because Cameron Haskell was sniffing up on her at dance--."

"So, you're protecting her?" I laugh because it's silly. Cam is only a year older than Alyse and as far as I know he's not a drug addict or a serial rapist. Not that Trevor's raped anyone, but the guy is a walking pharmacy. "She's been pretty clear I need to stay out of her business, but–you're using condoms, right?"

"I'm taking my time with her, man."

"Uh-huh. Use a condom. You don't know where you've been."

He laughs. I'm looking out the window and see Tilly pull into the driveway. She gets out and so do Alyse and Lily. I think about going down to talk with them, but I have no business messing with a girl who is younger than my sister. I'm a hypocrite, but that's a bridge too far even for me.

"You going?" Trevor talks a lot and he doesn't really need to be sure you're listening. Unfortunately, I wasn't.

"Sorry. Got distracted by something outside. What did you ask?"

"Hil's having a party. You going?"

Just like that, I want something to drink.

"When?"

"Tonight. Starts at eight on his yacht."

I'm pretty sure that's his father's yacht, but whatever. All I need do is remind Trevor that I can't drive, and he'll come get me. He'll scare the shit out of me because he'll already be warming up for the party, but I could go have a couple of beers and ....
I don't remember the accident that smashed Cheyenne's face, but I remember my own pain following it. In the flinch that follows, I remember

Ben isn't going to go to one of Hil's parties. Neither of us like the guy, so while I'm invited, I probably wouldn't have gone even before I decided to quit drinking. That's just my cravings trying to trick me into another relapse. And, if Ben hears someone saw me at the party, even if I don't drink, he'll think I did and...yeah. I need to stay sober if I want to rescue that relationship.

"Naw. I have something going on. You taking my baby sister?"

"No. Hil has a strict adults-only rule for this."

"Okay. Well, have fun. I'll catch the next one. Give me some warning."

"Since when do you plan?"

Since I need time to talk myself out of being stupid?

"And, Trev –don't drive drunk with her. Please."

There's a long pause on the other end.

"Yeah. I get that, man."

I say goodbye, sprawl out on the couch and reach for the television remote. I'm a season behind on *Fear the Walking Dead*, so I spend an hour catching up on Al's character. I'm hungry then so I take the backstairs down to the kitchen. I'm at the lower landing when I hear them chattering.

Alyse hates the kitchen. She considers it to be the domain of servants. But here they both are, eating vanilla ice cream and fresh peaches that I'd be willing to put money down on that Lily had to slice. I'm actually surprised that Miss Prima Ballerina Alyse is eating fat. She's gotta be high.

"Having fun?"

"Don't be bossy." I think the expression Alyse favors me with is called a simper. It's a weapon used by manipulative chicks when they want to trick a guy into thinking they're harmless. Alyse isn't harmless. The longer I try to work on my inventory, the more I realize she's kind of mean. But I still love my sister. Maybe I need a buffer between us...like Lily.

"Any of it left?"

Lily looks guilty as she shakes her head and Alyse waves her hand toward the big Frigid Air. I open the freezer bin and there's no vanilla ice cream left – that's probably the empty container on the counter. I prefer chocolate ice cream anyway, so I pull out that carton and look in the fridge. There's raspberries. Perfect combination.

"Will he think so?" Lily appears to be continuing a conversation from before I entered the room. I sit down across from them, cutting a glance between them, wishing I could read minds like Rick.

"If you're talking about me, just do it to my face." I smile at Lily, knowing I can get it out of her. How do I know that? Girls can't resist me when I pour on the charm.

"Do guys like flowers or do they consider them sissy?"

This is seriously what girls talk about when they pig out on ice cream? Who knew?

"Depends on the flowers."

"The roses out back?"

Alyse rolls her eyes. Her pupils are incredibly dilated. What the hell is she on?

"I'd run the landscaper's Brushhog through those if I thought I could get away with it." Lily's eyes widened. "Alyse loves them, though, right?"

"They were Mom's."

"My case in point. You still haven't figured out who she is."

Lily's staring at me like I've grown two heads. Maybe I need to dial it down a little, but I can feel my mother's fingers on my chest, and I'm pissed off that Alyse is high. I meet Lily's gaze and realize that she is completely not high. Her hazel eyes are clear and full of questions.

"She's our mother." Alyse doesn't get it and I really need her to. Maybe one reason I drink is so I don't remember why Mom can't be here.

"Oh, yeah, get all nostalgic for the woman who left you when you were nine and never looked back. We rated as highly as the roses, so love and daydream about Mommy Dearest treating you like she loves you. She loves the piano she took with her, not you."

"That's easy for you, Peter, because she *does* love you."

In all the wrong ways, but I can't say that, not in front of a stranger. I close my eyes for a moment, take a breath and let it out slowly. We need a change of subject or this night goes south in a heartbeat. Shit is closer to the surface when I stop drinking.

"In answer to your question, Lily, I like flowers. I hate roses, but that leaves a lot of flowers to choose from."

"What's your favorite?" She clearly wants to change the subject to something innocuous as much as I do. Wyngate family drama Is best taken in small doses. I have never considered her question, so I grasp at the first straw to flit through my brain.

"Um, lilacs, I think."

"You know you can't cut them, right?"

Did I know that? Uh, yeah, now that she mentions it, I knew it. Don't know that I knew it for sure until this moment. It doesn't matter for the conversation though.

"That's one of the things I like about them. They have to be natural."

"What did you do with the roses I gave you the other day?" Alyse blinks at Lily. She's really wasted.

"Took them home and put them in a vase for Bram's homecoming. My mother loved them."

"Glad someone can appreciate them." Alyse wipes her face, smearing her mascara. When did she start wearing all that goop on her face? Lily doesn't wear anything other than moisturizer.

"Yeah." I agree. If I knew how to transplant rose bushes, I'd make a gift of them for her. They'd take up the Wexlers' whole back yard, but at least I'd not have to care about them anymore.

"I think I'm going to be sick." Alyse runs over to the sink and barfs.

"So lovely." I figure Lily's going to agree with me, but she joins Alyse at the sink and helps her wash her face. Alyse stumbles toward the stairs and then staggers into me. I sweep her up in my arms and carry her up to her bedroom. Lily doesn't follow us, so she doesn't see Alyse lay a kiss on my mouth as I put her into bed. "Stop." I push back from her. "Sleep."

"Why does she love you?"

"Mom?" Alyse nods. "Because she likes boys better. Since you're passing out, I need to go help Lily clean up the kitchen. Go to sleep."

I push off her grasping hands and head back downstairs, pausing on the landing to look in a mirror there to make sure there's been no makeup transfer. Lily has put away my ice cream bowl and is rinsing her and Alyse's bowls.

"Thank you." I grab a sponge and wipe down the table while she wipes down the counter. "What's she taking?"

174

"I don't know. This is the first time I've ever seen her like that."

I rinse and squeeze out the sponge. She does the same and we stack them in the wire basket on the back of the sink. I want to warn Lily that it'll get worse – that I started spiraling at fifteen and maybe she wants to cut her losses now, but I can't bring myself to say the words. I get my ice cream bowl out of the freezer.

"Should I go up there?"

"Not until she's fully asleep. I think you're a pretty good friend for putting up with that."

"She's my friend."

I nod, but I'm thinking of Ben, who put up with so much from me until he just couldn't take it anymore...couldn't take *me* anymore.

"What are you doing this summer?"

"Not much. I'm taking some correspondence courses." That sounds so much more wholesome than retaking classes so I can go back in the fall. Of course, I'm not going to admit that I just lied to her, so I provide an unasked-for bit of honesty. "I start driver's education courses next week."

She meets my gaze and I realize she knows. Maybe Alyse didn't realize how embarrassed I am or maybe Ben told her as a warning. I look down at the counter, shame washing over me.

"I had an accident last summer–someone got hurt. They took my license because I'd been drinking. If I pass the course, I can get it back sooner."

She hesitantly puts a hand on my fist.

"People make mistakes. So long as you know it was a mistake, it'll be okay."

"I do know it was a mistake. Not sure anybody else believes that I know that."

"Ben?"

I sigh.

"That obvious?"

"I noticed."

"What did you notice?" I regret the question because she takes her hand back.

"You trying to talk to him and then looking sad after. I asked Ben about it and he said you guys were like brothers, but...well, he's really angry at you and I'm not sure what you can do about that."

"I don't know. I've tried. He wants something from me, but I don't know what it is, and he won't tell me."

She looks sad but gives me an encouraging smile. Maybe she'll tell Ben. Maybe he'll give me a chance.

"Don't you have some friends who are also his friends who would speak up for you?"

Meaning she doesn't see herself doing it...yet.

"Right after the accident, a lot of people weren't talking to me. It hurt at the time, but I kind of understand now and they're being better about responding to me lately. I guess I'm a little scared to bring it up with them. I don't want to stir up any bad feelings. I don't want to force people to choose between us."

"So, you'll probably be invited to the same things, right?"

Sure. I'm invited to some kind of party on Hil Cavanaugh's yacht, but I'm not ready to be around alcohol and I'd have to ask someone for a ride, since I'm still grounded, so I'm here with a 15-year-old girl who is Ben's neighbor because I can't think of anyone else who might help me.

"I'm trying to stay away from parties right now." Wow, I'm telling the truth and barely thinking about it. Amazing.

"Because of the drinking?"

"Yeah. Our crowd drinks a lot. Even volleyball games on the beach must have beer. And I just can't right now."

Shit! Am I right on the verge of telling a stranger, this innocent girl, that I'm an alcoholic? Naw! No way! But I am hovering in the vicinity.

"I guess that makes sense. If Ben is angry with you for driving drunk and caught you drinking at a beach party, he might take it the wrong way."

True, but Rick would say that's really not the point. I don't want to scare her away, so I cast her an apologetic smile instead of going full confessional.

I scoop out the last raspberry swimming in melted fudgy deliciousness and rise to rinse my bowl.

"I'm sorry you feel all alone." Her words hit me like an icy wet towel. I turn from the dishwasher.

"I'll make new friends, but he and I were best friends since kindergarten. I think I could have hundreds of friends and still regret losing him. You got someone back in New England like that?"

"Marcie. We still text. But we weren't like that. We didn't go all the way back. Just through Junior High. I'd liked to have a bosom friend."

Alyse made me watch *Anne of Green Gables* with her – the entire mini-series. I really do love my sister. So, I smile at the reference.

"Alyse has always wanted an Anne to her Diana too."

"Really?"

"Yeah. She used to have a friend – Ella – but she moved away last year. Did you talk her into the new do?"

"No. She just showed up with that one day. It was –hmm, a rite of passage, I think. She said she'd keep the braid for her kids."

I grimace.

"I hate it."

"So, I shouldn't get my hair done the same way?"

Her bob is loose around her neck, just skimming her shoulders, longer than I remember from Spring Break.

"I like longer hair. I think most guys do."

"Why?"

"Reminds us of your differences, maybe."

"Our differences?"

The kitchen seems really small now. I'm leaning backwards against the counter and she's resting her hands on the counter about an arms-length away and it feels intimate, even though we're not touching.

"We – girls and guys – are not the same." Something's starting to rise to the occasion, so I straighten from the counter. "In her closet are pillows, sheets and a blanket for the futon. I hope you didn't have a night of doing girl stuff planned."

"It's fine. Thank you."

"For?"

"Talking. Good night."

She leaves me standing there in the kitchen. I like the pleasant feeling of the darkened room. The house isn't that old, but it has a lot of high-end features meant to make it seem like it's been here a long time.

Strange! Every night when the house gets quiet, I go down to check if the bar is unlocked. It hasn't been – and why would it be if Dad's not here – but I'm surprised to realize that I don't feel like drinking

179

right now. I pull my phone out of my pocket and consider hitting Rick's number. I run myself a glass of water and sit down at the table. I pull up his number and hit it.

"Hey," he says in that wary 'is this a drunk dial' tone.

"Hi. Eight days."

There's a long pause.

"Good for you. Dry or sober?"

That is always the question. I was sober for four months. I've been intermittently dry since Christmas.

"I think I want it to be sober."

"You been to any meetings?"

"My dad grounded me. The staff won't give me a ride anywhere."

"You're making excuses, Peter."

I sigh. I know that. Setauket's a haul on a bike, but I could do it.

"You're right. Tilly probably wouldn't tell him if I was going to meetings."

"Tilly *should* probably tell him if you are. And I'd bet if you called him and asked, he'd lift that restriction for that reason."

"I asked him to send me to rehab and he refused."

"It's not his problem, Peter. You're the one who has to decide to go."

"I did."

"And, let me guess. You chose to bring it up during a discussion of your grades, so he had a lot of reasons to be resistant."

Rick is psychic, so I'm not even surprised that he knows how things worked down.

"He has things he wants from me."

"And if you were serious about getting sober, you'd make different choices. Look, Peter, you know all this. You can't blame him for *you* not doing the work. It's good that you've made eight days dry and that you asked your dad for what you need, but there's a rehab twenty miles from you and you've got friends with cars. Same with meetings. I bet if you called Ben and said 'I need a ride to AA' he'd forget he's angry at you and give you a ride. Or if he wouldn't, his parents would. You're only alone if you want to be. So, this is all a matter of you deciding to do what you know you need to do."

"Yeah." I know it. It's not like Rick hasn't said this to me before. "Thank you for not hanging up."

"I wouldn't do that, Peter. But you can't play in the program and you know that."

"Yeah. How are things in New Hampshire?"

"Okay. I'm back at my old job. Did I ever mention Liana to you?"

"I don't think so."

"She lives near my parents. I asked her out. Tomorrow night."

"Cool."

"Yeah, we tried to date a couple of years ago, but I was still shaky, so it didn't go anywhere. You taking care of yourself?"

"Yeah. The bar is locked. I'm trying to eat three meals a day. Since I'm grounded, I'm just walking around the property. Alyse and I did dance stretches two days this week."

"Good. Add meetings in and you'll be more to the good. And, seriously, Peter. If you walked in the door of a rehab and put your insurance card on the counter, they wouldn't turn you down."

Tilly lets herself in the back door and startles when she sees me. She's dressed like she always is – navy slacks, light blue shirt. I don't know why she'd be out at 11 o'clock. Not on family business.

"I gotta go."

"You okay?"

"Yes. I just – I'll call you later."

"Sure. Hang in there and remember what I said."

"I will."

I hang up.

"Hey." Tilly scans the kitchen. "I expected a mess."

"I helped Lily clean up."

"She's a sweet girl."

"She is." I silently hope to God she'll use that sweetness on Ben.

"Alyse decided it was beneath her?"

I nod and shrug. I'm not about to tell Tilly about the drugs. I know I should, but I've been covering for Alyse for so long I don't know how to tell the truth now.

"You feeling restless?" I stare at her. "It's been kind of obvious this week."

"Um, he grounded me. I have a small cage to pace."

"Peter, if you need help, just ask."

I open my mouth to scoff, but I know full well Vic will give me a ride to AA if I have her do the asking. I know it. So why can't I get my mouth to make the request? What the hell is wrong with me? Stupid, I think. I fix my gaze behind her and force the words out.

"I need to start going back to meetings."

Done and she nods.

"Eight o'clock in Setauket?"

"Yeah."

"We can do that." She drops one of her capable hands on my shoulder. "I'm proud of you, Peter. I wish I'd been here the other night to make sure the bar was locked."

I startle, staring up at her.

"Sure. I'm supposed to be able to stop myself, but I can't. Not having access helps. Thanks for understanding."

She gives my shoulder a little squeeze and heads toward her rooms. There's a part of me that wants to follow her, even though I haven't since before my mom left. I hear the whisper of the bar, but when I stand, I let myself into the backyard to spend some time just being quiet so that maybe I can sleep when I finally go upstairs.

Unexpected News

Alyse

I can't believe Trevor acts like it didn't happen. I mean, yeah, it wasn't a big deal. Just a mistake easily taken care of, but he acts like it didn't happen at all. I guess it doesn't mean as much to guys and it could have derailed his plans. Never use a condom that's been in a drawer for a year or more.

We're at the country club, hanging out in the hot tub and I'm inexplicably trying not to cry and pretending I don't want to. This would be so much easier if Trevor would talk about it, but he won't. I'm wondering if Peter would be more sympathetic when a long, tall figure steps over the side of the hot tub to join us.

"Hey, man."

"Finn! Where have you been?" Trevor demands. I know Finn Conover from high school. He might not remember a freshman from his senior year. He's big and loud and looks a little like a Viking, with curly red-brown hair and eyes more orange than brown.

"You want the full answer to that?"

"Always."

"Got popped for DUI on New Year's morning. My stepdad decided I needed help, so he sent me to rehab and then I've been at this camp place since March."

"Wow! You okay?"

I try to arrange my face into something that could be taken for sympathy. He brought Peter home that night like a ragdoll dangling over his shoulder.

"Yeah. I'm actually better than okay. I'm leaving in August to go to Jacoby Bible College."

Trevor's staring at him like he's grown two heads and I think he might have grown three.

"Why?"

Finn wipes his face with a wet hand.

"Something happened when I was in rehab and — I just think my life will go better if I make a big change."

"But, *Bible* college?"

"Yeah, I know. It's hard to explain. If I try, it'll sound like I'm preaching, but seriously, I need it."

Trevor smiles. Dancers learn acting skills. He can fake it if he needs to.

"Whatever works, man."

"Yeah." Finn stands. "I just wanted to touch base. My sister's waiting for me to get dressed so we can head out to my dad's place. And, just so you know, I won't get weird on you or anything. It's fine to call me – just not for a ride because I don't have a driver's license until next January."

"Got it!"

Finn walks away and Trevor giggles into my hair.

"Wow. Pete and Finn both. At least Pete didn't get religion on top of it. At the rate I'm going, Ben will be the only friend I've got I can drink beer with and that's – oh, wow, ironic."

I snuggle against his shoulder. I want to grieve, but I can't. It was nothing. So why can't I let it go?

Disturbed

Peter

Eighty times? I couldn't have driven drunk that many times. I wasn't drunk every day. I didn't go to school drunk. I usually took a day or two off between drinking. And I've only been driving for two years. Yeah, I clearly drove drunk once and I shouldn't have. I feel sick every time I think of it, but no way did I drive eighty times. Maybe Trevor has. Or Finn. Those two are *always* drunk.

Wow, twenty-seven people a day die in the US from drunk driving. That's about 10,000 people a year. Nobody died in my drunk-driving accident, but she could have.

Okay, I already knew that one beer equals one glass of wine equals one shot of bourbon. And yeah, I'm not drinking and driving again. I'm more than two weeks now and not feeling bad. Yeah, some days I'm circling the bar and testing the lock, but I'm doing it less and I haven't actually tried to pick the lock. I don't know how to pick a lock, but they make it look easy in the movies. I bet I could do it, but I haven't tried.

I went to meetings every night this past week and I called Rick last night to talk. He still says I should go to rehab and he's probably right, but he agreed I could get back to working on Step 4. I should probably tell him about Cheyenne's messages. I need to get to the amends part of this process because I need to help her understand that I'm sorry. I didn't mean for it to happen. There's got to be some redemption possible. Right?

The instructor, Abigail Lawrence, asks me a question, but I'm thinking about Cheyenne, so I don't hear her.

"Excuse me?"

"What age did you start drinking?"

I'm the youngest person in the room, so I guess it's a legitimate question. I don't like being put on the spot, but Rick would tell me I should always be honest.

"Before junior high."

"How often have you driven drunk?"

"I don't remember doing it at all ... except ... I didn't mean to that night." I promised myself I would only have one beer that night, and I don't even remember drinking that one. From my BAC, I'd had way more than that and according to some people at the party I drank at least a half-a-fifth of bourbon.

"So, why'd you do it?"

"I don't remember." Some of the older people in the class now stare at me. At least a couple of them look sympathetic. Others seem skeptical.

"So, which came first – the drinking or the driving?"

"I can bet the drinking. There was a party."

"And you just decided to get behind the wheel of a car?"

"I don't know. I drove someone else's car, so it wasn't as simple as I was drunk, and I had keys. Someone had to have given me those keys."

Abigail tilts her head. I don't know what that means, so I wait.

"I'm sure it's difficult if you don't remember, but from my perspective, that whole 'she-gave-me-her-keys' schtick sounds like an excuse."

I drop my gaze to the tabletop. Abigail moves on to harass someone else about why they're here. There are about 15 of us. Apparently, a lot of drunk drivers live in this part of the Gold Coast. Alcoholics come from all walks of life, but most of the folks in this room could be parents or older siblings to my friends. I haven't seen any of them at an AA meeting. Am I the only one who knows I have a problem?

Abigail is throwing photos up on the screen – wrecked cars where there's a good chance nobody walked away. I remember what Ben said about

191

pictures of Cheyenne. Maybe I should start with a picture of the car crash. My stomach feels like a block of ice. Abigail asks me to hold up as the class breaks for the day.

"You okay?"

"Yeah." I'm scared of her. If she flunks me from this class, I don't get my license back until August and there might be restrictions.

"You just looked like those photos disturbed you. Feeling guilty?"

"Yeah. I didn't mean to hurt her."

"So, someone got hurt?"

"We both did, but hers was definitely worse."

"It's good you feel guilty about it. One or both of you could have been killed."

I nod. Outside the windows, a beautiful Long Island summer day draws to a close and I haven't been in it. I wonder if Cheyenne gets to enjoy it. Ben's probably working. I'm silent for too long.

"If you're already blacking out for drunks, Peter, you might want to consider a full alcohol screening." She holds a card out to me.

Briercliff Manor Drug & Alcohol Treatment.

It has day and residential treatment and it's a 20-minute drive down the LIE.

I don't say anything. I just nod and slip it into my wallet. I want to say "I'm okay for now" but I keep hearing Rick whispering in my ear that revolving-door sobriety isn't working out for me. But I'm going to meetings and I'm 15, no 16, days sober coz you can count the day you decided to quit. I'm doing okay, even if I'm struggling.

"You might find it enlightening. You have a good evening. See you in the morning." Her smile appears sympathetic and a little sad. I escape for the day.

Missing My Best Friend

Ben

I miss Pete. Wes is too young to keep up with me on the bike. He really tries, but I'm constantly having to slow down to let him catch up. He's a great little brother, but I really need to connect with some people my own age. It's kind of weird, but we're not getting together like we used to and I'm beginning to appreciate Pete's ability to pull us all together. He'd have had a party by now – or suggested volleyball on the beach – or mountain biking at Laurel Ridge. Technically, he could still do that, but he's been flying below the radar since he got home from Yale. Maybe he's finally gotten the message that he can't fix stuff by pretending it didn't happen or maybe he's just given up.

I hate that second part. I hate that Pete and I aren't best friends anymore. He screwed up and he needs to own that, but maybe I shouldn't be so angry with him. I coast up into our driveway and Wes pants up beside me.

"You go too fast." He's only eleven and it's a long hilly ride from downtown. Maybe complaints are warranted.

"Get you in shape, man."

"It's not fun when it hurts." He rubs a calf where I can see a charley horse working.

Pete never complained. An athlete honed by the discipline of dance, he knew how to embrace the suck. I take a long draw off my water bottle. When I lower it, I see the bronze SUV pulling up to Lily's house. Tilly waves at me from the driver's seat and I wave back as Pete gets out of the backseat with Lily. No Alyse? My heart tugs painfully. She's a beautiful girl and I hate to think Pete might be careless with her. What happens when he can drive again?

As Lily walks up to her house, Pete casts me a forlorn glance, but he doesn't try to connect with me. He just gets in the front seat with Tilly and they drive away.

"You didn't even wave at him."

"He didn't wave at me either."

"Would you have if he'd done it first?"

"I don't know."

"So, you guys aren't friends at all anymore?"

"He needs to get some things straightened out before we can be friends again."

"Do you still want to be friends?"

Good question. There's an angel and a devil on opposing shoulders arguing their cases.

"I miss him."

"Then why aren't you trying with him? I mean, does he even know what you want from him?"

"I've told him. He just doesn't seem to get it."

"You mean like the time you were angry about my scratching the paint on the side of the garage and it took you a week to tell me that you wanted me to help repair it?"

"It's not the same thing, Wes. You were ten. He's an adult."

"Who looks like he doesn't know what you want."

"I've told him." I have. Pete can be clueless sometimes. I remember all the times I've needed to be very precise with him. I remember that day when Pam tried to clue him in. He didn't seem to get it. Maybe at some point, I just need to tell him the words I want to hear, but if I do that—will he learn anything from it or just parrot back the words I want to hear.

I miss him, but I don't know that I can trust him if he can't give a full-hearted apology of his own volition.

Secrets to Keep

Lily

Roses don't really have a fragrance. I never realized that before I sat in the Wyngate backyard with a hundred rose bushes in full bloom. They're beautiful, but I'm disappointed. No wonder Peter finds them wanting.

The lemonade smells heavenly. It's real. Someone squeezed lemons to make this beverage. I can imagine their housekeeper Tilly doing that. I wonder about her. It seems like she could be their mother, except she's not old enough to be Peter's bio mom. Peter clearly thinks the world of her, but Alyse hates her.

"Why can't she leave us alone?""

Tilly wipes down the patio furniture while we sit on the loungers soaking up the sun's rays. How is that bothering us? She's farther away from us than you can get anywhere in my house.

"We need to plan something fun." Life bores Alyse. She wants to go to Manhattan, which my parents would never agree to even if Tilly went with us as a chaperone, which is not what Alyse wants. She's trying to convince Trevor to take us. I'm contemplating how to explain to her that I'm not going to disobey my parents who are under enough stress right now. I haven't even met Trevor and the idea that we're going to go to this huge city by ourselves with just a 19-year-old guy – I don't think so. It sounds exciting, but alarm bells jangle.

"I like having fun. Maybe we could go to the beach." I'm hoping to distract her.

"Mt. Calamity Beach Park. Done and done. Or.... Have you been to Fire Island?"

"What's that?"

"Barrier island to the south. It's amazing!"

"Is it like Long Sands?"

"What's that?"

We talk about the differences. Fire Island sounds interesting. I tell her Thursdays work best for a full-day outing because Bram is in therapy all day.

Tilly heads toward us with a pitcher of lemonade.

"You guys might want to use some sunscreen. The UV index is pretty high today."

I already put on sunscreen because I knew we were hanging out in the backyard and the Wyngate yard faces Long Island Sound. I thank her for the lemonade while Alyse makes faces behind her back. Tilly tells us lunch will be ready in about an hour. It's getting hot and I'm ready to hit the water at the bottom of the wooden staircase, but I don't know what Alyse will say about it.

"She acts like I'm ten, not fifteen," Alyse grumbles. "It's getting hot."

"It is. Our air conditioning is out, so my dad built a wading pool in the backyard. Bram and I spent yesterday afternoon soaking." We don't know what Bram remembers, but he showed his appreciation by dribbling water on himself.

Alyse's mouth twists slightly and then she smiles.

"Let's go down to the beach." She pops up and heads that way. I grab my flipflops and follow her, wondering why she never wants to talk about Bram. Even just the mention of him bothers her.

I've not been down to the beach before. I only know it exists because Peter pointed it out during my last visit. It's a small pocket of sand backed by a bluff and braced by rocks. I stare around while Alyse pulls off her clothes and gracefully walks into the water. There's a light surf. I join her in a moment.

"This is nice."

"Peter comes down here to swim in the mornings."

"By himself?"

"He's bored, feeling trapped. And he's a really strong swimmer, so he's fine. Swimming, he's fine."

"He looked like he felt better the other day."

Alyse nods, slowly walking deeper into the water.

"I think he had a flu bug for a while there."

I'm not going to argue because I don't know Peter. I kind of think Alyse is lying. She lies a lot. I'm beginning to realize she lies to herself more than she lies to others. So far, it's been harmless lies, but I can hear my mother saying, "lies will come back to bite you every time."

"I'm glad he's feeling better. Where is he?"

"He's got a class he's taking this week."

"Stuck indoors on a beautiful day like today. That stinks."

"He's getting pretty tired of our yard – even of this beach."

"Is that why he comes with you to pick me up?"

"That's some of it. I think he also likes you." She winks at me.

"He seems to like Bram too."

She turns her eyes out to sea. The way the beach is situated, you can see a bluff across the way then a long sweep of ocean.

"Maybe you could stay another night. I can get Trevor to come over and we can do something fun – just the four of us."

"I can't. My mom needs a break sometimes, so I'm staying with Bram while Dad takes her to a movie."

Something flickers under Alyse's surface, but then she smiles.

"Maybe next time."

"I don't suppose Peter would be allowed to relocate to my house. Bram is asleep by 8 pm."

"Oh, no, I don't think Tilly would agree to that. My dad is pretty mad at Peter right now."

"What exactly did he do?"

"Low grades on top of some other stuff."

The other stuff being DUI, which Peter seems to really regret. I don't know why she can't just say that since Peter admits to it.

Alyse dives under one of the small waves and emerges about ten feet away, treading water. I didn't bring shampoo, so I decide not to get my hair wet, but I swim with my head up to join her. I can imagine Peter enjoying it out here in the mornings.

"This was a great idea." Alyse points out to the ocean where a sailboat is skimming along. "I should talk Ben into taking us sailing."

"Ben has a sailboat?"

"Yeah. I don't know how much he gets to use it when he's working, but he and Peter used to go sailing all the time."

"Peter sails too?"

"Well, Ben's sailboat used to belong to him. He sold it to Ben a few years ago."

"Why?"

"Because he got the speedboat and he didn't have berthing space for both. He's got a really nice Malibu."

I have no idea what that is. I look up at the sun.

"I think it's probably getting close to lunch."

"So? Tilly can wait."

Wow, being rich lets people act like children.

"She's paid to wait on me." Alyse laughs at my expression. "When I go to college, she'll lose her job and have to go do something not nearly so easy — like wait tables or clean motel rooms."

"But doesn't she do other stuff for you?"

"Because my father pays her to do it. She's got no other skills. She's a maid."

I never really thought of it that way before, and I'm not sure it's a reason to look down on Tilly. Someone has to be here to drive Alyse to her dance lessons and make sure she eats. Not that she eats enough, but she's at least got the opportunity to do so.

Alyse turns in the water, stares out at the ocean.

"You ever wonder how far you could swim before you couldn't anymore?"

Uh...what?

"Why?"

"Just thinking. Let's go in."

She strikes out for the shore and I paddle after her. She rubs a vigorous hand through her hair to knock off the water before gathering her clothes from the sand.

"I'm glad we're friends." I straighten from squeezing water from my hair. "There's lots of people who want to be my friend, but most people don't want to just hang out and *be* friends. You know?"

I nod. Lots of others would love to be caught up in Alyse's draft, but they don't like her that much. I think that's called an entourage and they're not just for rock stars.

"I really like you, Alyse."

I'm not sure what else to say to her, though there's a little voice echoing in my head that I should tell Tilly about what I thought Alyse said to me out there in the water.

"I like you too, Lily, which is why I tell you stuff I wouldn't tell anyone else."

Now I'm obligated to not say anything. I don't know what to do. She links arms with me, and we head up to the house.

Self-Analysis

Peter

Abigail calls it the FAST test. I'm familiar with it because Rick asked me these same questions way back when.

"How often do you have eight or more drinks on one occasion?"

Answering in my head, I think "never", but Rick explained to me that there are 25 shots in a fifth of whiskey. I drink half the bottle, at least, almost every time, so "weekly" is the correct and terrifying answer. Yeah, maybe I don't drink weekly because I'm only 18 and I already know I'm an alcoholic, but just about every time I drink, I drink like that. That's three points.

"How often during the last year have you been unable to remember what happened the night before because you had been drinking?"

I want to say "never", but that's a lie. It's more like – if you spread them around – monthly. That's two points.

"How often during the last year have you failed to do what was normally expected of you because of your drinking?"

The scary thought is "almost daily", but I've been sober a lot during the last 10 months, so – monthly. That's two points.

"Has a relative or friend, doctor or other health worker been concerned about your drinking or suggested you cut down?"

That's all been in the last year. People really didn't bring it up until Europe. Well, that isn't really true. Ben freaked out over my walking a balance beam over a hot bed of coals once. Except I don't remember that. Might Ben make something like that up? See Question 2. I wince at the not-so-fun "Most Likely To" list that went around in which someone nominated me as "most-likely to need a liver transplant." I got the official "most likely to succeed" category too. I guess it all depended on how well you know me.

Add four points. That adds up to 11 points, 12 if I'm honest – but I don't want to be – which is a problem in itself. No matter how I do this test, I'm a hazardous drinker. Good thing I've stopped drinking.

But then there's the second test.

"How often do you have a drink containing alcohol?""

Pretty danged often.

"How many drinks containing alcohol do you have on a typical day when you're drinking?"

A lot.

"How often do you have six or more drinks on one occasion?"

Every time I drink, just about.

"How often during the last year have you found that you were not able to stop drinking once you started?"

Pretty much all of them.

We already covered Question 5 on the earlier test. Drinking makes me unreliable. Ditto Question 6. That not remembering thing is a theme with me.

"How often during the last year have you needed an alcoholic drink first thing in the morning to get yourself going after a night of heavy drinking?"

Only in the European time zone, but nearly daily there. Well, yeah, I *wanted* an alcoholic beverage before finals this spring and I suspect I would have passed the classes if I'd tossed back a slug before those tests instead of taking them hungover.

"How often during the last year have you had a feeling of guilt or remorse after drinking?"

I don't want to answer that question. I admitted to alcoholism about nine and a half months ago and since then, drinking makes me feel guilty.

"Have you or someone else been injured as a result of your drinking?"

I keep circling this drain and I hate it. Yup, I have a drinking problem. But I'm working on it. Yeah, treatment is available. Rehabilitation centers, AA, other programs. There's one called Rational Recovery that is like AA for people who don't believe in God. I don't really believe in God, but I also don't not believe in God. I just sort of ignore the whole "higher power" aspect of it. Rick says I ignore something that might help me stay sober, but I can't believe what I can't believe. Then there's that weird memory of walking that aisle at camp so many years ago. What was that about? Too much junk food and not enough sleep? Everybody else did it? It felt right at the time and then I went home and .... I don't want to think about Mom and Sam and the rest of that summer.

A lot of people just quit drinking on their own and substitute exercise for drinking. Or woodworking. Or religion. Finn's going to Bible school makes sense now. Alyse laughed at Finn, but I kind of get it.

I need to find something I can substitute for bourbon. I need to do something else when I want to get drunk.

The class is over. I put in my 40 hours and I'm getting my certificate. I'll get my driver's license back in a couple of weeks and Dad said he'd lift my restriction as soon as I completed this class. I'm getting an A in one of the courses I'm repeating and probably a high B in the other. My life is normalizing. But there's still this issue of not drinking because I know I need to stop. I want my independence back, but I never want to risk someone again.

So, while I wait for Vic to pick me up, I open the Big Book on my phone and read the Step 4 section again. I can do this. I can.

Communication

Lily

Bram became much more interactive in the last few months and is now home full-time, though going to therapy a lot. He can walk with a long leg brace and a walker if someone helps him stand, but he seems to prefer the wheelchair at home. He's still not talking, but he shakes his head for yes and no, not always accurately.

Peter sits beside him trying to draw the same picture with his left hand. Since Bram is probably never going to talk again, the therapist suggested art might be a way to express himself, but Bram is righthanded and the stroke paralyzed his right arm. When Bram demonstrates frustration with what I'm trying to show him, Peter sits down and takes a colored pencil up in his own left hand. He's doing a little bit better than Bram, but he's not brain-damaged and he might understand the instructions better.

The amazing thing is that Bram is trying to copy him.

"Bram, this is hard." Peter speaks his admission in a measured way, not as if he's talking to an idiot but as if he's slowed his tempo down a half-beat. He starts every sentence with "Bram" which gives my brother time to focus for whatever follows. Peter drops the pencil and flexes his fingers, then rubs them with his right hand. Bram smacks Peter's hands.

"Bram, don't do that."

"Lily, it's okay. He can't massage his own fingers. I can see that would be frustrating if someone else does it." Now he faces Bram who doesn't know what we're saying and looks ready to explode. "Bram, it's okay. Do you want to draw?" He indicates the pencils Bram discarded.

Bram blinks at him. His lips part, then crease into a tight line, pulling up on the left. Then he shakes his head.

"Tired?" Peter pantomimes like he's falling asleep. Bram nods.

"He's not supposed to take a nap for another hour."

"Maybe he's just tired of doing this project. Let's try something." Peter gets up and gets the backgammon set from the bookshelf. There's a photo on the wall of Bram playing backgammon with my older brother, taken only a few weeks before the stroke. Peter doesn't miss much. "Bram, do you remember this?"

Bram frowns at him.

"Bram, can you play this?" Bram freezes as if paused. Peter opens the little suitcase and puts it in front of him. He plucks the instruction manual out and lays the set-up diagram so Bram can see it. Bram hesitantly picks up one of the white pieces and places it on one of the points. It's correct, but that might be an accident. Bram reaches for another piece and places it correctly too. He tilts his head to look at the diagram and gets the next one correct, then pauses, frowning. Peter encourages him and he sets up the entire board according to the diagram. He's slow, but he's clearly processing. When he's done, he pulls a happy half-smile and then rubs his left temple.

"That means he's getting a headache. His right eye still tends to get strained easily."

Bram shakes his head at me then gestures at Peter in a very nonspecific way. Peter picks up one of the dice cups and drops in a brown die and a white die and then gestures to Bram.

"Roll to see who goes first."

Bram clumsily shakes the cup and rolls. The white die is 6 and the brown die is 5. Bram stares at them, finally casting a distressed look at Peter and then me.

"He can't count and doesn't recognize numbers." Peter didn't know. It's not his fault.

"Well, that sucks. But I looked aphasia up on the internet and it said he might or might not recognize numbers and he can count. He just maybe needs to remember how."

"You are sweet, but the therapists have tried and--." A knock on the screen door going into the garage demands my attention. I go to find Ben standing there. "Hey. How are you?"

"Good. Can I come in?"

"Uh, sure." I open the screen for him. "Peter's visiting."

"Yeah, I saw his bike."

Peter shows Bram how to count on his fingers. When they get to five Bram looks confused.

"Maybe ... this way." Peter folds his thumb down. Using his thumb as "one", Bram silently counts out each finger to five and then folds his thumb down. He smiles again then moves his white piece, five and then six spaces. "Strong opening move," Peter tells him.

Bram rubs his left temple again. Peter notices but rolls and makes his own move. He isn't cheating to lose. If Bram truly remembers how to play, that would be insulting. Ben hasn't said anything. Bram rolls again and Peter helps him count the die and shows Bram his possible moves. He lets Bram make the choice of how to move. Now Bram rubs his temple again.

"Bram, you're tired. I'm going to write down where we are, and we can finish the game tomorrow." Peter pantomimes to the best of his ability and Bram nods, giving him a lopsided smile. I'm nervous of leaving Peter and Ben alone, but Bram needs to lie down.

We converted the den to his room when we bought the house, so I leave the door open so I can overhear my guests while I get Bram settled.

"What are you doing here?"

"Went out for a bike ride and just ended up here. Since I knew you wouldn't talk to me, I figured I'd visit Lily and Bram." There's an edge to Peter's voice that says teaching a brain-damaged kid to count is less stressful than talking to his best friend.

"You look like you've done that a bit."

"I've said 'hi' to Bram a few times when Alyse and I were picking up Lily."

"You're good at it."

Peter doesn't reply audibly. I think he might be touched by Ben's compliment.

"I just can imagine what it must be like for him."

There's an awkward silence before Ben speaks again.

"What are you doing these days?"

"Well, I just got off being grounded."

"For what?"

"Stupidity." Peter sounds embarrassed. "And I took a driver's awareness course."

"How'd that go?"

"I passed. My license is supposed to be reinstated soon." There's an odd silence that I think means I need to get out there soon. "Don't worry. I won't drink and drive again."

"Why am I supposed to believe that?"

I don't hear Peter's murmured reply. I turn down the light and step into the living room just as Ben replies to whatever Peter said.

"If you have a wreck when you're drinking, it's not an accident."

Peter's toeing the carpet.

"You have a point. I guess I didn't really think about the meaning of the word. Hey, Lily."

Ben frowns at Peter who smiles tentatively at me.

"You wore him out, but that's a good thing. Mom will be really excited to hear he can count now."

"He could count before. He just didn't know how to show you." I nod. Maybe Peter ought to be a speech therapist. He's figuring out things about my brother the therapists seem not to notice.

"So, I should probably get going. Dinner will be ready soon. Maybe I'll stop by tomorrow."

"Bram will be at therapy all day and I'm going to Fire Island with Alyse."

"Wow. Just two girls hanging together?" Ben looks uncertain.

"No, her boyfriend Trevor is driving us."

"Sounds like fun." Peter frowns like he's uncertain too.

"It would be except I'm going to feel like a third-wheel."

Peter nods.

"I haven't been to Fire Island all summer. This 'not-having-a-drivers-license' thing is confining – which is probably the point." He looks embarrassed again. "You ever hang out with Trevor before?" I shake my head. Peter cuts a glance at Ben. "Big personality." Ben snorts.

"Putting it mildly. Always the life of the party, though."

Peter's drifting toward the door. Ben glances at him.

"Can we talk?" Something flickers in Peter's eyes as he scans Ben's face. Maybe it starts as hopeful optimism, but it ends with wariness. "Maybe I could drop by tonight."

Peter's thinking, weighing the offer, almost as if he's afraid to hope.

"I...can't tonight. I've got somewhere to be."

"Tomorrow night, then?"

"Um, I don't know." His hand flutters up to scratch a shoulder. "I've got this meeting I'm going to every night. Don't think it's a good idea for me to skip it right now." He shoves his hands into his jeans pockets. "Maybe Saturday or Sunday, during the day?"

Ben's frowning. Peter seems ready to take flight and flutter around the room. I don't know how to help him.

"Yeah." Ben sounds uncertain, like he knows it's his turn to reply, but he's not sure what to say. "I'll text you."

Peter nods, shrugs, turns to me.

"I'll see you. Maybe, I don't know, day after tomorrow?"

"He'll be here."

"Cool. And, Ben, it's not that I don't want to talk. It's just that I've got some stuff going on and...I just...yeah. Text me."

He's gone then, leaving Ben standing there with a scowl.

"So, what's up?"

"Is this really the first time he's been here on his own?"

"Yeah – well, since Spring Break. That's when he met Bram. And he's been with Alyse a few times when she's picked me up or dropped me off. Alyse says it's his way to get a break from his cage."

"Pete hanging out with Bram seems...." Ben frowns at his thoughts. "Maybe that's unfair. He's always been really good with Wes. He'd get irritated with Alyse tagging after us, but Wes was always welcome...by him, not always by me." He chuckles. "Do you know what he does every night?"

"No. We didn't really talk. Crosstalk frustrates Bram."

"Of course. Just remember what I said about him. Okay?"

I nod. I had kind of forgotten about Ben's warning. Peter just doesn't seem like that kind of guy. Ben scans the artwork attempts on the table.

"Bram almost had it here."

"Peter drew that."

"Left-handed?"

"Trying to sympathize, I guess. He really is good with Bram." I gather up the backgammon board, stashing Peter's notes inside. "Hopefully, he won't have to start all over again with this lesson. The doctors say Bram's memory is dodgy."

"I think you need to worry more that Pete won't show up to continue. He's not the most reliable person on the planet."

"Is that just stuff you realized after you stopped being friends?"

"No. I actually knew that when we were friends. I let it go because he was a friend and I thought he'd get better."

I don't know what to say, so I don't say anything. Ben's gaze dwells on my face for a nervous-making time and then he turns toward the kitchen.

"Well, I should go grab a shower. Nice to see you."

As Ben heads out of the garage, I realize he stopped by because he saw Peter's bike. I'm torn now because that's just plain mean to keep Peter from having friends now that Ben doesn't want to be friends. My phone buzzes.

> ALYSE - Trevor points out you're going to feel like a third-wheel tomorrow. Fire Island is not to be missed, but I don't want you to be bored. Dad lifted Peter's grounding so I could ask him if you're okay with him coming.

Ben's warning filters through my head, but Peter working with Bram also comes to mind. How much danger could he get me into on a sunny beach in the middle of the day?

> LILY - I'm okay with that if he is.

American Bohemia

Peter

I'm sleepy as hell as Mel Grey's red SUV turns into Bay Shore Bean. Trevor borrowed it so we could all go in the same car without having to rely on Vic. Trevor's Fiat has something they call a backseat, but not even the girls could share it comfortably. The girls could sit in the backseat of the Jag, but I can't drive yet so Trevor worked out a substitute. According to Alyse, Trevor invited me on this outing, but I must admit I jumped at the suggestion immediately. I'd agree to go to Fire Island with a group of nuns. Anything to relieve the boredom.

The dock is mostly deserted. It's a weekday and it's too early for anyone but fishermen. You'd think Trevor would want to sleep in since he's usually partying every night, but he's actually an early riser, although I'm pretty sure this dawn start is my sister's goofy idea. Dancers are just too disciplined.

Lily looks good. I know. She's fifteen. I shouldn't be thinking that her blue swimsuit is just right. It covers her girl's figure just enough to suggest those curves will become more dramatic soon – maybe tomorrow. She's covered it with a darker t-shirt and white shorts, but those just show her tanned legs, which are still long and trim.

Alyse wears a red-and-white striped bikini under her red shorts and matching sleeveless t-shirt. Her black pixie ruffles in the wind as we settle down for the short ferry trip. I sip my coffee, hoping I wake up soon. Not drinking is still messing with my sleep cycles. I kind of feel jet-lagged, but in truth, I only got about four hours of sleep because I kept waking up.

"You want some?" Trevor opens an Altoids box with several orange capsules inside.

"No, thanks." My pulse starts to flutter. I don't want Adderall, but it makes me want something and that's concerning.

"Just because you had a bad experience the first time doesn't mean you will this time. You're taller, bigger."

"And I still don't want to feel bipolar. Thanks anyway."

My coffee cup is almost empty. Trevor might be an enabler, but he's not a pusher. The box goes away. Now that I'm closeup, I can tell he's popped at least one Adderall already. I guess I don't blame him since he drove. I don't know if he still takes it for ADHD. How can you tell when you've always got something on board? I'm beginning to realize how hard it must have been for Ben to see me buzzed *all the time* and never knowing when I'd crossed the line into wasted.

The wind picks up as the ferry pushes off the dock. Lily dons a sweatshirt and Alyse looks frozen. I shrug out of my jacket and drop it over her shoulders. Trevor's forehead creases. *Yeah, that's how you're supposed to treat your date, man.*

Lily's brought a backpack that I expect I'll end up carrying. She's not wrong. A blanket, towel and sweatshirt are not a bad idea, but they all weigh a bit and it all adds up. By the end of the day, she's going to regret every ounce.

"So, what are the plans for the day?"

Trevor rolls his eyes. He's not much into planning and he'll roll with whatever comes his way. Alyse likes to plan, so I figure I'll give us something to talk about and maybe it will wake me up.

"Breakfast at that place. You know the place. The really good egg sandwiches?" Alyse sucks at remembering names, I've noticed.

"Rachel's. Great coffee too." Lily nods like she approves of that. I notice she doesn't drink her coffee very quickly. Alyse is already out and I glance over at Trevor and see he's topping his cup off from something in his jacket. Way too early for that and I'm glad I hate rum. I can do this whole sober-fun thing. I can.

"Fire Island has great food." Trevor is covering, trying not to draw attention to doctoring his coffee. It's seven in the morning, for heaven sakes.

"And the beaches are to die for." Alyse's eyes widen and I realize she's probably had an Adderall too. Not Lily though. She's as fresh as new-fallen snow.

"Just so long as we get breakfast first. I'm starving." Lily sips some coffee while Alyse launches into a verbal tour of the island and all the fun she has planned.

I lean my head back and smell the salt air. The Great South Bay glitters in the early morning sun and the wind makes my eyes water. Gooseflesh covers my arms. Alyse owes me for giving up my jacket.

I might have dozed off if it weren't for the wind. I open my eyes before we get to the dock and we walk out into American Bohemia. Seriously, slouchy beach houses, boardwalks and bicycles, zero cars. My last visit, mountain bikes ruled. Ben isn't much into shopping or eating egg sandwiches. We ate, but we pumped into the sand dunes before the next ferry arrived. Trevor would be up for something like that, but Alyse hates anything natural and — well, I don't know what Lily might like. She's young enough that *she* might not know what she likes. I can take one day of walking around on boardwalks and hanging out on the beach. Anything different from our yard feels like heaven.

Rachel's Bakery is a half-story-up beach-shack of a place that is on the way to the beach. Well, everything in Ocean Beach is on the way to the beach. We climb the stairs into this bright, friendly atmosphere with a greenhouse dining section beyond the bakery cases, nets hanging from the ceiling with Japanese glass floats, dried starfish and seashells caught in the twine. There's this beachy milk-paint white on the walls and ceiling and wide pine floors scuffed by decades of sandy feet.

I'm starving by now, so I order an omelet and a croissant and the largest black coffee. Alyse fusses at Trevor for ordering the Bran Pancakes. He's nowhere near getting fat, but she's got that dancer's mindset — even as she orders an egg sandwich. I watch Lily try to be casual about breakfast, but I think she's shocked by the prices. She orders a single croissant, which I suspect means she'll be starving by midmorning. I add two of the biggest breves they have to my order and ask the server to put a double scoop of whey in one of them. Alyse frowns at me. I roll my eyes at her and she wanders over to the table.

"There's no picnicking on the beach?" I try to get out of the way of the overweight woman with the Bed-Stuy accent asking the question because she seems crabby, but she's apparently asking me.

"There's laws against it."

"Why?"

Why would I know? I don't live here. Maybe because people make a mess and it attracts more seagulls? Or maybe.... Seriously, I don't know.

"You're from the mainland, aren't you, honey?" The woman behind the counter gives me an apologetic smile, saving me from having to disappoint this woman. She doesn't act like she takes disappointment well.

"I am." Her gaze shifts to the woman and I step back.

"The town council voted to not allow eating on the beach. Not even ice cream or cookies, which are allowed on the boardwalk and paths."

I escape. Lily laughs at me.

"Maybe it's the tan and your hair is still tousled by the ferry ride. You look like you spend a lot of time on the beach."

"The joys of being half-Greek." My mother's Mediterranean complexion meant acne in junior high, but I still have a vague olive tone even in late-winter and I've had lots of opportunity to sit on our private beach or in the back yard this month. Boredom makes beautiful tans.

"I've got the same parents and look." Alyse holds her arm next to mine. She's got a vaguely olive tone, but I'm naturally darker. "I still have to use sunscreen."

"So do I."

"In March!" She hisses at me and shrugs out of my jacket to sit down. I confiscate it and tuck it into my own backpack along with my water bottle and sunglasses. Trevor has his arm against Alyse's now. He has WASP complexion, though his hair is naturally dark brown, frosted silver. He did that for *The Troll King* three years ago and he's not changed it back. It's a commitment. I tried bleaching my hair in boarding school and it's painful.

"I forgot sunscreen," Lily mutters. I pluck my tube out of the side pouch of my backpack to hand to her. "Why do you carry it if you don't need it?"

"It got left there from that one sunny afternoon during Spring Break."

"Which was the last time he needed it."

Alyse isn't wrong, but I don't know why she's busting my chops. I take a long draw on my coffee. Maybe the caffeine will help me not be testy with her.

"Remember that time we went to Cherry Grove?" Trevor just spiked his coffee under the table. I can smell it on his breath.

"Oh, yeah, that was — interesting." I slide my eyes Lily's direction, warning him that he might shock the youngster. Trevor has no boundaries.

"We pull up to the store there — we're on bikes — and, I shit you not, twenty gay men immediately descend upon Peter like seagulls on fish. They thought he was incredibly *yummy.*" Trevor exercises his vocal talents fully here, sounding just like a stereotypical gay man – dark and effeminate --and I suddenly flash back to Cormorant Island, my first date with Cheyenne. I shouldn't be here with Lily. It's too late to back out now, but I should know better. For just a moment, I wonder what might happen to hurt her.

"Remember the one guy who just kept following us?"

Trevor's telling a funny story. My looks definitely get attention. Bold women stuff business cards in my pants in hotel elevators and once during Dad's campaign a woman old enough to be my mother left her key card next to my plate at a fundraiser. Gay men usually just look me up and down, but some of them can't take "I'm straight" for an answer. That time in Cherry Grove, I wasn't even sixteen yet, and not as comfortable with my masculinity as I am now. He'd get my message now.

"So embarrassing. I wasn't trying to lead him on. I really wasn't."

The waiter brings our food and we tuck in. I pretend I mistakenly ordered the second breve with the whey and give it to Lily. Trevor starts teasing Lily about her braid, which is too short to stay neat in the wind. It's also too long to just let blow in the breeze. She'd be eating hair all day.

"You should cut it. There's something so liberating about it." Alyse emphasizes her point by flipping a hand through her short do. Her hair's not as curly as mine and the hairdresser did a good job of taming the cowlicks. I need to get her name.

"I had mine short until this year. I want to try long for a while."

"It's so much work."

"How could braiding your hair be work?" I really want to know. It was the world's simplest hairstyle. She could get out of bed in the morning and not even need to brush it.

"Maybe just above your shoulders."

Apparently Alyse doesn't think I deserve an answer. Trevor says her change of hairstyle surprised him too.

The beach dazzles as we approach it a half-hour later, the white sand reflecting the southern sun, casting the world in golden light. Fire Island is only about a half-mile wide. The north shore faces the Great South Bay and is lined with buildings. There are a few blocks of beach houses to the south and then there's the star attraction – the beach. Alyse drops her bag in the sand and starts to kick off her clothes. Although it doesn't matter because I'm here, I glance around for the lifeguard station. No need to be stupid and the FI police are strict about their rules. Trevor skims off his shirt revealing his taut abs and dancer shoulders. He and Alyse hit the surf while Lily and I spread a blanket and rescue their clothes from the sand.

"Spontaneity makes the party." I more slowly remove my shirt and stash my sandals in my backpack. My feet are tough. I won't need shoes until the ferry tonight.

"I like that about Alyse."

"Trevor too, although by the end of the day, you might wish you'd come with less exhausting people."

I settle down on the blanket. Lily settles too.

"It's a little too early after eating, right?"

"That's my thought."

"By the way, Bram counted a bunch of stuff last night."

"Yeah?"

"The doctors all say his memory probably isn't good, but he used that finger-counting thing you taught him and got it right."

"That's good. So, what do they do in therapy?"

"They're working on his walking and using his arm today."

"Not speech?"

"They're kind of giving up on that."

"Why?"

"It's been over a year since the stroke and they've managed to teach him 'hi' and 'Mom' and he can't string them together."

"Wow. That's gotta suck for him."

"Yeah. I don't know why he responds to you though. He doesn't with most people."

"Maybe it's because I don't believe he doesn't understand. I didn't know it when I met him, so I wasn't preprogrammed."

"Maybe. Ben's brother Wes asks about him sometime. My parents are reluctant because an 11-year-old might not understand Bram's issues."

"Wes is a cool kid. I'd give him a chance. Maybe have him over some day when I'm there and he can see that Bram does interact if you give him time."

"Yeah, maybe. I'll suggest it to Mom. Thank you for agreeing to come today, by the way."

"Yeah, third wheel syndrome, it's painful."

She laughs. I smile in response. Because I'm nearly a year younger than most of my classmates, I didn't catch on to girls as soon as they did, so I've experienced third-wheel syndrome. I'm glad I could help her avoid it.

"So, this is a barrier island?"

"Yes. The whole of the Great South Bay is protected by this and then there's Jones Beach that way and the Hamptons that way."

"It's gorgeous."

"It is. You ought to come back sometime and see more of it. There's way more than just this town."

"Yeah, but how do you get to it?"

"Biking mostly. Fat-tire bikes. You can rent them."

"Sounds like you've come here a lot."

"Yeah. Ben and I discovered it when we were freshmen and then a lot of our friends joined us. My dad rented a beach house here that summer and we were here for the entire vacation."

"He hasn't done it since?"

"He got distracted by running for governor. If I hadn't screwed up, I probably could have done it this summer."

"You mean with the DUI?"

"Yeah." It's uncomfortable, but it's the truth. I'm struggling to accept the whole truth-telling part of AA, but I don't really want to lie to Lily. "I'm trying to get a handle on that now. I really screwed up."

We're silent for a moment.

"Maybe you needed to do that to find your way."

Well, that's kind of her. We're getting too personal, so I push up from the sand and suggest we get wet. She doffs her outer clothes and we stride into the surf. Alyse sees me coming and throws her toned body at me. I allow her to pull me down into the water. It occurs to me she is here with Trevor and holding me down to the sand in an unsisterly manner, so I toss her off me and then scoop her up to deposit her in Trevor's arms. He laughs and I smell the rum on his breath and really long to find a drink, but I splash Lily instead and quickly forget that I'm thirsty for something other than saltwater.

A Good Guy

Lily

Wow, everything here is so expensive. The ferry ticket and breakfast left me with just enough cash for lunch, meaning I can't buy the necklace even though it's gorgeous – tiny seashells separated by chunks of something that looks like amber but probably isn't. I didn't expect for so many places to only accept cash and I haven't yet seen an ATM. I sigh and admire the earrings Alyse is buying.

"I'm starving, girls!" Trevor calls as we come out of the shop.

"Where to?" Peter shopped with us while Trevor went to find a bathroom. Peter's not wearing a shirt or shoes and it's driving me crazy. He's in amazing shape, though you can tell Trevor is more disciplined in his workouts.

"So, when you going back to Joffrey, man?" Peter asks Trevor as we start walking along the Grand Promenade again. There's nothing grand about it. It's a boardwalk interspersed with concrete paths.

"I don't." Trevor's mouth twists. "It wasn't a good fit. I'm trying out for a troupe in the City, though. Dad's trying to talk me into Columbia, get my degree on."

"Cool. I wish he'd rub off on my father."

"Yeah, friends, right? Not always on the same page, even after knowing each other since – what, third grade?"

"Something like that, yeah."

"Do you really hate Yale that much?"

"No, but it's that whole 'not-having-a-choice' that gets to me."

"Stop talking about sad things." Alyse makes a face. She's very hyper currently. I'm scared for her. What is wrong with her?

"Were we sad?" Peter and Trevor cast questioning looks at each other. Trevor laughs first, but Peter's is just as genuine.

"CJ's!" Trevor bellows. Peter's stride grows noticeably slower as we approach. The sign outside the door announces that it's "The Home of the Rocket Fuel." I looked up Fire Island on the Internet and CJ's is supposedly the place to party. That concerns me because none of us are of legal drinking age – though that doesn't seem to be stopping Trevor or, I suspect, Alyse.

Before I can ask if there's someplace that isn't a bar to eat at, Trevor and Alyse disappear into the crowd. Peter pauses, donning his shirt, then staring at the entrance, licking his lips.

"I'm – just need a minute." He breathes out heavily. I stand there waiting. He's only eighteen, so how many bars could he possibly have been in and, yet, Ben warned that Peter is a heavy drinker. Surely, he's not afraid he can't control it – not at eighteen?

"Let's go." We dive into the crowd that is spilling out the open door. We push through an almost monolithic clutch of human flesh, smelling of cocoa butter and what I assume is rum. They're laughing and moving to the beat of the music and everybody has a glass or bottle in their hand. For a moment, I lose sight of Peter's back, but then I almost run into him as he's come to a complete stop, trying to negotiate around a group of fit men all dancing to the beat. He fumbles his hand back to catch mine, giving one of the guys a weird smile and drawing me along. We emerge on the far side of the room where Trevor appropriated a table for four. A waitress is already there taking a drink order.

"No!" Peter's face pinches. "No Rocket Fuel for me, thank you." The waitress scratches something out. "I'll have a lemonade."

"Iced tea," I say when she looks at me.

"Chocolate martini." The waitress gives Alyse a skeptical look, but Alyse produces a driver's license that seems to satisfy her. Peter stares at the tabletop until the waitress disappears into the crowd, then leans toward Alyse.

"Whatever you drink after this better be non-alcoholic."

"Seriously, big brother? Like you've never gotten blotto on Fire Island."

"I'm not a hundred-pound girl and look how well that worked out for me. I'm not saying you can't drink at all, but you've already had a couple and trying to keep up with Trevor is just plain stupid. You don't want to have to go home because you're puking."

"He's right, luv. Take it easy. Drinking is a marathon, not a sprint. You're not drinking?" Trevor directs that question to Peter.

"I'm not and please don't try to sabotage me."

"Never. You know better than that. It'll leave more rum for me ... and you have a nasty history with rum anyway." Peter grins but he looks embarrassed too.

The menu is pricey. How in the world do these people afford a day here? I'm thinking I'll just order an appetizer, though the CJ's Burger sounds great. When the waitress returns with our drinks and to take our meal order, Peter says he's treating me.

"You're babysitting me. I should pay you for that."

I can't afford lunch or dinner if I don't accept his gift, so I smile and thank him. We order four burgers and an extra order of chicken fingers and another round of drinks, substitute iced tea for the chocolate martini. Peter is in the middle of telling a story where Trevor did something phenomenally stupid when a waiter comes over with a tall glass that matches Trevor's.

"Trev, I said no."

"It's not me. I have no want to watch you puke the afternoon away. Seriously."

"The man in the blue shirt sends it your way." The server nods his head in that direction. Peter glances over. Is that the same guy who stopped our progress on our way in? He's young, handsome, and staring at Peter like some guys stare at Alyse.

Peter sighs and shakes his head, points to his lemonade and passes the Rocket Fuel to Trevor, who winks at the gift-giver.

"What's that about?" Alyse asks.

"He always attracts at least one." Trevor thinks it's funny, or he's drank so much rum he thinks everything is funny. "I need to drain the lizard before the burgers get here."

He springs up and heads into the crowd, presumably in the direction of the bathrooms. I'm glad Alyse and I stopped at one of the public bathrooms earlier.

Peter licks his lips, staring at Trevor's abandoned drinks. He breathes out heavily, then delves in his wallet and hands me a driver's license.

"Hang onto this." I frown at it. The information is correct except he'd be twenty-three. I thought the police confiscate your driver's license when it's suspended. So now I frown at him. He laughs nervously. "Yeah, best forgery money can buy, but I don't want to use it, so just hang onto it for me. I think I'll be okay, but don't let me wander off. If I say I have to go pee, escort me to the bathroom door." I can't help staring at him because this is what Ben warned me about, only different. "C'mon. I know Ben warned you off, but I'm not – I'm trying to stop, and I just don't trust myself right now. I need a little help."

I nod because he seems genuine. I secure the card in my Velcro shorts pocket with my cash and ATM card.

The burgers are delicious, and I'm stuffed. Alyse only ate about half of hers, but Trevor and Peter split the other half and polish it off. Now we're headed toward the register to pay the bill and that guy gets in the way again.

"Where have you been all of my life, beautiful?" I blush, but his gaze rakes over me to dwell on Peter's lower abdomen. "Don't tell me you're wasting that gorgeous package on *that*."

Peter smirks and snorts.

"I don't swing your way, man. Sorry to disappoint, but I'm straight."

"Naw. You need to be honest with yourself, man."

"Whatever. Our friends are waiting." Peter steps around the man and draws me behind him. After he pays the bill from a roll of twenties, we meet Trevor and Alyse on the boardwalk.

"How do you do that, man?" Trevor asks. "I always want to kick 'em in the nuts."

"You probably don't get hit on as often as I do. Let's walk to Point of the Woods."

Trevor and Alyse look at one another while I shift gears from why gay men hit on Peter to the island sights.

"What's that?"

"It's like the original gated community," Alyse explains. "Literally fenced. Come along. Let us enlighten you."

We start walking eastward, Peter and I trailing behind Alyse and Trevor who dance and sing and generally make a spectacle of themselves. Peter's right about them being exhausting. If I'd come with them alone, I would be thoroughly worn out by now and maybe a little scared by how much they're drinking.

"At least he's a fun drunk and keeping Alyse from becoming a bitch. I hope you're having fun."

"I am, although – don't you worry about her?"

"I do, but – it's pretty common in our school, you know?"

"The rich party set. I've heard. Alyse talked about having parties, but she hasn't' done it yet."

"Yeah. I don't think Tilly's going to help her with that, and I won't either, so …." He shrugs. "She can help Trevor plan one, maybe." He lays a long-fingered hand on my forearm. "Hold up a minute."

"They're going to leave us behind."

"They can only go so far before they run out of path. Just take a pause."

He turns me toward him and pulls something out of his pocket – the necklace I admired.

"Fire Island is expensive and Alyse should have told you that, but she's kind of careless sometimes. So, you should have a good time and not worry about how much it costs because my dad's really rich and he reinstated my allowance, so …." He slips the necklace over my head.

"But you are doing me a favor by being here."

"We're doing each other a favor. I've been pretty lonely the last month at home and I needed an adventure, so I'm grateful to be invited. But I needed someone who wasn't getting drunk along because it's hard to say 'no' when you're the only one. And I like treating my friends. I don't do it very often, because it tends to make people uncomfortable, but I'm not going to miss the money nearly as much as I would have regretted not coming today."

"Thank you." I touch the necklace. We continue down the boardwalk.

"You have friends, right?"

Peter sighs, takes my hand.

"Yeah, but – I'm starting to realize how many of them were either Ben's friends or just hanging around me for the benefits."

"Benefits?"

"Rich people can afford some cool stuff. When my dad grounds, the cool stuff gets locked up and – well, somedays I paced the backyard forty times just to keep from listening to the clock tick. And even though I'm off restriction, I can't throw a party and get everyone together because that's what got me into trouble in the first place."

We come up to a chain-link fence that bifurcates a beach.

"What is this?"

"Point of the Woods. This is where the regular people live and over there is the exclusive zone where regular people aren't allowed."

Trevor and Alyse are on the other side of the fence, still laughing and singing.

"Um, what happens if they get caught there?"

"Arrest maybe." I cast him a distressed look. He grins. "Trevor's dad owns a house so probably nothing."

"Are we going over there?" He frowns now. His expressions change like the wind. Something moves behind his eyes. Is it fear? Dread.

"Do you need to?" I'm curious about this gated community, but not so much that I would make him go somewhere that he doesn't like.

"No." A change of subject is in order. "Where did you stay when you summered here? It's called summering, right?"

"It is." The light comes back into his eyes. "It's a couple of blocks back." He moves in that direction.

"We won't miss them?" He turns back to me, gently takes my hand.

"Trevor's probably looking for the spare key right now so they can use the bathroom."

"How do you know that?"

"Trevor and I have been friends since before Ben and I were friends. Just not as deep."

"You really miss him."

"Yeah. But maybe we'll talk on Saturday or Sunday and things will be better." He looks sad. We walk in silence for a while. He's substantially taller than me, but he strolls so I don't have to match his stride.

"What happened?"

"I don't know. Well, I do, but .... I had an accident – a wreck – and someone got hurt and ... I don't know. I was in the hospital, pretty drugged for the pain and I guess I said something ... something

246

wrong, because Ben decided we weren't friends anymore. He said I could fix it if I gave it time and if I stopped drinking and ... I'm trying, but I don't seem to be able to get him to even listen to my side. Yesterday, he finally told me to stop calling it an accident. He's right that it's not an accident because I was drunk, but I didn't mean to have that wreck so 'accident' seemed like the right word."

"Sounds like word games, yeah."

"Yeah. I get that he's trying to teach me something, but – I really did some dumb things this winter because I didn't know what he wanted. Why couldn't he have just said that?"

I don't know the answer. I guess I could ask Ben, although I have no idea how to bring something like that up.

Peter turns us down a side lane. We stop before this great beach house with several additions and decks galore. Parts of it are shingled gray and parts are clapboard painted in eye-popping Caribbean yellow.

"There's a swimming pool around back and you're a five-minute walk to the beach. Great place to spend the summer." He smiles at a fond memory. "I dragged Ben along and he got a job at one of the beach shacks. And then Trevor would pop over every day he didn't have a dance intensive and we'd hang out until Ben got free. Lots of beach time and mountain biking and just hanging out." Something sad creeps across his face.

"And then?"

"We went back to Port Mallory and Dad decided to run for governor. Things have not been the same since."

He turns toward the beach and we walk slowly down the concrete path.

"How do people get furniture into these houses?"

"Mostly in the winter. You can drive 4-wheel drives then."

We walk into the sand. Trevor and Alyse are nowhere to be seen. The Atlantic breeze lifts the hair off my forehead and Peter's usually carefully trained hair curls damply all over his head. He helps me spread the blanket and we sit down. I feel overheated, itchy, awkward sitting next to this beautiful boy with the arresting green eyes. He leans in and gently kisses me. I respond, kissing back. In the movies, things escalate at this point, but my first kiss ends sweetly, with him gently easing off.

"You are way too young for me."

"There's less difference than between Alyse and Trevor."

"Yeah, and he is breaking the law. He's having sex with a minor who is more than two years his junior. I'm not going to be that guy, right?" I stare at him. "Much as you tempt me – nothing's happening that direction until you turn sixteen."

That's good. I mean, I have this hope I'll be a virgin when I get married, but most girls will choose at some point before then and you do think about it on your first real kiss. I'm so not ready to say "yes" to that, so I'm glad Peter has limits.

"And, by the way, if we're still hanging out then and I'm pushing you further than you want to go – just tell me 'no'. I never want to be one of those guys who talks a girl into something she doesn't want to do."

"You're not, though ...." My face flushes red hot. Peter grins at me.

"A virgin? No, but I don't think it's a bad thing. If I could go back and do it differently – with a girl I cared about – not drunk off my ass – I would."

Trevor and Alyse climb the fence, handing her laden bag over the top. People stare at them, pointing, remarking. Trevor sets the bag beside me, so I can see the bottle of Bacardi hidden there. His father must keep a bar in the house. Peter sees it too and snorts, shaking his head.

"Let's go swimming, Lily. You two try not to go unconscious, okay?"

I strip off my outer clothes, stash my lovely necklace in my backpack and then we walk hand in hand into the surf.

Fateful Choice

Peter

By the time we finish dinner at Flynn's, I'm starting to want to punt Trevor into the Great South Bay. If this is what Ben's been dealing with the last couple of years, I'm not surprised he's not talking to me. Trevor is a big personality anytime, but drunk, he's mega-sized. It's funny as anything when it's not scaring Lily, but he is scaring Lily and other people are starting to stare.

We've already missed the time I wanted to leave so I could go to a meeting, but now we're headed for the last ferry to the mainland. Alyse needs to pause to puke, which I can't argue with since I've watered the bushes on Fire Island at least a few times. There's a saying here about falling off the boardwalks. You will! It's a given. The first puke session Lily holds her, and the second one Trevor does it. I'm starting to really regret coming.

Then Lily stops to stare at a gathering of three deer. I pull her into my chest to keep her from stepping off the trail.

"I don't want to have to do a tick check on you."

"Right." She whispers, awed by the undulates cropping branches beside a beach house. They roll liquid brown eyes at us, wary, but used to an audience. It's like dinner theater where the cast eats the food.

"And we still need to make the ferry," Alyse remarks. You got to hand it to Trevor. He's got water in his backpack, so she can rinse her mouth. "Unless we're staying at your house."

Trevor smiles a lazy grin at her.

"Nope. Dad's renting it, that's why we just used the cabana."

"Right. I forgot." They giggle. They didn't just use the cabana. That bottle of rum came from somewhere. Alyse is as drunk as he is. They've both had way too much rum.

"Do you have a learner's permit?"

Lily blinks at me. The dock is in sight and the ferry hasn't arrived yet, so we're good.

"No, but I did practice driving up in New Hampshire with my dad."

"That doesn't really help me."

"Especially since I can't drive stick."

"Oh." I sigh. I know what I'm going to have to do. As we walk out onto the dock, I grab Trevor's arm and unclip his keys from his backpack.

"What the hell?"

"Sorry, man, but you can't drive."

"I'm not that drunk."

He's slurring. He *is* that drunk. Is this what happened when I took Cheyenne's keys last summer? Did she think I was more sober that I was? I bet I didn't think I was *that* drunk either.

"Then how are we getting home?" Alyse finally asks when we're all sitting on the ferry. "You can't drive."

I plan to call Vic as soon as we have cellphone service, but when we get to the mainland, he picks up to remind me that it is his regular night off and he's in Long Island City visiting his kids. We arranged for Trevor to drive all of us because Vic had the day off. I try dialing Tilly, but her phone goes straight to voice mail.

"Now what?" Alyse asks me.

"Get in the car." I look at Lily. "Give me back my ID. If we get pulled over, hopefully they'll fall for it."

"I gotta get the car home," Trevor mumbles. He's passing out before we even leave the parking lot.

"I'll call your dad."

Mel Grey's cell goes to voicemail too, so I don't have a choice. I didn't become a bad driver when I lost my license. I'm just legally not allowed. If we get pulled over, Lily hasn't had anything to drink, so it'll be fine. My ID will hold up and I know for certain I'll blow a zero. I spend an inordinate amount of time walking around the car making sure all the

253

lights work, adjusting the seat and mirrors, and assuring my passengers are buckled in.

I drive with the window down to assure Trevor and Alyse don't puke in the back seat. I'd forgotten how much I enjoy driving and as we approach Port Mallory, I almost wish I could keep going along the Gold Coast out to Orient. But it would be foolish. If I get caught, I might not get my license back for years. I drive directly to my house and park the SUV in the circle.

"You don't need to go home, do you?" I'm asking Lily while I scoop up Alyse to carry her upstairs.

"No, I planned to spend the night anyway. What about him?"

"I'll get him into one of the guest rooms. Don't mention my driving to anyone, right?"

"Oh, right. You did the right thing, though. He shouldn't drive when he's been drinking."

"He's pretty much always a little tipsy, but he shouldn't drive drunk."

The house feels empty, which is weird. It's almost midnight. Thank goodness Alyse doesn't weigh anything. These sessions of lugging her to her bed are becoming far too frequent. I at least usually manage to make it to my bed under my own steam. I settle her and go back for Trevor, leaving Lily to sort herself out. Trevor is all wiry muscle that feels very solid against my bad shoulder, but I manage to make it all the way up the stairs and into a guest room with him.

I stand there rubbing out my shoulder, thinking how much I hate this room. It's the one where I found my now-stepfather having sex with my mother. But it's the closest to the top of the stairs, so it suits my purposes and I pull the covers over Trevor, just because I'm not an ass. I go back to lock up the SUV and retrieve our bags. In the hall outside Alyse's room, Lily thanks me. I'm yawning when I reach my room, but I know I should make a call.

"Hey."

"You okay?" Rick asks.

"Yeah. I got through another day sober. I missed a meeting, though, so I figured I should call."

"Why'd you miss the meeting?" I explain it to him.

"Sounds like Trevor and Alyse are risky to hang out with."

"A little, but I had the good sense to put temptation as far from me as possible." I explain what happened at CJs.

"So, do you think maybe you should have paused before accepting that as your lunch destination?"

He's got a point. Although everywhere on Fire Island seems to serve alcohol, CJs glorifies it and I knew that the minute Trevor suggested it.

"Yeah. It's good that I recognized it, right?"

"Sure, but you put the burden of your sobriety on a teenage girl. And why are you still carrying around fake ID?"

"That came in handy when I had to drive."

"Which you shouldn't have done. Come on, Peter. It might have been the safe thing to do, but it wasn't the smart thing to do. I'm thinking you can afford cab fare across Brookhaven."

"Yeah. Just didn't think of it, I guess."

"You need to learn to do that. The beach wasn't a bad idea, but Fire Island – isn't that like Party Central?"

"You have a point. It wasn't my outing and I wanted to help Lily out, but you're right, I probably should have avoided Fire. But the good thing about Trevor is, as soon as I said I wasn't drinking, he held me to it. I got a little weak with the bottle there, but when he saw me looking at it, he said 'you told me to tell you no.'"

"That's putting your sobriety on someone else, man. Someone who has a drinking problem of their own. Have you told anyone about Alyse yet?"

"I should. I don't know why I feel... I don't know."

"You don't want her to be mad at you."

"Something like that, I guess. Maybe afraid nobody's going to believe me."

"Yeah, well, it sounds like you need to love your sister enough to risk that."

"I do. I just – I told Dad *I* needed help and he didn't listen."

"That's because you timed it, so it sounded like you were making an excuse. So, how's Step 4 going?"

"I'll email it to you. I think it's mostly done."

"Yeah okay." He sounds skeptical. I'm doing better, but I admit I'm not breaking any records completing Step 4. Step 5 looms after and that scares me. I'm afraid if I start telling my inventory to someone, *all* my sins are going to come out, including ones I've been sitting on for six years.

"Well, it's late. Peter, make the meeting tomorrow night. I get needing to blow off some healthy steam after being cooped up for a month, but don't let yourself lose momentum, okay?"

"I know."

We hang up and I stare around my room. I enjoyed myself today and I did it sober, so why do I still feel like I'm standing on a fence about to slip and rack myself?

Keeping More Secrets

Lily

Peter overtoasted my bagel, but he remembered I like milk with my breakfast, though he made coffee, so I add a splash to my milk.

"New meaning to 'would you like some coffee with your milk.'" His green eyes twinkle in the morning sunshine here on the patio. "Any sign of life from Alyse?"

"She said, and I quote 'I think I threw up my stomach.'"

"Rum. Trevor left about half an hour ago, looking like hell. I'm not missing the hangovers, that's for sure."

"Kind of wondering how I get home without her."

"It won't be a problem. I saw Tilly's car in the garage, so she apparently came home while we were sleeping. Here, have some grapes and cheese."

He moves the platter closer to me. The bagel suggests he doesn't really cook much, but fruit and cheese look nice together on a plate.

"Tilly can give us both a ride and I can spend some time with Bram. By the way, congratulations on not getting sunburned yesterday."

"I think I can thank you for the great application on my back."

"I enjoyed that a lot." He's darker than yesterday. His teeth flash white watching me drink my milk.

"What?"

"You seem to really enjoy that."

"Don't you?"

"I like the taste of milk, but I can't drink a lot of it."

"Why not?"

"Mediterranean DNA, I think. My uncle Matt said it just tore up his stomach, but I can drink about a half glass without getting gas. And, usually, in a mocha or something it's fine."

"But cheese is okay?"

"Yeah. So's yoghurt. Doc told me once that my Greek ancestors probably drank a lot of goat's milk, but cows are kind of a northern European thing."

"I never knew that. It's a better excuse for not drinking milk than some people have."

"Oh, the poor cows." He turns the word "cows" into a lament. "They suffer soooo much. Yeah, I don't feel sorry for the cows ... or the goats. I also eat meat. I like meat."

"Me too. You know how skinny Bram is?" He nods. "The doctors say he's protein deprived because he can't really chew meat. We're trying to find ways to increase his protein intake through soft foods. Soy sounded like a great idea until we learned about its side effects."

"Man boobs. I've heard that. I think I'll just stick with trying to get him to talk." He looks through the open patio doors. "Tilly's up."

She comes out a minute later in her usual work garb. Apparently, he'd set the third setting for Tilly because Peter gestures to the plate and coffee cup.

"I brought sugar out just for you."

"Thank you." She takes the third seat.

She doesn't look different, but he's got his head cocked like he's trying to figure something out.

"I got your messages. My apologies. I spent the evening playing cards with some girlfriends. I figured Trevor would bring you home. How'd you'd get here?"

He clearly knows he can't lie since he parked Trevor's car in the driveway.

"I drove us." She looks over the rim of her mug. "I know. I shouldn't have, but it seemed like the most sensible solution. Trevor really couldn't drive."

"Well, you didn't get caught, but if you had it might have been another two years before they'd allow you to get your license back."

"I know. It won't happen again."

She nods and gives him a tight smile. I consider satisfying my curiosity.

"So what game were you playing?"

She startles, blinks at me.

"Uh, it's called Bunco."

Peter slides his gaze sideways at her and lifts an eyebrow. I guess he knows she's lying. Or maybe – I mean, I would guess she might be dating someone and doesn't want her employer to know. Peter seems thoughtful as he finishes his coffee.

He's the one who gathers the plates to take them into the kitchen and put them in the dishwasher. I can see why Tilly might like him better than Alyse.

"Where's Alyse?"

"Sleeping off the effects of too much sun." Peter's voice doesn't betray his lie in the least. "She just wouldn't listen to me."

"Sunburned?"

"Not bad, but mostly just sun-exhausted. Trevor won't be sleeping on his back for a few days, however."

"Well, it looks like you took good care of Lily and yourself."

"I am past needing sunscreen, so I won't burn and, yeah, I think I was a very good escort. What do you think, Lily?"

"You were. I really appreciate it too. I need to run up and get my bag."

"We'll meet you at the car." Tilly dumps some dish powder in the reservoir and turns on the dishwasher. I start up the stairs. "How was it really?"

"I had a good time and I didn't drink, so I could drive when Trevor got stupid."

"That boy? I don't like that he's dating Alyse."

I pass out of distance for hearing them. Alyse frowns at me when I come into the room.

"Good, it's morning?"

"It is. How are you?"

"Ugghh."

"Yeah. Peter says rum hangovers are the worst."

"Great! You headed home?"

"I am."

"Did we embarrass ourselves last night?"

"Mildly. Give me a call when you feel up to it. Peter told Tilly you got too much sun."

"He's a good brother."

I agree and leave to let her sleep it off, not entirely sure that it's a good thing the Wyngate siblings lie for each other.

Apology

Ben

Pete suggests we sit in the backyard when I drop by on Saturday. He's clearly been doing just that – a glass of iced tea on the table and *The Dragon Bone Chair* laying open on the chaise lounge. He's brown, which makes the emerald of his eyes pop like jewels. He pulls another chair over so we can talk.

"Just working on your tan, huh?"

"Yeah, I wasn't really allowed to go anywhere for a month."

"He grounded you and Tilly didn't help you wriggle free?"

"She's not been so easy since – since." He looks away, mouth tightening. Shame? Maybe. "Look, Ben, I'm really sorry for what happened. I know it doesn't change anything, but I didn't mean for it to happen."

"That doesn't forgive it."

"Then how do I redeem myself?"

Alyse comes out of the house.

"Ben!" She's too loud and too quick and she's got her legs wrapped around me before I can even react.

"Alyse, leave him alone. Leave *us* alone. We're trying to talk."

"Oh, poor, Peter, not getting *his* way."

Annoyed a second ago, he now just looks sad. I put Alyse on her feet. It's way uncomfortable for her to drape herself on me like that. I'm a guy and she's a girl and there's nearly four years of difference in our age.

"I spent all day Thursday with you. Give me a break here."

Alyse is great at pouting, but the pixie cut somehow messes with the expression.

"What's with the hair?"

"Just looking for a change. Can't a girl do something different when she's at a pivotal point in her life, when she makes big decisions?"

"Sure, Aly." Pete's frowning. "What big decisions?"

"You don't have any idea. I'm not a little girl anymore. What would you say if you knew?"

"Don't know because I don't know. Enlighten us?"

"Don't want to."

I realize with a jolt that Alyse is drunk...or high...or both. Her pupils are huge. Pete catches her arm and leads her toward the living room doors, speaking with quiet ferocity in her ear.

"Don't you tell me what to do. I'm not having drunk driving accidents. And Trevor and I will do what we want. You have nothing to say about that. Maybe instead of having a stick up your ass all the time, you should actually try to have a good time once in a while. Have a drink. Smoke some weed. Stop being an asshole."

"Aly, just go away. Please. I'll talk to you later. I want to talk with Ben now."

Tilly comes out of the doors and takes over for Pete who comes back to me and sits down, dropping his head into his hands. He doesn't look like he's having fun.

"You okay?" I shouldn't care, but I do, and I still want to repair the friendship. He breathes deeply and sits up straight.

"I don't know. I guess."

"She like that all the time now?"

He nods.

"I kind of think maybe I caused it."

"How?"

"By going away to college, by screwing up Christmas, by not foreseeing that Trevor likes her."

"Trevor? Oh, no! I mean – *way* too old for her."

"And a walking pharmacy. We all went to Fire Island on Thursday. Alyse asked me so Lily wouldn't feel like a third-wheel."

"Lily with three drunk people – yeah, that couldn't have been fun."

"*Two* drunk people. I've been sober for thirty-five days now."

He says it like it's an accomplishment, but Cheyenne's wreck was ten months ago. He reads my expression.

"I had four months in December. And, I've had weeks here and there since. I came home for Spring Break to try and get sober then and it worked until a big party in the dorm. It's not as easy as it sounds."

He's not wrong. Everybody drinks in college. Even I still enjoy an occasional beer with pizza. Grandpa Jack's diagnosis comes to mind.

"You're an alcoholic?" His gaze comes up to meet my eyes and his mouth tightens. I anticipate his rejection and my reaction.

"Yeah." He says it reluctantly as if he's embarrassed. "Probably not a surprise to you."

"Kind of surprised to hear you admit it." He nods.

"It's not fun to admit. And I still don't remember Cheyenne's accid – wreck, so I don't really know how to apologize for it. But I am sorry for what must have at times been an embarrassing friendship."

"When you got back from Europe?" Those few weeks in August were heartbreaking.

"Yeah." He lets his breath out really slowly. "Remember that last party before I left?"

"Right after your uncle died?" The tenor of that party felt different. I'm not the only one who thinks so. Pete always threw great parties and he kept good control over all the elements, but that party went south fast. He got drunk early and way drunker than I'd ever seen him before. His shoulders hunch and he speaks to his hands in his lap.

"I ended up in the hospital with alcohol poisoning and, um, I probably got hepatitis then. Only nobody told me, or they didn't know, and then I went to Europe where I drank *a lot*. I didn't know why I was getting drunk so much easier. My liver couldn't handle it."

"You okay now?"

"Liver function's okay. And as long as I don't drink, it'll probably stay okay. But that's what killed my uncle, so...." I didn't know or I wouldn't have put so much pressure on him. Now he makes eye contact. He seems sincere. "You setting up those barriers – it was good in a way. I needed someone to talk to who understood and there was a guy at Yale. Maybe I wouldn't have talked to him if I hadn't felt so alone. So – I'm not ready today, but if you wanted to show me those pictures of Cheyenne.... Just – I need some more time."

I nod. Sadness dwells in his eyes. I'm torn. I want to believe him and yet this wouldn't be the first time he's lied to me. Pete sees my doubt and sighs.

"I don't know what else to say. I guess now I have to show it."

He stuns me. He's apologized a lot for things in the past, but that he knows it has to go further than words seems...different. Better...maybe.

"I need to go. I sort of believe that you've changed – or that you're trying to, but I don't *believe* it yet and – I don't want to be mean."

"Sure. I guess I can't expect for more."

"Not yet. Maybe we can get together again, talk some more." Pete nods. He still looks sad, but I feel like we're leaving it at a good place considering everything we've been through. He walks me out to the portico as if he wants to suck up as much of our friendship as he possibly can. Pete always formed the center of our group of friends, but he also needed me to keep the parts from flying away. He's not complaining about being left out, but I sense it's there. I wish I could help him, but I'm not ready right now.

"See you...sometime." Pete sticks his hands in his back pockets. He sighs and turns away. He's trying not to be grabby and desperate. And I'm going to let him do it because.... How do you fix it after you've damaged trust to that extent? I know it won't happen today.

Dad

Peter

I wake up Sunday morning to find Alan came for a visit. Can you visit your own home? I don't know. I come downstairs expecting coffee and a bagel on the lawn and instead find he's having a mimosa and frittata on the patio. I really didn't like mimosas when I drank, so I don't feel tempted by his glass and I enjoy the food. Alyse doesn't join us.

"You got really good marks on those makeups."

"I didn't have a whole lot else to do." And the locked bar helps, but I don't say that.

"And you passed the Driver's Ed class?"

"It was sort of Pass-Fail. Look, Dad, I'm sorry about being stupid last semester. When I drink, I get dumb and I'm getting dumber with every relapse."

"But you're okay today?"

"Thirty five days."

"Since the day I grounded you?"

"That was thirty-three days. The withdrawal starts about a day in."

"Are you okay with that?"

I hesitate, Rick's advice echoing in my ears. I know I need to go to rehab, but I don't want to disappoint my dad, so I don't say it. It's more than thirty days. I'm going to be fine. The fact that I want a drink several times a day and I can't be trusted with an unlocked bar isn't a sign that I need more help. Everybody goes through this.

"Yeah. The worst part's over."

"Good. So how was Fire Island this year?"

"Nice. We had fun. I mean, it's beaches, right? I'm thinking of suggesting Trevor, Ben and I go back from mountain biking later this summer, although I'm also thinking of taking a dance class during next month's intensive."

"It's a good way to stay in shape."

"That's what I'm thinking, and I really enjoyed dance. I just let those guys at boarding school talk me out of it."

Dad hasn't touched his mimosa since I sat down and he's frowning at it now. If I brought up rehab, would he agree or yell at me for being weak?

"I really misjudged with sending you to boarding school."

He did. He didn't know about Alyse, but he could have talked to me. I'd have taken home schooling with a tutor. Boarding school felt like punishment with a whole dorm infested with blossoming alcoholics.

"I need to get back to Albany. How is school going, really?"

Dad gathers his plates and the mimosa. The smell of it wafts to me and my mouth immediately goes dry. He's staring into my expression, forehead creasing.

"School's going okay."

If he asked me to carry the glass, what would I say? I am so not ready to have an adult beverage in my hand. I carry my own dishes and the coffee pot into the kitchen. He dumps the mimosa into the sink while I load the dishwasher. We chatter about the weather and Alyse's dance classes. I've gone to watch a couple of them, but I feel Miss Rebecca's anger toward me when I'm there and Mrs. Sims has avoided me entirely.

"But you're going to go back there to dance?"

"Yeah. I guess I'm not ready to admit I can't fix it."

"Maybe you can. I'm still funding the transition to a non-profit. They should at least be polite to you to your face and that may be all you can hope for in this circumstance."

I nod. I walk him out to the driveway. He flew in sans bodyguards and grabbed a rental car. I can't think of any governor in a hundred years who would be that bold. He dons a Carhartt jacket over his jeans and a gimme-hat from the Ducks and Skeeters and gives me a hug before he goes. He doesn't really look like the sitting Governor of New York in that disguise. He looks like he's about to go fishing with Granddad Mike.

"You have a good week or so. If you keep up the good work, I'll let you have the Jag back after you get your driver's license reinstated."

"I only have the one last test to do, so --. Thanks."

Alan drives off. I go back into the house. Alyse must still be sleeping and I don't know where Tilly has gotten to. And like a magnet, the bar drags me into the den. I stand there a moment, savoring the memory of bourbon, but then I glance at the mantle clock. Lily said her family would be back from church around one thirty and by then Tilly will be back with her key that keeps the demons away. I head for my bike in the garage.

Hot Licks

Peter

Bram remembers backgammon and manages to insist we play. He still needs help with the possible moves, but he's counting on his fingers. I definitely would win if I played to my fullest, but I skip a few good moves and show him how to execute his better plays. He's confused by captures and gets a little frustrated by them, but after the fourth one he begins to remember how they work. In the end, he wins by five pips, two moves. He's tired after one game, so that makes it easy to draw Lily away. Frazzled by caring for Bram, Madalyn doesn't do due diligence as a mom. She lets her 15-year-old daughter go bike-riding with an 18-year-old man.

Okay, I'm beginning to realize I'm not as mature as my ID, not even my *real* ID. I think I'm maybe sixteen. I lost a lot of growing up time. Assuming I stopped maturing in boarding school that would be three years, so fifteen. Maybe I like Lily because we're the same maturity level. It also helps that she's underaged so can't legally drink and I can't scratch the sexual itch with her without risking becoming a sex offender.

We ride into Port Mallory and head to Hot Licks Ice Cream, which is the definition of treating a girl right. It occupies a double section of a strip mall with wide front windows, a long freezer case of open ice cream containers, and a collection of mismatched tables and chairs that remind me of an old soda counter. The creamistas (as the owner calls them) serve cones, bowls and assorted other goodies in about two dozen flavors a day. Lily's never been, so I get to play the expert. I'm simple. I like their chocolate which is this multilayered treat that only appears simple, but I've tried most of the other flavors. She says she likes strawberry, so decides to try blackberry shower.

"I love how you never flinch from Bram. When he started to get frustrated, you just found another way to communicate it to him."

"Helps that I'm a artist. If I can envision it, I can draw it and that sometimes bridges the gaps his lack of words creates."

"I noticed he's trying to draw more. He's really bad at it, though."

"Not everyone has natural talent for drawing, but I'm betting he'll get better at it because it's a necessity for him."

"And you think Wes will understand what you're going for?"

"Wes is a cool kid. And them being the same age might help too."

We eat ice cream for a bit.

"Your sister got me to take a single introductory ballet class this afternoon."

"And how was it?"

"Fine. It's a beautiful art and I felt like I had two left feet and three arms."

"It's a sport and you have to condition for it, but you can take an introductory course and in about a month, start to feel like you have the basics down."

"There sounds like so much to learn. First position, second. It's just – wow."

"That's why most people start dance when they're four or five. But Miss Rebecca started as a highland dancer who discovered ballet at 16. Within a year, Joffrey offered her a position. So, it's all in how motivated you are."

"And you're taking a class next intensive."

"Yeah. Intermediate ballet. Just to see if I can get my conditioning back. If it seems possible, I'll take a similar course in New Haven."

She smiles at me, her eyes glowing.

"I can imagine you in tights lifting Alyse over your head."

"Alyse would be easy. I could do that now. She weighs like 95 pounds. It's taller girls that are hard.

Even if they don't' weight that much, it's like a balancing act. I'm in awe of Trevor's strength and control."

She nods. Trevor's not as tall as me, so the strength and control he shows is even more impressive.

"We should head back before my mom wonders where we are."

Ben's working on his car when we coast up into Lily's driveway.

"Hey." He's grunting at me. That's better than frowning, so I slow to say "hi."

"What are you two up to?"

"I took her for ice cream. How often do you change oil on this thing?"

"*Checking* the oil, *not* changing it. You know she's only 15, right?"

"We're friends. Nothing more. We like some of the same authors and bicycling. And I'm not drinking, so I won't be stupid."

"Is that really over?"

"It's not a simple yes-no answer, Ben, sorry. I want it to be over until I get thirsty and then I sometimes don't know what I want."

Ben looks to where Lily is coming out of the house with lemonades. I notice it's three glasses, not just two. I take the lead one and she hands the second one to Ben. She apologizes that it's not fresh-squeezed and I assure her I don't care. You can buy fresh. Tilly does, but it's expensive and unnecessary. Ben laughs and the momentary comfort recalls good times of hanging with Ben in this very spot, asking dumb questions about his auto repairs and not absorbing anything he said.

"I probably should have listened to you when you were talking about car repair."

"Really? I knew you weren't listening."

"Sorry. Kind of a jerk. Maybe you'll give me lessons again sometime."

Ben nods, but his gaze is on Lily. She's not my girlfriend and I'm not going to get jealous of Ben, but they do live next door, so they interact more than she and I do. Ben and I have never really fought over a girl. That doesn't mean I'm not bothered when she laughs at his jokes.

"I should probably go. I'm trying not to make Tilly serve dinner late on my account. Next time I come by, though I want to try something with art."

"Day after tomorrow," Lily says. "And come earlier so he's fresh. Like, between 10 and noon."

"Wow, I'll have to get up at a normal time." I dead-pan it, but Ben knows my humor and smiles, so she quickly recognizes it as a joke and grins. "I can do that. Thanks for giving me something to do. Nice to see you again, Ben."

I push off and coast into the street. The renter at my dad's property waves at me from the mailbox. I wave back. I don't remember her name, but it probably doesn't matter anyway since we'll never interact. I put Ben and Lily in my rearview and ride home wondering if Ben and I can ever mend our fences.

Art Talk

Lily

Wes sits back and watches while Peter shows Bram watercolors. I always thought of watercolor as those kind-of-washed-out impressionistic paintings, but Peter has a lot more control over the medium than that. Using an underlying sketch of our house and thicker paint, he's doing a realistic painting with his left hand. Bram sucks at drawing with his left hand, but he's copying Peter fairly well doing a kind of paint-by-number version.

"Yeah, you're getting it." Wes mostly observed in the beginning but interjected a comment or two as the exercise went on. I can tell from Bram's half-expression that he's trying to understand Wes but struggling to do so. Familiarity helps and Peter's frequent visits bridged that gap for him. "Isn't there a tree here?"

Wes gestures to the left side of the front door. Peter told me last night that he planned to leave the tree out for simplicity sake. Bram's mouth pulls down on the left corner.

"Simplicity helps, Wes." Peter doesn't sound at all judgmental. "Remember, he's brain-damaged. You can't overwhelm him."

Bram puts his good hand over his left ear, face growing red, pushing the project away from him a moment later. Peter taps him on the arm and holds up a conciliatory hand, circling it in a soothing motion.

"Wait." He gestures letting something rest on the table a moment. Then he grabs a pencil, takes a third copy of the house sketch and sketches a tree over it. Bram's face relaxes. He tries to reach another pencil, can't, pulls his feet off the leg rests and levers himself to standing, bracing himself on the table to reach the pencil. His limp right arm draws up hard against his chest, the hand fisted. He sits back down and scowls at the sketch pad, then draws stick figures, showing the really tall one and the other male talking back and forth while the girl *my longish hair gives it away* standing off to the side and a really short guy *maybe sitting* with dizzy swirls around his head.

"Too much talking confuses him?" Wes' interpretation shows why Peter believes he'll be a good friend for Bram.

"Yeah. He's brain damaged." Peter points to the swirls around the Bram figure's head. "But here's the thing." He sketches again, showing a tall figure talking with a figure in a wheelchair with swirls around his head. Then he draws the same tableau without the swirls.

"Then." He gestures over his shoulder. "Now." Bram smiles, nods. Peter indicates Bram's sketch, erases the swirls. Gestures for in the future. "Tomorrow." Then Peter does a quick sketch of a Bram figure and a Wes figure. "You and you."

Bram gives Wes a weighing look. Wes grins.

"We can try." He makes a gesture like he's trying to push something up a hill with concentration and then grins again and holds out his left hand to Wes, who laughs softly and meets him in a handshake.

"You're a genius." Peter laughs at me.

"So not, but I don't want to go back to school and have him lose what progress he's made because I'm gone. Trust me. Wes will be a great friend."

"I believe you. Now if you can just convince my mom."

I hear the screen door on the garage close then.

"Convince me of what?"

Peter gestures for her to be quiet and to watch Wes and Bram together. Wes has somehow learned how Bram counts and he says "One, two, three, four, I declare a thumb war", extending each finger, then braces his hand on the table. Bram frowns, but then counts out four fingers and they grapple for thumb supremacy.

"Did you see his lips?" Mom barely speaks above a whisper. I didn't, but Peter smiles at her. "He didn't voice them, but it looked like he said 'one, two, four, and war.' We've got to get him in for an evaluation. Peter, you've done some amazing work here."

"I just saw a kid who needed someone to try and reach him." I've seen that look in his eyes sometimes. He's remembering something. I walk him out to his bike.

"What made you so sure Bram was in there?"

He licks his lips.

"When we were kids – my mom went through a really deep depression. At about 18 months, Tilly came into our lives. Nonverbal and a total wild brat. Alyse, not Tilly. Dad wanted to take her someplace for autistic kids."

"Alyse isn't autistic."

"Probably not, no. But Tilly didn't leave her there anyway. She saw a human being inside who just hadn't been properly raised because her mom was catatonic, and her father was busy. Tilly used to make me help with games designed to make Alyse talk. And, I guess that's where I got the idea." He loops his lock around the frame of the bike. "I gotta go. Wes is going to want to do more physical things with Bram and that's not a bad thing, I think. Maybe have your mom talk to his physical therapists so Wes isn't pushing him too hard."

"Sounds good. You've been a really good friend, Peter."

I do sometimes wonder about him as a boyfriend, though. He does occasionally call me on the phone and then the ice cream "date" the other night, but he's not tried to kiss me since Fire Island and he's yet to ask me out on anything official. Yes, he's too old for me and he's acutely aware of that, but I almost wonder if he's not interested in me *that way* since he's not showing his interest.

He puts a hand on my shoulder while those thoughts go through my mind.

"Thanks for being patient with me, too. I'm still just trying to feel my way through this summer, come back from last year – take my time with you. Your birthday's in November, right?" I nod. "If you don't have to beat the boyfriends off with a stick at school, we'll see how your parents feel about my taking you out then."

"And if you don't find a girl at school, right?"

He blushes.

"Yeah. There's some things I need to do differently next year. I got to get going. I promised Tilly I'd help her move some boxes this afternoon."

"Sounds good. Thanks for that." I jerk my thumb over my shoulder where we can hear Bram's spastic laugh and Wes' gentler chuckle. Peter grins, swings a long leg over his bike and pushes off down the driveway.

Photos

Ben

Pete said we could talk if I picked him up at a meeting in Setauket. I don't realize what it is until I pull into the parking lot and a memory washes over me – my grandfather brought me here a few times when I was a kid. He'd buy me a milkshake and attend a meeting and I'd play in the bushes outside while he attended a meeting. Then we'd go do something fun. My granddad is one of the best people I know, but my father says there were times, way back, when Granddad was a jerk to everyone around him. Then he got sober, found Jesus and developed a woodworking addiction.

So, there's hope for Pete, if he's willing to try and he seems to be willing right now. I still don't like that he's hanging out with Lily, but he seems to be mostly working with Bram and Lily insists he was sober on Fire Island. I kind of sense she's lying about something, though, so I want to keep an eye on both of them. That means mending my friendship with Pete, so I'm around when things go south, so I can protect Lily from the disaster that follows Pete going off the rails.

Pete's tall, so I spot him right away in the crowd on the wide front porch of the Alano Club. I refrain from hurrying him with a text. If Grandpa Jack is right, Pete needs this. Still, I'm only there a few minutes when Pete breaks off a conversation with a man and weaves through the crowd to slip into the car.

"Thanks for picking me up. Not having a driver's license is kind of a pain."

"Vic doesn't drive you? Or Tilly?"

"They do, but it's nice to give them the night off occasionally."

Pete really is pretty nice to the staff at his house. There were a lot of rich kids at Port Mallory High and most of them treated their drivers and housekeepers like trash. Pete is always courteous and sometimes downright generous.

"I know you have to be to work in the morning. You want to stop for – I don't know, pie or something?"

"I'm full from dinner, but if you want to stop at Hot Licks, an ice cream cone would be cool."

Pete laughs and I realize I've just made a pun. He's always loved to play with language. We drive downtown where the area is lit by white Christmas tree lighting and the shops are all open on this sultry night.

"How is Cheyenne?" Pete spoons up some chocolate ice cream from his waffle cone. He's never asked me so directly.

"All of her bones are back in place. She has another surgery to repair scars in August."

Pete sighs, puts his spoon back in the cone.

"I'm torn. I feel really bad about what my stupidity did to her." He heaves a shuddering sigh, mouth twisting. It takes a lot to make him lose his appetite for Hot Licks chocolate. "I don't want you to be mad, but my sponsor says I should tell you. Cheyenne--she—well, she PMs me. It started a while ago. I don't want to be angry about it, but I don't really know how to feel about it."

"Remorseful ... guilty ...?"

His full lips tighten, and he swallows.

"That and alone and attacked." He catches his bottom lip between his teeth. This discussion scares him. Maybe he's afraid I don't want to hear how he feels. Grandpa Jack says Pete has a right to emotions. "Can I have more than one emotion for this?"

"Yeah." His fear of alienating me pulls on my heartstrings. "You're allowed to have feelings." But he's not the victim here. "You kind of ruined her life, though. She's never going to be the same because of what you did."

"But what did I do, Ben?" His hoarse voice barely rises above a whisper. "I still don't remember the wreck, but according to the lawyer, there was something wrong with the car – steering, I think. Even if I'd been sober, I couldn't have avoided the tree. I'm not saying – I *am* responsible. I know that if you drive drunk, you're responsible. I just – I didn't mean to hurt her, and I couldn't control that something broke on the car while I was driving."

"Except you were drinking."

"Yes, 100 percent, I shouldn't have been driving under the influence."

He's got a point about the mechanical issue, and this is the first I've heard of Cheyenne PMing him. Someone should probably make her stop. Pete's doing what he's supposed to be doing. He shouldn't be harassed while doing it. I'll call her parents when I get home. We eat ice cream for several minutes, mostly talking about Bram and Wes, who just met a few days ago, at Pete's instigation.

"I'll be going back to school in the fall. Bram needs a friend who understands him. Wes – he's a cool kid. Very kind-hearted."

He pops the last of the waffle cone into his mouth. He's thinking about something. I can tell by his profile as he stares out into the park we've stopped in.

"So, do you have pictures of her?" I blink at him. "My sponsor said if I did this, I should probably do it after a meeting. Tilly's locked up the bar, so – now's as safe a time as any to upset myself."

I hadn't really thought about it before, that Pete might feel like drinking during times of high stress. Of course, Alyse did tell me he drank himself into a stupor after my encounter with him at The Rinx on Christmas Eve. Maybe his reluctance to see the harm he's done is self-protective rather than avoidance of responsibility.

I open the slide show of Cheyenne on my phone and hand it to him while I drive. Pete takes a deep steadying breath and looks at the first one.

"Fuck!"

I don't interrupt as he goes through the entire slide show. There's more than just the damage to her face. I recorded her struggles in rehab as she tried to recover from the medically-induced coma. I'll have to show him the videos later. By the fifth photo tears slide down his cheeks.

"I'm so sorry this happened to her." He sounds like he's swallowed razor blades. I pull up into his driveway. "I really didn't mean to do that. And I get why you were so angry with me."

He puts my phone on the console.

"You going to be okay?"

"Yeah." He pulls out his phone. "I'm going to call Rick, talk to him about it. Thanks for showing me." He's still crying.

"You're sure?"

"I am. I gotta go."

There's a part of me that hates that I'm leaving him alone to deal with the remorse and guilt on his own and then there's a perverse part of me that thinks he deserves it. I'm not sure which part of me is going to win this tug-of-war with my heart, but I suspect it matters.

Guilt

Peter

I'm still crying when Rick calls me. My plan for dealing with the pain of seeing Cheyenne's injuries sucks because Dad's home again, talking with Mel Grey out in the garden, all grandiose gestures and raucous laughter and the fucking bar is unlocked. Tilly gets it. Dad doesn't and I'm not coping well tonight.

"How are you?" Rick knew I meant to talk to Ben tonight and he's psychic. I probably wouldn't have called him.

"I ruined her life. She was going to Joffrey and I put her in a coma."

"Ben showed you pictures, huh?"

"Yeah."

"And you didn't call me."

"We just finished a few minutes ago." I sink onto the floor behind the bar, my back against the wall.

"You make the meeting?"

"Yes. Doesn't feel like it."

"A part of being sober is feeling pain, man. Do you feel like getting drunk?"

"All the time."

"But you haven't so far?"

"Nope. But I don't know how this gets better. I can't fix what happened to her."

"No but feeling the guilt of it moves you a little closer to being able to redeem it."

"How?"

"Step 4. I got your email. I can't say it's the deepest moral inventory I've ever read, but you at least made a start. So, take the first thing on your list and write something about it and when you think you're done, send it to me. And call me in the morning. Don't choose to stay in pain alone."

I hear his words, but he's just spinning platitudes. Yeah, life wasn't easy for him when addicted to opioids, but he never hurt anyone like I did. He doesn't know what it feels like. I say goodnight and just sit there staring at all the pretty bottles. Dad and Mel come into the den and I expect Dad to ask me what I'm doing, but I guess he doesn't see me. I'm sitting in the shadows staring at my prettiest poison. It's a metaphor of my life.

"Criminal justice reform is a libertarian principle, Lan. You could rewrite the history of this state by championing it."

"And risk not being reelected."

"Maybe, but not necessarily. I think there's a lot of people who secretly think that our justice system is criminal and needs to be reformulated."

Dad sets his empty glass on the bar. They neither of them see me sitting here in the shadows, and I don't draw attention to myself.

"Let me get my phone and I'll give you that number for Shay McMasters." Grey sets his glass down next to Dad's and they both move toward the entryway where I saw Grey's jacket hanging on a hook.

I look up at the half-full glass with its creamy caramel goodness. Like me, Mel likes bourbon. I listen. They're still talking. It's just the one half-glass and just for tonight. It's not like I'm taking a bottle to my room. My hand flutters around the glass as Rick's voice whispers in my ear. I can hear them laughing in the foyer. Any minute they'll come back, and I'll have to explain what I'm doing. Explaining won't fix this agony in my soul. I knock it back in one smooth swallow, set the glass on the bar and slip out the patio doors so as not to be caught by my dad.

I'm not drunk, but my tears dry in the mild breeze off the ocean. The storm in my gut quiets. There's something to be said for just one drink. I'll get back to sobriety in the morning. I know I need to confront the accident, but for one night, I need some space from it. I'll go to my room and sleep and it'll be better in the morning.

Alien Possession

Lily

The stars sparkle like diamonds as I stand out in the backyard. I really need to google to find out what flowers I'm smelling. I breathe deeply and let it out slowly. As I open my eyes, I see something out of my peripheral vision and turn to see Ben standing in his own yard, staring up at the sky too.

"Hey." We say it at the same time, which makes us laugh. "Psych," Ben says.

"How are you?"

"Don't know. Worried."

"About?"

"I just might have made the wrong decision with Pete tonight." I wait because I have no idea what to say. "He asked to see photos of Cheyenne and I figured that was a positive step, but now I'm worried about what he might do while he's upset."

"Did you tell him that?"

"I tried. He said he was okay, that he'd call his sponsor, but – I probably shouldn't have left him until he had the guy on the phone."

Peter struggled not to drink at CJ's. Can he handle not drinking when he faces his past?

"I don't know." I don't know how else to answer. I could call Peter, I guess.

Ben takes a couple of deep breaths. I wait because I don't know what to say.

"How's Bram?"

"Good. He pulled himself up to standing in therapy yesterday."

"And that means?"

"Um, it's one of the things that has been keeping him from walking on his own."

"Oh, yeah, that makes sense. So, he won't have to use the wheelchair anymore?"

"Well, he has a long way to go before that, but yes, it's a – a milestone. Now that he's figured out the body mechanics, he just needs to get strong enough to do it all of the time. He's still rebuilding muscle after the coma."

"How long was he comatose?"

"Four months of deep coma, but even at Spring Break they were saying he might still be at a reduced level of consciousness."

"And now?"

"They think he's fully awake. He's more interactive, trying harder to understand. There's less staring off into space as if he has no idea what's going on around him ... although global aphasics don't really understand what other people are saying, so he probably doesn't really know what's going on."

"Pete seems to do pretty well with him."

"He's good with body language and aphasiacs sometimes understand voice intonation even when they don't understand the words. Peter's really good with voices."

"He is." Ben smiles. "He can do impersonations."

"So, are you guys friends again?"

"I think we're moving that way. It's going to take time to trust him again." He sighs. "When he gets his driver's license back – just – make sure he's sober before you get in the car, right? I would hate if something happened to you and I didn't say anything."

I nod, because I think he means well. Peter seems pretty determined not to drink and drive again but given his history he kind of deserves Ben not trusting him. Ben's still staring at me.

"I will."

He sighs, sounding relieved.

"I should go. I meant to do something for Pete tonight and then I got weird and came out here and sort of forgot I need to make a phone call."

"I have laundry to fold and put away. Have a good evening."

I pause inside the garage and dial Peter's number. It goes to voice mail after three rings. I text him.

LILY – You okay? Ben mentioned you might be upset.

I don't get an answer. In the house, Bram's had a seizure and Mom and Dad are trying to sooth him. He only recently realized that his right side will suddenly start writhing and it bothers him. It's got to feel like an alien force takes over his body. I can't help, so I go to my room to put away my laundry. My phone lights up.

"Hey." Peter sounds a little stuffy, like he's been crying. "I'm okay. Just standing on the beach trying to calm down."

"Okay. You need to talk?"

He laughs.

"I don't think it would help right now. Thank you for calling me though. I'm just going to sit here and watch the waves for a while."

"Of course. Try to get some sleep."

"Yeah." He sniffles and then he swallows audibly. "How are you?"

"I'm good." There's a long silence.

"Bram doing okay?"

"He just had a seizure."

"Oh, poor kid! So, does he have to go to the hospital?"

"No. It's a Jacksonian seizure. Just his right side. No loss of consciousness. It upsets him more than anything."

"Yeah, it would. That helps. My life's not that bad."

"Glad I could help."

He doesn't chuckle. He sniffles again.

"It does help. But not much is going to help tonight. And that's probably the way it should be. I did this thing. I've got to face it."

"Doesn't mean it doesn't hurt."

He grunts.

"But shouldn't be feeling sorry for myself."

"Maybe give yourself one night."

Now I hear him chuckle. There's a long pause. I don't know what more to say.

"So, I should go. Dad's here, so I probably can't sleep through breakfast. Have a good night."

I almost say "You too" but that isn't happening.

"I'll pray for you." That feels weird to say. I used to be such a Sunday School girl, but she's been mostly absent since Bram's stroke.

"Thank you. Good night."

He hangs up and I finish putting away my clothes. What else could I do for him?

Hatred

Ben

The living room stands silent. Wes went upstairs to research Bram's conditions, which I marvel over. He's 11 and it's like he's grabbed hold of a passion we never knew he had. Bram's needs somehow ignited something within him and Pete both. While I feel sorry for Bram and pray for Lily and her parents when I remember to, I don't have a passion to rescue him or even an inkling for where to begin.

I sit down on the love seat and dial Kevin Theriault's number. I haven't really spoken to him since Cheyenne got out of rehab. I usually talk to her mother Maxine. The phone almost rings to voice mail before he answers.

"Ben? How are you?"

"I'm good. How's Cheyenne?"

"Doing much better. She's in some pain from the scar correction but the plastic surgeon says she's healing nicely."

"Great. I hear she's texting people, so that part must be getting better too."

"Much! They say she'll probably make a full recovery in that area. She's frustrated by the foot drop. She wants to dance again and it's hard for her to accept her leg will probably never allow that."

"Yeah, it's totally unfair. She was a beautiful dancer."

"She was."

"Um, Mr. Theriault – what happened to her was horrible and I'm still mad at Pete for it, but – you should know since there's a restraining order against *him* – she's been texting him, saying some pretty mean things. He's trying to stay sober and it's shaking him up. And I think he's a little scared that the cops might think he's somehow encouraging it. He admits he texted her back in the spring when it first started, but he hasn't lately. I just think – you guys should know."

"Good for her, busting his chops like that."

I blink into the dimness by the television.

"It just seems to me that nothing is helped if she guilts him into drinking again."

"And I hope that kid puts a bullet in his brain. I get it – he was your best friend, but I have no sympathy for him, and I think you should just cut your losses with him." There's a pause while I try to think of what to say to that. "Well, I gotta go. You keep in touch. Cheyenne is starting to accept visitors more these days. Give her mother a call before you drop by, make sure it's a good day. Bye for now."

He hangs up and I groan, almost wanting to throw my phone across the room.

"What's wrong?" Mom stands in the opening between the kitchen and the living room. I tell her. "Well, there's two ends to that conversation. If you can't get Cheyenne to stop texting Peter, you can get Peter to stop accepting her texts."

"Pete says he feels like he's not being repentant when he does that."

Mom smiles, shaking her head.

"He's a glutton for punishment, I must say. I'll call Tilly and tell her what's going on. She can overrule Peter and reduce his stress level in one easy step."

"Thank you. I felt bad about leaving him tonight when he was upset, but if I can fix this problem for him, that's good, right?"

"It is." Mom picks up her cell from the charging station. "Don't worry. Tilly will take care of it."

Reinstatement

Peter

There's an envelope with the DMV logo on it by my plate when I come down the next morning. Dad smiles at me as I tear it open. Except for some special insurance which Dad's already taken care of, there are no restrictions on my license, and I slip it back into my wallet. I don't feel like smiling. I'm aware of the obligations that come with that license now.

Dad holds up the keys.

"You did well on that final, too. The Jag is yours, but you need to realize that it's also a deadly weapon. You're getting it back, but under no circumstances should you drive after drinking and the car needs to be here at the house by midnight every night."

Oh, for fuck's sake! I'm not twelve. He has a point about drinking and driving and I'm never doing that again, but a curfew? What the hell?

"Or I can keep the keys for another month."

"No. You're right. I won't be drinking anymore and if I do, I won't drive. And home by midnight."

Unexpectedly, I taste bourbon as I sip my coffee. That half-glass shouldn't have affected me like that, but I woke up wondering if the bar was still unlocked. Under no circumstances should I drink. Alcoholic! Remember? Do you hear me, Peter? Don't drink.

"So, did you ever settle that strike at Christmas?"

"Really? Do you not pay attention to the news?"

"I – no. I was busy flunking two classes and drinking and drying out."

Dad rolls his eyes at me. Yeah, saying it aloud does make me feel like I'm an idiot.

"We settled in April. The bridge is back on the back burner – again."

"Is that good or bad?"

"Do you have an overwhelming need to drive to Connecticut?"

"Ferry works for me."

"There you go. And the seamen don't want the bridge. It's a complicated argument. Some people really present great reasons for the bridge. Then the environmentalists get involved – and they don't agree."

"What do you mean?"

"Well, there's the environmentalists who are against the bridge because it might affect tides and currents and then there's the environmentalists who hate the ferry and then there's the environmentalists who object to commuting all the way around through New York City."

"They're all bad for the environment?"

"They say so, but they don't agree. It's almost as if they think we should all just walk where we need to go."

I laugh with him.

"What are your plans for the rest of the summer?"

"Uh, I don't know. Take a long drive. Drive myself to AA." I shrug. "I probably do need to find stuff to do. Maybe I should take another course."

"You could do that now. I spoke to Yale Friday and you've been fully reinstated, but you'll be on probation in the fall semester. As long as your grades are Cs or better, that'll drop off after the holidays."

"That means I can only take twelve credits, right?" Too much time on my hands is not a good thing.

"You might need to take an extra semester to make up for it – or a summer correspondence course."

I nod. I know I screwed up and this is working out as well as it could. Now I just have to admit to Rick that I relapsed last night. Relapse? Yeah, barely a gulp, but I shouldn't drink alcohol– period. Rick's advice that I go to rehab washes through my mind. If I asked Dad now, would he say yes? I could do a 28-day program and make my first class at Yale. Dad and I talk about the weather and I walk him to his car.

I need to start work on the second part of my Step 4. I put my foot on the bottom step and my phone buzzes.

CHEYENNE – I'm still limping. I'll never dance again. Asshole.

I stare at the screen, gaze caressing the words. I did that! There's no redeeming it. I'm at the bar without even thinking about it. The full glass of bourbon goes down smooth. I reach to pour myself another glass and my hand stalls. I don't want this. I promised myself I wouldn't. I need to be smarter than I have been in the past.

Passing through the dining room into the butler's pantry, I grab a jar with lid. A small supply will help ease the pain when she texts, but it won't be enough for me to get drunk. I can ration it. I won't drink all the time and that'll be okay. And Tilly will lock the bar again, so I won't have access. Best of all possible solutions.

I'm headed up the stairs when Tilly walks into the den with her keys jingling. She doesn't need to know. I'll go to a meeting tonight. I'll get back on track. It's just a momentary stumble while I deal with some real pain.

Blocking

Alyse

I hated Cheyenne all the time we were in dance classes and I warned Peter she would hurt him when he started dating her, but nobody listens to me. We're sitting in the dining room eating breakfast on a misty morning when Tilly asks for Peter's phone. He turns it over as if there's nothing on it that might get her exercised. Maybe there isn't. Peter doesn't seem the type to watch porn on his phone.

Tilly unlocks the phone and scrolls through the icons.

"Helen Anderson called me and said Cheyenne Theriault's been harassing you. My God, Peter! Seriously! What is *wrong* with you that you let her do this?"

"I hurt her. Seems like the least I can do since Dad won't let me do anything else."

Peter pushes back his plate and coffee cup. I think breakfast might be over for him.

"Thread deleted; contact blocked." She puts Peter's phone face down on the table. "Listen to me! You made a *mistake*. You're paying for it. You don't do anything wrong by protecting yourself from her. She's angry and that's not a wrong emotion, but harassing you is. So, I've taken care of it and you're not to unblock her again. Do you understand?"

Peter nods. He picks up his phone and scowls at the screen. Tilly offers him maple syrup. He swallows tightly and then smiles and pulls his plate toward him again. He's going to be okay. Now the question is – will I?

Responsibility

Peter

I didn't drive the first day I had my driver's license back. I had alcohol on board when I sat in the driver's seat and I couldn't talk myself into turning the key. I kept rerunning the photos of Cheyenne's ruined face in my mind.

Instead of driving, I decided to take a long walk and call Rick. I told him about my relapse, but not about the jar I'm sipping from. Halfway down last night, I estimate the sips will run out tomorrow night—long enough to ease the withdrawal symptoms. I won't start counting the days until the jar's empty and I won't drive with even a swallow on board.

I woke up this morning to Tilly wanting to protect me from Cheyenne and I decided not to take any sips. Instead, I drove to Long Island City. I stopped at a noon meeting in Setauket on the way back, but I didn't feel like going home yet, so I drove all the way out to the Hamptons. I had a lot to think about. The topic focuses on taking responsibility. Yeah, I so need that topic today. Is it right or wrong to block Cheyenne's calls? I have no idea and I must look at it from every angle possible during that long drive.

I drove at or slightly above the speed limit, keeping pace with the surrounding traffic. I guess I got it out of my system. Now I'm sitting alongside the road where I drove Cheyenne's car into a tree and ruined her life.

I don't remember much of that night. I hosted a party. I wasn't going to drink – or keep it to a beer, maybe two. I remember drinking the first beer and then.... I stare into the impenetrable abyss of a blackout, unable to call forth anything more than a few seconds of pain and red-and-white flashers across the dash as I tried to draw in a breath. The next thing I clearly remember is my dad telling me about the accident. How I got from the one beer to blackout drunk driving Cheyenne's car into a tree is a complete mystery to me. Maybe she knows. She says I did it deliberately, but Mr. Barnes says I had no ability to steer when I hit that tree. It couldn't have been deliberate.

My head hurts. Could be I'm remembering how it hurt for days after the wreck. Could be pent-up pressure from unspent tears. I'm not sure what I'm supposed to feel, so I just sit there rerunning those photos through my head.

What am I supposed to do with this huge wad of guilt? It's another month, six weeks before I can offer to make amends. And in the meantime...? I wipe a hand down my face. A tear trails after. Wouldn't crying be feeling sorry for myself? I'm not the one that got hurt. I just don't know what to do that makes amends. Saying I'm sorry isn't enough. How do you take responsibility for something you can't take back?

I don't know and that's the problem.

Patterns

Lily

Ben's got his shirt off, washing windows on the back of his house. I'm going through a box of quilting squares my mom hasn't had time to think about. Maybe I could put together the log cabin quilt she stopped working on when Bram collapsed in the school yard last year.

Of course, I'd need to get my mind off Ben. I've seen both Peter and Trevor without shirts and they're both more muscled than he is, but there's something about the V of his torso and the light stripe of hair running down from his naval into his shorts. I really need to stop thinking about it because I'm kind of dating Peter and that's probably a no-no – something akin to cheating in a platonic relationship. Right? I have photos on my phone of Peter from Fire Island. He's taller and thinner, but his abs are more defined. And then there's Trevor – always standing with either Alyse or Peter, of course. That kid has no body fat.

I've mixed two different kinds of blocks into the same pile. Distracted sorting! I separate them. Mom suggested I arrange them into the finished quilt layout, using the sunroom floor. Since we're not using the room when it's this warm outside, I could leave them in place and just work a little at a time. I could even set up the sewing machine there. She seems excited that I'm taking over her project. I don't know how I feel about it. I'm not nearly as good at quilting as she is.

Ben dumps his bucket and preps another one, his butt to the sky facing my direction. Does he not realize what he's doing to me? Probably not. Ben has never been more than older-brother friendly to me. I shouldn't be having thoughts about him like this.

My phone buzzes. It's Alyse.

"Hey."

"Hi you. You busy tonight?"

"No, just working on a project for Mom, but I have all summer."

"You want to come spend the night?"

"Sure, so long as it's okay with my mom. I spent all day with Bram, so it probably is."

"Trevor and I'll pick you up in an hour. Ring me back if she says 'no', otherwise we'll show up."

"Yeah, okay. Any idea what we've got planned?"

"I'll let you know when we pick you up. Hey, wear that sundress."

"Really?" That dress feels a little special for hanging out at Alyse's house.

"Yeah. I promise, you'll be happy you did."

Okay. Well, Alyse loves spontaneous activities, so I guess I can just go with that. I hang up and gather the quilting blocks I need into neat stacks to carry inside. The others go back in the bin.

"Done already?" Ben asks.

"Alyse invited me to spend the night."

"Have fun? Remember what I said about Pete and cars, right?"

"Of course. She said Trevor would give me a ride."

Ben hesitates.

"Trevor likes to drink too. Just – you know, pay attention and say 'no' if you don't feel safe."

"Right. I'll do that. Thanks."

"Have a good evening."

I nod and head for the open door of the sunroom. I'll set up the sewing machine tomorrow and see how far I get on this project. Meanwhile, Ben's chest and stomach muscles strain as he hefts the bucket and a part of me that I'm only just becoming aware of melts.

Best Friends

Peter

It's a beautiful sultry summer evening while Ben, Wes and I wash my car in his driveway. After my long drive yesterday, I stopped feeling like a cop would pull me over. Andy Harmon invited me to a big party in the Hamptons, and I know that is not where I want to be, so I came over here to hang out with Ben tonight. Wes always liked washing my car for some reason. I'm starting to feel like my life might straighten out, even though I screwed up and I know I must get back on track. My cell phone rings.

"It's Finn." Finn and I used to be tight, but I haven't heard from him since New Year's Eve.

"He's out at his dad's Hampton place for the summer," Ben remarks. Meanwhile, my phone is still ringing.

"Hey, Finn. What's up?"

I'm glad he's reaching out, but I can feel myself bracing for a rebound.

"Hey, Pete--Peter. Um, your sister came to my sister's party."

Okay, Finn Conover calling from a party and he sounds sober...I'm not aware of any universe where that's allowed. He's a bigger lush than I am.

"I just wrestled Trevor's keys away from him, but the girls are stuck here because I can't drive, and neither can he."

I want to say "Screw Alyse" and leave her wherever she's allowed Trevor to take her, but the plural noun piques my curiosity.

"Who is with Alyse?"

"Some chick named Lily. She's the one that clued me to Trevor being beyond the bend even for him. Since he got kicked out of Joffrey, he's been spun."

Ah, so that's how it went down? Not surprised, really.

"How screwed up is Alyse?"

"You should come, man." He sounds slightly worried. I've not touched anything since before lunch and I'm feeling good, but....

"I don't know – party, not my thing right now."

"Yeah, Trevor said you were sober these days. Me too. Six months."

"Cool." He's at a party, so how sober can he be?

"Um." Ben's staring at me from over the roof of my car, his keys in one hand, a questioning expression.

"Yeah. Ben and I'll come and get them. Can you try to keep Alyse away from the bar?"

"She's not drinking – at least not now. Not sure what she's on, but I kind of feel like I need a chastity belt and, you know, she's way too young for me."

"We'll get there as soon as we can."

Ben tosses the towel he used to wipe my rims to Wes.

"Tell the folks – uh, just tell them I went out somewhere with Pete."

I never said her name aloud, so I don't think Wes will get Lily in trouble. Ben just somehow knows they're together. I repark the Jag at the curb and get into Ben's Jeep.

"Finn's dad's place?"

"Yeah."

"Lily okay?"

"According to Finn, she's far wiser than Alyse, who is seriously fucked-up."

"You maybe need to tell your dad. I mean, if I'd told him about you – your drinking -- years ago, nobody would have gotten hurt – including you."

I taste bourbon for a moment, but I can't very well ask Ben to stop at a liquor store and I left my fake ID at home for just these sorts of temptations. I'm taking little sips from that jar and I'll be out by bedtime tomorrow night and then I'll get back on the wagon and stay there. I even made a noon meeting today. I felt guilty going with something on board, but I can't seem to dump the jar and a half shot every four hours or so is not getting me anywhere near drunk. Still, I'm paranoid about driving with anything on board. I biked to the Wexlers for my time with Bram before coming home to get the Jag for the trip to Setauket. I would have blown way below the legal limit, which of course doesn't matter when you're only 18. After the meeting, I just decided to come here to see Ben, extending my time between drinks. I admit, I kind of hoped to see Lily too, but not enough to go up to her door and knock. Odd, Lily didn't mention plans to go to the Hamptons with my sister.

"What are you thinking?"

"Just worried about them. How'd you know Lily was with her?"

"I stopped by this afternoon and Mrs. Wexler told me she left with Alyse. I'm going tomorrow to tell her that Trevor and Alyse are bad influences."

"Could you – look, yes, Trevor is a bad influence. If I could figure out a way to break them up, I would. I tried the Bro Code and it didn't work. He's my friend but he's off the chain and someone must do something. But – just don't – don't cost Alyse the one good friend she has. That's not going to help her with whatever has her spun up."

"Lily's safety matters to me, man."

"It matters to me too – a lot. And, I'll tell my dad – or at least Tilly – about Alyse. Something's wrong. She wasn't like this at Spring Break. And, if I hadn't been dealing with my own shit the last month, I probably would have been a better brother.

Southampton is an hour's drive from Ben's house and he's not inclined to break the speed limit. I'd have definitely gotten us there faster in the Jag, but the backseat is tiny, so someone would have to stay behind. He frowns out the windshield for a while.

"Mrs. Wexler said you were there this morning working with Bram. I liked those paintings. How is it you're a better artist than him even with your left hand?"

"Um, probably my eye is better and – um, I read something on the Internet about some of the conditions that go with global aphasia – that's his diagnosis. It causes a lot of problems with perception and stuff."

Here on the Port Mal Road, he can risk a glance at me.

"Wow – you really get a kick out of working with him, don't you?"

"Yeah. It's weird. I started just being nice for the sake of Alyse and Lily's friendship, but – yeah. I can see him in there, trying to find a way out and – I just want to help that."

He returns to frowning at the road in front of us and I don't know what that means, so I try texting Alyse, but don't get an answer.

"Do you know what she's taking?"

"No idea. I tried to pump Trevor, but he sent me back to her and she's not telling. I kind of think it might be interacting with bipolar."

"Coz of your mom?"

"Yeah, and – it's not like I've tried a lot of drugs or anything, but the few times I've experimented – I think substances and my body are a bad idea and – she's up, she's down, she's cycling. Could just be whatever she's taking but given the family history – that's beyond me. Alan needs to take some responsibility."

"He really shouldn't have left you to raise her, that's for sure." I've felt sometimes like a substitute parent. I just didn't realize others saw it too. "I think you're a good older brother, Pete. You don't always make good choices for yourself, but you care about Aly. I know that. But you're only 18. She needs adult supervision."

I feel this warm glow of pride. I *am* a good brother. Ben doesn't know the pot that got me suspended from school in sophomore year belonged to Alyse. I took the punishment – the semester in boarding school that really got me drinking like a fish – because I love my sister maybe more than I should. Maybe I should have snitched on her then to avoid today ... for both of us.

I'm yawning as we drive through the hamlet of Southampton and head toward the beach houses. We've been to parties at Finn's dad's place so we both know the way. Cars park bumper to bumper along both sides of the road. Ben puts his Jeep in 4-wheel drive to get off the road at the only place possible, through the ditch, parking in sea grass by the neighbor's property.

"Hope you're up for a hike." With that, he starts walking toward the music echoing through the night. A party is a bad idea for me right now, but maybe with Ben and Finn I can manage this. I hope.

Party Central

Ben

There's a smell to Pete that reads anxious. I gave up chocolate for evangelical Lent back in freshman year and I remember the struggle to say "Thanks, no," when someone offered me chocolate. The thing is—I don't like chocolate. That's why I chose it. I didn't think it would be hard to give it up for forty days. Pete likes to drink. He *loves* parties. Heck, *I* loved his parties. Now I've brought him to Party Central. It must be like hanging out in the chocolate factory when you gave up chocolate for a never-ending Lent.

"You going to be okay with this?"

He swallows audibly.

"Don't know. Don't let me out of your sight." His eyes flash white in the thin moonlight. "I'm not kidding. Don't let me out of your sight. I can't be trusted here."

Okeydokey, just so we're being honest here. He's still walking toward the house which blazes with lights and throbs with music. We turn into the driveway. Mr. Conover's house is huge white and metal with several outbuildings and lush plantings. His garage is bigger than my house. The main house makes Pete's house look small. The driveway is clogged with cars.

"I'm surprised you weren't invited to this."

"I was. Andy Harmon texted me about it and Trevor mentioned it. I decided to hang out with you."

He raps on the door to the carriage house and, after a moment, the door opens. Macaria Berber grins at us. We went to high school together and Macaria is a regular in the party scene.

"Heydee-ho. Finn asked me to stay here with Lily."

"Where's he?"

"Alyse made a jail break. He went looking for her."

"That sounds like a dumb idea." Pete looks tense as a small E string. Macaria appears sober. It's been a long time since I've seen that.

"He's on Antabuse. He's got a good reason not to drink." Uh, okay. I have no idea what Antabuse is, but if it helps Finn resist drinking, that's a good thing.

Lily appears behind Macaria, her face streaked with tears.

"I don't know what's wrong with her, Peter. It's like demon possession."

Macaria slips an arm behind her back.

"I'll keep her here while you go look for them."

"Thanks." Pete looks toward the house, sighing. "You ready?"

I start walking as my answer. Half our graduating class rocks out with Solo cups held high, right at Pete's nose level. He looks pale under his tan as he scans the crowd, pushing a cup away from his face. He points toward a cheering sound spilling out of the billiards room.

"Betcha that's Alyse."

We start walking. Pete has height on most of the crowd, so he cuts a wavering path through it. I follow behind him. I want to suggest I go check another cheering crowd by the pool, but I promised Pete I wouldn't leave him alone and I've seen plenty of evidence that he needs me to listen to him tonight.

We stall at the double open doors to the room because of a wall of people cheering at a show occurring on the pool table – Alyse with no shirt on, unzipping her skirt while Finn tries to talk her into coming down from the table. Pete stands there a moment, mouth hanging open.

"Holy shit."

What he said. I push up next to Finn.

"Aly, you don't want to do this!"

I think my voice carries, but I don't think she hears me. Pete appears on the other side of Finn.

He strips off his hoodie while I grab Alyse's blouse off the pool table.

"Sorry about this, man." Pete aims that at Finn before he sets a knee on the pool table so he can grab one of Alyse's gyrating arms. He pulls her down into his arms, scoops her up into his hoodie, then looks down into her flushed face. He twists onto his butt so he can get his feet on the ground. Alyse smiles up at him.

"You came!" She grabs his face in her two hands and lays a big kiss right on his lips. The muscles of his neck strain like docking chains as he pulls back away from her. The crowd stops cheering suddenly as his gaze sweeps them, daring anyone to comment. Finn leads the way out as Alyse starts singing a ribald song in an off-key voice. She flings herself backward in a stripper's pose and nearly racks her head on a door post. Pete struggles to get her back into his arms.

"Aly, cut it out!" He pinions one of her arms, but she brings a leg up and clearly knees him in the side of the head. He sets her on her feet but keeps his hand wrapped around one of her biceps. "Fine, you can walk. Come on."

She stumbles as he moves toward the driveway. I grab the hoodie to keep it from slipping off her shoulders and take her other arm, so she won't get away.

"Where are my shoes?"

"Maybe with your bra." Pete's pissed. Grandpa Jack says reformed drunks are sometimes less than kind to unreformed drunks. "Stop fighting me." She takes that as permission to sit down.

"I'll do what I want."

Pete's got a death grip on her wrist, so she's not going anywhere he doesn't want her to go and the look on his face says he'll leave bruises if he must. I pick her up to get her moving, but Pete still doesn't let her wrist go. We leave the crush of the party behind. Finn waited for us.

"Just so you know, I didn't plan this party. I was hanging out with friends in Sag Harbor and didn't know about the party until I got home a couple of hours ago. I didn't know she was here until Lily came banging on the door."

"Apparently, Monica learned party-planning from you." Pete's tempers are quixotic, and he can go from mad to joking in a second. I've always admired that about him. "You collect keys *before* things get out of hand. Any idea where Trevor is?"

"Passed out somewhere, maybe. He was pretty pissed at me – giving me that whole 'you can't judge me' speech. I figure guys like us *can* judge drunk drivers. We know what would have kept us from driving drunk."

"Yeah, that's not exactly what happened to me. We'll have to swap stories--."

Alyse twists out of my arms to splay on her hands and knees on the pavers. Pete has no choice but to let go of her wrist or risk breaking her arm. She scrambles up to her feet, but Finn grabs her around the waist and keeps moving toward the carriage house.

"Let me go! You can't do this! It's kidnapping!"

"It's my house, sugar. I'm evicting an uninvited guest – a drunk and abusive uninvited guest."

Alyse rips the air blue with a string of swear words that would rival Trevor at his most drunk. Finn's as tall as Pete and looks like he's been spending his sober time working out, so Alyse can struggle all she wants, she's not getting away. She ups the ante by biting him on the bicep.

"Ow!" Finn grabs her wrist and twists her face forward as blood runs down his arm in thin trickles. "Please tell her when she comes down from whatever this is that she should never come here again."

"No problem," Pete tells him. We've reached the carriage house where Macaria and Lily stand on the porch. "Thanks for letting me handle this and not just calling the cops on her. If you find her shoes, could you ask Trevor to return them?"

"Sure, or I'll swing them by myself."

"I've got them." Lily holds a pair of four-inch heels that match Alyse's bright red blouse that's in my hand.

"I'll still swing by sometime. Should be over your way next week. Can you get to your car with her or do you need to bring it around?"

Macaria stares into Alyse's face. Aly's drooling and her eyes are glazed.

"I think she needs to puke. She's taken too much of something, which comes with hanging with Trevor." Finn and Mac bare Alyse into a nearby bathroom and then we hear puking.

"You okay?" Lily's searching Pete's face as he stares after the trio.

"Kind of want to go find a really strong drink right now." Pete runs a hand down his face. "I'm okay, but this is a hard place to be."

She knows that about him. How did they get so close that he shared that with her? Finn comes out of the bathroom.

"Mac will get her cleaned up." I hand him the blouse, figuring Macaria can also dress her. I have no idea how I'm going to purge the memory of Alyse's breasts. It's a visual I don't need. Now that I think about it, Pete got over seeing them pretty danged fast. Alyse kissing him comes to mind.

"I'll go get the car." Pete holds out his hand for my keys and I automatically reach to give them to him. Pete's hand hesitates in his own reach. "Remember what I said about I can't be trusted. Still true."

"We've got her." Finn points to the door. "Go get the car and I'll bring her out to you. About how long?"

"I'll text you."

Pete rubs the back of his neck as we walk toward the car.

"I should have left you in Port Mallory, shouldn't I?"

"No. I would have come on my own and gotten myself into trouble. I. Can't. Be. Trusted."

We swing wide around giggling in the bushes. Sounds like two girls going at it. Pete sighs heavily. We reach my Jeep and I back out through the ditch to the road. Pete gets in.

"Thank you for being willing to do this. I couldn't do this alone."

"Yeah. I'm sorry I didn't understand before."

"You just knew that I hurt her. I get it. Let's get Aly."

Finn opens the door to bring the girls out to the car and Alyse makes a break for it. At least she's got her shirt on now. Pete's out of the car in a heartbeat and catches her in a few strides. She kicks at him. He lifts her off her feet and smacks her butt once with the flat of his hand before tossing her over his shoulder.

"I'm done, Aly. Stop being a fuckwit."

Now she's crying and begging him not to hate her. He looks torn as he buckles her into the backseat. Lily buckles in on the other side.

"Don't hate me," Alyse whimpers.

"I don't. I couldn't. Aly, you're my sister and I love you, but I can't let you do this to yourself."

"You don't know." She wipes snot with the back of her hand. "It's so sad and I feel like death."

Pete leans down and hugs her.

"We're going to get you some help." Macaria sighs, leaning back against the wall beside the carriage house door.

"What?" I don't want to jump to a conclusion about what she thinks she sees.

"He's never going to tell his folks. He does denial better than anyone I know. Still the boy most-likely to need a liver transplant." I remember she contributed the addendum on the "Most likely to..." list.

"It's been more than a month." Why do I feel like I'm lying? She lights a cigarette and takes a deep drag before speaking again.

"Has it? Maybe I'm misreading him. Or maybe if you spend time with him, you'll see how long he can go between maintenance drinks."

Pete closes Alyse's door and glances my way. He needs to get out of here, so I move toward the driver's seat while Pete thanks Finn for his help.

Alyse weeps quietly in the corner of the backseat as we head home.

Party Favors

Lily

I haven't eaten since lunch and my stomach growls. Ben asks me if we need to stop for food. Peter looks back at me.

"She needs to get home." I don't want to be the center of attention here. Alyse is asleep now.

"Naw. She probably could use some food to help her come down. Any idea what she took?"

"No. Here, I have her purse."

Peter accepts the small leather clutch and with a grimace he opens it and sifts through the contents. He pulls out an Altoids box. Everybody knows the orange of Adderall. I don't recognize the blue pills, but Peter sighs when he sees them.

"What is it?" Ben asks.

"Clozapine, I think. They use it to keep my mother on the planet in the summer months."

"Where would Alyse get that?"

"Don't know." His hand dips further into the purse and pulls out a small vial with white powder. "Shit!"

"That would explain a lot, right?" Ben's trying to drive and look at Peter's discovery at the same time.

"Yeah, the bipolar-ish behavior makes a lot of sense now. Let's get them some food. It might settle the craving I'm having right now."

"For?"

"It's always the same thing with me – bourbon – although I'd take any alcohol but scotch right now – and red wine. That gives me migraines."

Peter puts everything back in Alyse's purse, then stows it in the front.

"What are you thinking?"

"Not yet. Can't think when I want a drink."

Eats on the Montauk Highway promises great food and a relaxed atmosphere. Peter shakes Alyse until she wakes up and makes her come in with us. She objects to the fries he orders for her.

"You need carbs, or you're going to crash and trust me, that's not any fun."

There's an old Wurlitzer in the corner of this diner and it plays *The Bus Stop*. An old disco tune, It's one of the songs my dad's taught me.

"I love this song."

Peter holds a hand out to me. We're the only ones in the place, so after a few bars of the song, he uses the narrow space between tables to spin me into a partnered version of the classic dance move. For such a tall guy he's graceful and he makes me feel like a princess late arrived at the ball. To go

340

from earlier in the evening begging Finn to rescue me to this is surreal. How long before midnight and I must try not to lose my glass slipper.

Realizations

Alyse

I pry my bleary eyes open. My head pounds and my mouth is dry. Peter's not sitting across the table from me. He's dancing with Lily and she's got this enraptured look on her face.

They neither of them know anything about life and I'm sick of putting up with Peter's shit. He thinks he's better than me and he's not. He's just got Mom's admiration and Dad's ear and Tilly thinks he walks on water. Sure, he got bumped down a peg when he crashed Cheyenne's car, but he's back on top again. Look how the little Pollyanna stares at him. So naïve. I'll show her one day soon.

"You all right?" Ben's sitting beside me.

"Where's Trevor?"

"Not sure. Passed out at Monica's party, maybe."

"You left him there?"

"He can drive his car home tomorrow. How's your head?" He pushes a coffee cup into my hands.

I sip it. Way too sweet. I say so. "Pete's our hangover expert and he said drink it."

Peter brings Lily back to the table and she sits next to me.

"How are you feeling?"

"Bitch!"

"Hey!" Peter's annoyed. "If it weren't for her, you'd be sitting in a squad car by now and with drugs onboard, Tilly would have to call Dad."

"I'm sorry. You don't know." They don't and they never will. The choice I made was the wrong one and yet I can't take it back so I can't tell. I wipe tears.

"Her stash of goodies." Ben's looking at Lily, forcing her to meet his gaze. "You didn't participate?"

"No. I took a sip of beer once – tasted like fizzy pee."

They both laugh and Peter adds.

"Pretty sure it *is* carbonated piss. It explains why it passes through you so quickly."

He used to make those observations for *me*. The food arrives. I'm not eating those fries.

"Trust me. The Adderall and coke – you burned way more calories than is on this plate. Starches blunt the hangover. Eat." I tighten my mouth. "Don't make me make you."

There's a glint in his eyes and I remember the bite of his fingers on my bicep. My wrist isn't bruised, but my ass still stings. I eat some fries. Peter tucks into a burger, his hands shaking as he prepares it. Ben's watching him sideways with a thoughtful look on his face, but I can't spare thought for it because I need to run to the bathroom again to puke.

BJ's Way

Peter

Four days and I haven't told Rick about my detoxing technique with the jar. He wasn't surprised I relapsed, saying he could kind of sense it coming when I shut down on him the night Ben showed me Cheyenne's photos. He reiterated my need to go to rehab and we talked about Steps 1 through 3, but he let me go back to working on the first item on Step 4 – what I owe Cheyenne. It keeps circling back that I owe her not to keep putting other lives in danger.

But I also owe Ben amends and I'm trying. We're on BJ Way at Mountain Laurel and we stop to rest because my shoulder is hurting. It's been sore since that night at Finn's house. I must have tweaked it and didn't notice in the heat of the action.

"I told Tilly about Alyse."

"And?"

"Um, she's grounded for a while. Tilly's taking her to a doctor. She's pissed at me."

"Tilly?"

"Alyse." I laugh then sober, shifting my water bottle from my shoulder and stretching the joint. "Tilly said she'd call Dad."

"Why don't *you* call him?"

"He doesn't really listen to me." I want to change the subject. "Your birthday's coming up."

"Yeah, Big 19."

"You know I can't throw a party for you this year? That feels weird."

"I don't need you to throw me a party, Pete. You need to do what's right for you. You'll come to the sedate one my parents will throw, right?"

"For sure. Trevor called, by the way. He admitted the other night was completely his fault."

"Yeah, but it'll happen again next week."

"Maybe not. He got into that dance troupe in the city, so he's on the wagon for now."

"Can he just quit all that stuff cold turkey?"

"I have no idea. I can't quit bourbon just like dropping a rock, so --. I told him to stay away from Alyse or he'd be going to New York with a broken leg."

"Do you think he'll listen?"

"He says he will. He's leaving in a few weeks anyway." I rub a hand through my hair which is curling from sweat. "Tempts me to do a birthday party for you just so all of us can get together one last time."

"And, if you relapse, then what?"

"I get back on the wagon. I've done it often enough that I'm getting kind of good at it."

It's on the tip of my tongue to admit I relapsed over those photos, but I don't want to alienate him. As it is, he's frowning.

"You were doing the whole 'I'm not drinking' thing the night when you and Cheyenne had the wreck. Somehow you ended up driving drunk."

"Yeah, I don't know what happened that night."

"Because you were drunk."

"I also had a concussion, Ben. The steering broke. I don't know how that happened, but the cops said I couldn't have avoided what happened after it did." Ben looks ready to explode and I'm not sure what to say. Rick would say to not apologize for something I didn't do. Rick says a lot of things. "Ben, I can't go back and change it. Will you just give me that, please? The accident, the wreck, was my fault, but not entirely and I can't change what happened. I'll do better going forward."

He swallows hard, stares out into the trees. I hold my breath.

"Yeah. I get it."

"So, do you know – something happened with Alyse since Spring Break. The only thing I can figure out is that she started dating Trevor. Has he said anything?"

Lela Markham

"Not really. He's been weird lately – since he got fired from Joffrey, but also since he started dating her. Drunk more."

"So, it's not just me noticing because I'm sober and sensitive on the subject?"

"No, I don't think so. He's different. But I was up in Dartmouth and so, I wasn't here to see what happened. I can ask around. Ask Lily maybe."

"She says she doesn't know anything – which sounds a lot like me and Alyse when we cover for one another."

Ben looks up at the sky.

"I think it might rain. We should probably get going."

"Yeah. I'm headed to the Wexlers to visit Bram anyway."

"What's on deck today?"

"I'm going to try and teach him chess." Ben casts me a skeptical look. "Well, if it doesn't work, he still pretty good at backgammon and, if it works, then he's using his brain on another level. That can't be a bad thing."

"I just don't know how you're going to explain it to him. Global aphasia means he doesn't understand what you're saying."

"I think he understands some. Anyway, let's go."

We race each other out of the forest. The storm turns west before we get the bikes loaded and the afternoon continues to be gorgeous and muggy.

Strategy

Peter

Bram frowns the whole time as I set up the board. According to his mother, he knew how to play before the stroke, but most things can be assumed wiped by the brain damage. Using pantomime, I suggest he set up his own side of the board. He does the pawns just fine, but then struggles with the power line. He keeps twisting his head like he's having trouble seeing the whole board – which Mrs. Wexler says may well be true. I move the board over a little so it's more fully to his left. He still struggles. I hand him one piece at a time, and he does better. Good to know. Don't overwhelm the brain-damaged kid.

I came prepared for the complexity of the game. I know we're not going to play a game today. I'm reminding him of the moves and figuring out a way to communicate with him. Chess isn't counting. Chess is two dimensional strategy and that means he must both think more and communicate more.

I draw pictures of each piece as we "discuss" the moves. He has a tendency to nod when he thinks he has something and then to stubbornly cling to the same wrong move, but I remain patient with him and in the half-hour allotted for this experiment, he figures out that he's White and that his bishops move diagonally and can't hop other pieces. I promise I'll be back. Then we play a game of backgammon, which he legitimately wins, though only because I couldn't cover a piece and he put me on the board when his home field was well covered.

We high-five. He motions toward the window. I don't know what he wants so I start playing 20 Questions. He shakes his head or gives a one-shouldered shrug for every question. I grab paper and pencil and roll him up to the table. Frowning furiously, he stick-figures a deer, a tree and himself in the wheelchair on a deck.

"Who saw this?"

He draws another stick figure, then grabs a colored pencil and puts red hair on it.

"Your Mom." His mouth tightens. His throat contracts. I wait, knowing he won't manage it, but giving him time to try.

"Mmmmaaa."

"Hey, you spoke!" He smiles, joy lighting up the half of his face that works normally, even seeping over to the right. "You keep that up, man. You'll be a real chatterbox by Christmas."

He gives me that look that says I've just spoken Chinese to him, so I use "talking-hands" to show he'll be talking a lot in the future. He sobers, touches his throat, nods and leans his head forward. Personal sign for "I hope so" perhaps.

Now he motions at Madalyn that he's exhausted. While she puts him to bed, Lily provides me with a glass of iced tea. She's wearing the necklace I bought her, and it looks good on her.

"His occupational therapist suggested they test his language skills. She believes she's seeing improvement."

That pleases me. Maybe my own life is all screwed up, but I'm doing something right here and I enjoy the feeling. And per my agreement with Rick, I am not substituting sex for booze. It's okay to be friends with a girl, but no falling in love or lust and no sex. He's right about the clarity. My head is clearing even with the relapse last week.

"Does that mean more speech therapy?"

"Maybe. We think he's understanding us more too. Of course, they don't care about that unless they see it. They say we're just getting better at interpreting his non-verbal communication. I think when I'm a speech therapist, I'm never going to say that to anyone."

"It's gotta to be hard to read the mind of someone who can't talk. I mean, it is hard – but even for professionals."

"Well, even Jemmy says he noticed improvement before they did." Jemmy's her older brother, who I've not met. "You'd think professionals wouldn't want to discourage us from getting him talking again by telling us it's unlikely to happen."

"Yeah, that's--. Maybe they stumbled over too much information. I didn't know what the odds were, so it didn't stop me."

"Maybe."

"I also don't have a lot of other patients all with different demands. I was just one bored guy who saw a challenge he wanted to overcome. So, you're thinking about becoming a speech therapist?"

"Might as well go with something you have a lot of experience at."

"There's a lot to be said for passion." I glance around to assure Madalyn is still busy. "Do your parents know about the other night?"

"They know about Trevor. I didn't tell on Alyse."

"Thank you."

"I didn't do it for you – or for her, really. I did it because she's my friend and I don't have a lot of those."

"Yeah. Next year at school, make some. Alyse likes exclusivity. She was always jealous of my friends. But it's healthier for you if she's not the only one."

Lily nods. She's maybe not as naïve as I assume.

"I gotta get going, take a shower before dinner."

"Can I catch a ride with you?"

"To my house?"

"Alyse asked. It'll save my dad having to drive me."

"Ah, yes, of course, although Alyse could have just asked Vic to come get you."

"That always feels so weird."

"It is weird. We're not a normal family. Be aware of that in your friendship with her."

I expect her to ask, "What about in my friendship with you?" but she doesn't. I reward her cordiality by driving at a safe and sane speed all the way home.

Party Planning

Peter

Why the fucking bar was open this time is a mystery, but I'm proud of myself that I didn't drink. It was, thankfully locked again the next morning. So far, my fake ID remains in my sock drawer, so I'm not tempted to buy alcohol for myself, but that bar is like a siren's call and I really struggle to say "no". Thus, my anxiety when Alyse announces Trevor is throwing Ben a 19th birthday party. Trevor's parties are notorious for overserving and letting people drive away drunk. Add in the pharmaceuticals, and they're a mess. Fun! Way fun! But he doesn't anticipate problems like I did, and he's not got any adults in his corner like Tilly. I swear, that woman could invade a small country, grab their treasury and execute a strategic withdrawal before that country's army knew she was there.

"Aren't you still grounded?"

"No, it was for one week. That's tomorrow and the party is next week."

"And, didn't I tell you to stay away from Trevor?"

"We haven't seen each other. We just talked over the Internet."

"And planned a party – which I'm assuming will have alcohol, drugs, uncommitted sex and possibly dancing bears."

"Well, that would be entertaining. I thought dancing clowns instead – or dancing older brothers who don't know when to back off. Seriously, you're no fun sober." She frowns. "Or are you intermittently dry?"

"Shut the fuck up! You have no right to judge me after the other night."

She blushes, but then scowls at me.

"Thanks for siccing Tilly on me, by the way. Were you hoping she'd get distracted from watching after you?"

"I was worried about you. I still am."

"And I'm fine. Trevor leaves in a couple of weeks and I'll go back to being boring old Alyse."

"Or maybe you become addict Alyse."

"That's not how it works, Peter. You have to use it for a long time."

"That's alcohol, not cocaine, not Clozapine. Didn't you read the drug pamphlet they gave you at freshman orientation?"

"Please, stop. I'm fine, but she's making me go to a counselor just to be sure."

"Good. I guess they learned something from me."

"They?"

"Tilly and Dad."

"You say that like they're a couple."

"They kind of are, aren't they?"

"You remember that?"

"Remember what?"

She frowns at me.

"Never mind."

"Well, I do mind. Ben said he didn't want a big social gathering for his party."

"He doesn't want you to plan it because you can't stay away from the kegs, but he wants one. Of course, he does."

She's got a point. I can't handle my liquor and I should stay far far away from any of Trevor's parties. But it's Ben. It's a moral conundrum. I dial Rick because that's what I'm supposed to do – consult with my sponsor. Right?

So, I tell him.

"Peter." He sounds like he's sighing. "Your friend Ben would totally understand if you couldn't make his party because you checked yourself into rehab. And don't give me any shit about your father. You're 18, dude. Just do it and your dad will get onboard afterward. Because if you go to that party, we're back at revolving-door sobriety and I told you, I'm not on board for that."

359

I'd still have time for a month program before going back to Yale. I've done more than a month and recently. I could get away from all the pressures and just concentrate on learning to be sober. But then I'd miss Ben's party and waste half the summer indoors. I don't have to drink. I got through four months in the dorms without drinking. I can do it at Trevor's house. He'll probably even help me with that.

I can do this. It's a week away and if I'm sober between now and then, I can be sober for the party. I can.

Turning A Corner

Alyse

Trevor's here with his father and Tilly won't let me take him upstairs. She's so bossy! Peter's tense as a bow string and repeatedly beating Trevor at pool before dinner. At least he's interacting with us. He's been avoiding me for days now. He almost seems angry about my planning Trevor's party. He goes for long drives, swims, goes to the gym and is generally boring. He joins us for dinner but announces he has somewhere to go afterward.

"A date?" Grey asks. I like Trevor's dad. He's so relaxed and non-judgmental.

Peter fiddles with his spoon.

"I'm headed to a meeting."

"A meeting for what?" Dad sips his wine.

Peter stares at him like he's never seen him before.

"I'm trying to stay sober, Dad, remember?"

Grey's wife looks up from her phone and blinks at Peter.

"How old are you?" Carolyn is half Grey's age. I think she's younger than Tilly who joined us at the table after she served the food. She's always done that when it's just us – well, for a long time, but she now joins us when we have guests. I know she and Daddy are having sex, but something seems to be changing in their relationship and I hate it.

Peter stares at her. He recognizes Dumb Blonde Syndrome when he sees it. I wonder how much it costs her to get that perfect yellow Lab tint. And, I realize she can't be as young as Tilly because she has a daughter my age. She's got a great plastic surgeon.

"Eighteen. I'm going to head out now." He leans down and whispers something in Tilly's ear. She nods and pats his forearm.

"What was that about?" Daddy never seems to wonder about Peter and Tilly, though I sometimes do. Peter can make her do anything he wants. Maybe Dad's finally waking up.

"He just asked me to do something for him. I'll tell you about it later." She gazes at the wine glass by his plate and Daddy cocks his head like an idea has just occurred.

"He's struggling tonight?"

She nods.

"Alan, you need to agree to come onto my pod cast." Grey sounds so enthusiastic about that prospect.

"I could possibly call in. What's the topic going to be?"

Trevor links hands with me and we head out of the dining room. Tilly clears her throat.

"You two are not allowed to be alone right now. You know this, Alyse, and your father is the one who decided that."

"This is so unfair!"

"Life is often unfair. Stay on this floor and inside the house and it'll be fine."

I sigh. Trevor settles on the bottom step of the stairs.

"It's okay."

"Is it?"

"Yes. I screwed up that night and your family is concerned."

"Peter didn't need to tell them."

"He probably did. You got a little out of control and I cut out on you. Peter did what he had to do."

"He's gotten really judgmental since he stopped drinking."

"Lyse, he loves you. Just – give him a little bit of a break. He didn't want to tell them, but I think you probably needed them to know. Peter didn't do so well with drugs when he experimented either. Adderall made him incredibly manic. From what Finn told me, it made you even worse."

"I just wanted to feel."

"I know. How you doing with that?"

"I talked to the counselor the other day. I guess it'll be okay. How are you, really?"

363

"I'm good. Haven't had a drink since that night. I'm going to adopt that as a rule for ballet too. I'll party for, like, Ben's birthday, but cool it if we're not celebrating."

I nod. How I acted that night scared me. I'd never admit that to Peter. I barely remember what I did, but what Peter described does fit some of Mom's behaviors when she's off her meds. Well, he says that. I've never actually seen one of her manic episodes. The counselor agreed it could be a sign of bipolar – or just a sign that I overdid.

"Your dad doesn't seem mad at you."

"No. He's never mad at me." He smiles, laughs nervously. "No, he talked to me about it. He threatened me with rehab."

"Really? That doesn't sound like him."

"He's usually more libertarian than your father, but – I guess Finn talked to him. That night is pretty foggy, but I remember enough that I know I wasn't acting like myself." He sighs. "I convinced him I could clean up on my own and I'm doing that. It was a whacked few weeks there."

"Yeah."

We made a wrong decision and we can't take it back. It would have ruined our lives, but now there will always be this sadness.

I'm deep in my thoughts when he leans in for a kiss. He didn't drink wine at dinner so I can taste roast beef on his breath. I have a brand new diaphragm and no way to use it.

"I wonder if they'd let us be alone in the billiards room. I mean, it's all windows."

"Let's go." His eyes crinkle a little, so I kiss him. "Better to beg forgiveness than ask permission."

He nods.

"Do you even play pool?" he asks as he follows me toward the pool table.

"No, but it beats listening to politics. And, you play, so you can teach me."

"Apparently, I don't play that well. Peter just ran the table four times."

"Show me. Maybe next time I can surprise him."

Trevor cocks his eyebrow when he realizes that he must *show* me how to play pool and that has some decided benefits to it.

Briercliff

Peter

My head pounds and thunders with the beat of the rain on the roof of the Jag. I have no idea what happened last night. I came home from my meeting feeling confident. Dad and Grey were still talking away, but they'd moved their confab to the billiard room where they played with Trevor and Alyse. Tilly and Carolyn chatted in the kitchen.

Dad left the damned bar unlocked *again*. It felt like I'd never been to a meeting. I didn't stop at Go. I didn't call Rick. I grabbed the whole decanter of Four Roses and took it to my room. A lone shot of bourbon resided in the bottom of the bottle when I woke up this morning and that settled my stomach enough so I could function. The bar remained unlocked, so I put the empty decanter back in its place. Let them figure that one out when there's an admitted alcoholic in the house.

Briercliff looks friendly – a central fake-colonial administrative entrance and two wings to the side with more modern glass and metal style about them. There's green lawns and mature trees and I'm sure if it weren't pouring down rain it would be a lovely place to spend a month. As soon as I stop feeling like I'm going to hurl, I'm going to take care of that.

I've got my speech mostly worked out. It's short and to the point. I've got a DUI prior and I've been working on sobriety for a year now and I can't. I'm just not able to stay out of the revolving door. Simple enough. I believe it. They'll believe it and my dad will get onboard later. I reach for the door handle. My phone buzzes.

CHEYENNE

I unblocked her number after Monica's party. I don't even bother to read the message. They're all the same. I ruined her life and I deserve to suffer. I do. I am. I did. I wipe tears. I'm screwing up with everybody and I don't know what to do about that. Even Rick is about to write me off. If I were calling him rather than driving here, he *would* write me off. Ben's just now talking to me and he would be so disappointed with my getting drunk last night. It wasn't even a controlled drunk. I passed out before I swallowed the last bit. Even Trevor is, supposedly, doing better than me. Finn's got more than six months. There's a guy at the Alano Club who celebrating 42 years. I'm pretty sure he's Ben's grandfather. I only know him as Jack and we never talk about how we know each other, but I'm pretty sure that's the case.

I blot my tears on my sleeve and reach for the door handle again. My phone vibrates again. I almost don't look because it'll just be Cheyenne again, but then I do.

> LILY - Has Alyse told you why she's mad at me?
> I invited her to barbecue at my house.

Damn! Damnit! Why do they always have to call me? Alyse is ruining the one friendship she truly has and there's no one I can call to ask for help. I need to walk in that door, but I can't. Someone must fix this – fix Alyse – and there's no one else available. I can come back in a few days. I'll have some sober time and I'll be past the worst of the withdrawal symptoms. I won't have to embarrass myself in front of strangers. I start the car and steer toward home, a purple bullet slicing through the gray rain.

Uncertainty

Ben

W hat are you doing?" Lily's butt is sunny side up in her backyard, her hands in the dirt by the fence. She straightens, laughing. She's wearing well-worn jeans and a tank top that shows off her young figure.

"My mom says there's lilies growing here, and she wants me to separate them so next year, they'll bloom."

"There were lilies growing all along the fence. They might not come back though because the yard guy last summer mowed them, and my mom claims that if you mow the stems the bulbs don't regenerate or whatever."

"Dang!"

"Might not be right though. If you notice, we don't have a lot growing in our yard because Mom has a brown thumb. Ask Geneva across the street. She is a master gardener. She can give you all sorts of tips and she's one of those people who enjoys talking about it." Geneva also probably will give Lily some lily bulbs.

Lily brushes the dirt off her fingers and grabs the top of the fence which is about shoulder-level on her.

"Good to know. Mom used to grow a lot of flowers back in Manchester before ... well, before. She doesn't have time now with Bram. So, I figured I'd at least do this. She says it's all in knowing what can grow and what needs love and what prefers to be neglected."

"Geneva knows how to do all that."

"I'll go say 'hi.' So, someone tells me you're having a birthday party."

"Too many birthday parties. Mom and Dad are going to do one here at the house *on* my birthday and then I just heard that Trevor has one planned for Saturday."

"Oh? Isn't that the 3rd?"

"Yeah, which is fine because there'll be a bunch of people back home for the regatta on the 9th. Trevor's got good timing. It's just I still have a sour taste in my mouth over that thing at Finn's place and – well, the last time we all gathered together for a blowout, Pete wrecked Cheyenne's car."

"Yeah, he mentioned that. He's nervous about it too."

"You're over there more than I am. Have you seen any signs of him drinking?"

"No, but I'm not sure I'd really recognize the signs unless he was drunk. Alyse says the bar's always locked now and she has been normal-acting ever since that night – well, except for when she got snippy about my inviting her to the barbecue. That was weird."

"Not so weird. I warned you that she can be fickle. So long as you're doing things she wants to do, she's fine, but ask her to do something like hangout in the same yard as your disabled brother--."

"Really? You think that's it? Because Peter seems to come here to hang out with Bram."

"I noticed that. They're definitely not the same person. You'd think Pete would be the more damaged because he interacted with their mother longer, but Alyse is starting to act like her." I spent a month as Pete's tagalong on a Greek family vacation before the divorce and Laren Wyngate scares the hell out of me.

"That's the drugs, right?"

"Or the bipolar. Her personality – capricious, don't give a crap what you think, selfish, entitled. Pete can have that streak, but I'm beginning to realize that's who he can become when he drinks. It's not who he is when he's sober. Or at least not who he wants to be."

Lily stares off at the trees in her back yard. I wonder if she minds that Pete enjoys helping her brother as much or more than hanging out with her. I know girls who would be jealous, but Lily doesn't seem to be coded that way.

"So, anyway, I've half a mind not to go to my own birthday party."

"Oh, you shouldn't do that. Peter asked me to tag along to keep his attention away from the beverages. He said there's always great dancing and I got a little taste of that the other night. So, you shouldn't skip your own birthday party since he and I are both going because of you."

That sounds like Trevor – guilt Pete into attending and then guilt me into coming too. I would just as soon go camping on the 3rd and spend it out until I have to be to work Monday morning. But Pete would take it personally and that might stall mending our relationship. Are we mending? I know I had fun the other day when we were mountain-biking, but then something will happen – he's late meeting me or he doesn't answer his phone – and I'm right back thinking he might be pulling one over on me. Maybe I should ask him to go camping with me. I could maybe take a couple of extra days.

"What are you two up to?" Pete's actual voice cuts right through my reverie. I turn toward him. He's come up the side of the garage where I see his bike leaning. Why's he back to riding his bike when his wheels have been restored?

"Talking about the care and feeding of lilies."
There it is, something dark moving in the depth of
his eyes as they twitter from me to Lily and back.

"He's making a pun. We're talking about actual
lilies." She spreads her hands to indicate the flower
bed at her feet.

"Oh. Something grows there?"

"We think so. Lily is going to consult with
Geneva."

Pete frowns at me again. Seriously? He doesn't
know the tenants' names.

"The woman who rents your dad's place across
the street."

Pete casts a glance that way.

"Is that her name? I don't think I've ever talked
to her."

"Really? She's lived there a couple of years."

Pete shrugs. There it is – that streak of *I don't
care*. I can't smell it on him, but I guess I never
really could. If my theory is correct, he's drinking
again. But I so don't want him to be.

"So Alyse and I have a bet going. Are you going
to show up for your own birthday party?"

"How much does she lose if I don't?"

"Just my pretend-willing attendance at a dance
afterparty. Which won't be so bad this time because
I'm taking a couple of exploratory sessions starting
on July 15."

"You're getting back into dance?" He's said before that drinking crowded out dance, but that's a revision from when he said he got teased at boarding school. Which is the lie? One or both. Hard to know when dealing with an Olympic liar. I just know he's been doing better, and I just don't know that I trust him yet.

"Jazz and hip hop. I'd need to get in a lot better shape for ballet and I don't have enough time."

"You thinking of dancing up in Yale?"

"Maybe. There's a couple of private studios. I can't take a class at Yale. Since I'm on academic probation, I can only take twelve credits, so I don't have room for a credited dance class."

That sounds like he's sober. Damn it! I just wish I knew. How did things get so screwed up that I can't trust my best friend not to lie to me?

"Sounds like a good way to fill your evenings."

"And burn nervous energy, of which I have a lot right now."

There! Sober! Maybe the bike-riding is an attempt to burn nervous energy. But ....

"So, are you actually coming to the party?"

"Sorry."

"It's fine. I had to give Trevor an answer, so I asked Lily to be my plus-one."

They fist-bump each other. Pete never had female friends in high school. He didn't date much either. He preferred hanging with guy friends and if

376

there were girls around, they always seemed to gravitate toward him. He just never got close to any of them until Cheyenne and things turned out badly for her. I *want* to believe he is just being friends, but I worry that he's morphing into Trevor.

"Yeah, I'll definitely be coming. Maybe we should carpool. The parking at Trevor's always sucks."

"I've already got Vic lined up. You can catch a ride with if you want. You should bring a date even. You and Pam still seem friendly."

"We don't hate each other, but it was never more than a summer for us. You're not dating anyone either."

He nods then hums a few lines of one of my dad's favorite songs – Easy Come, Easy Go. His last relationship didn't turn out well. I could see why he might want to take his time.

"Well, I promised Bram another chess lesson and to let him kick my butt at backgammon again. We better get to that before he's too tired to do anything."

Lily laughs, bids me a good afternoon and follows him to the garage. Maybe I imagined that flash of jealousy or maybe I need to examine myself about the flash of jealousy I feel right now as they disappear together. The fact is, I don't trust him with Lily and someone who cares about her safety needs to be there for when he does something dangerous.

A Party Worth Having

Lily

I've never seen Peter so relaxed. He's laughing and joking, and he gets all the inside discussions. The Andersons' backyard is lit up with tiki torches and Christmas lights and they've got a firepit going. There's about 20 people here, which proved to be too much for Bram. Mom took him back to the house. She came back out after about half an hour carrying the nursery monitor.

"He was okay with going to bed, but I don't think he's tired, so I just want to make sure he doesn't try to get up and falls."

"We'll take turns going in and checking on him," Dad assures. I nod. Peter rises from a chair.

"Is Bram okay?"

"The cross-talk frustrates him." Mom uses that as a standard explanation, though truthfully, we really don't know why he gets agitated.

Peter accepts the explanation. Nobody is dancing, but there's music, so on the way to the food table, he spins me in a loose waltz. I'm sloppy. He knows exactly what he's doing.

"How are you doing?" He's been odd the last few days – distracted, looking like he's not sleeping.

"That obvious?"

"Not here. You really feel comfortable here."

"Yeah. Thanks for helping Ben and me to make up."

"I didn't really. But, really, how are you?"

"It just comes and goes. I didn't sleep very well last night. And the night before Dad was there with everybody."

"Alyse said Trevor was there."

"Yeah. It just ran late, and I didn't get to bed."

And when I called him in the afternoon, he sounded like I woke him. Ben's warnings about Peter's drinking keep creeping into the corners of my mind.

"Anyway, tonight's a celebration. Have you met everybody yet?"

"No, I don't think I know most of these people."

We load our plates with food. Trevor's here, but without Alyse. His half-sister Kristen is tall with straight blond hair to her waist and the palest blue eyes I've ever seen. Peter is across the way in what looks to be a deep conversation with Ben's grandfather Jack, which leaves Kristen and me alone at the food table.

"So, you're Lily."

"Yes?" How come she knows me?

Kristen laughs.

"Trevor and Peter both talk about you like you walk on water. Nice to meet you. Congrats to the girl who grounds the Wyngate twins."

I'm confused.

"They aren't twins."

"They might as well be. They're very close – like twins. Peter has never found a girl before that Alyse didn't hate, so congrats on that. Maybe consider a job with the UN if you can pull that off."

I thank her. Peter finishes his conversation with Ben's grandfather and joins us at the picnic table. I ask him where Alyse is.

"She's no longer grounded, but she's not allowed to hang out with Trevor, which if I read your parents' expression is true for you too."

"Yeah. I can't ride in a car with him ever again."

"Which is kind of ironic since he's not drinking anymore," Kristen says.

"You mean he's not drinking right *now*." Peter sips a water. Kristen winks at him and wanders away.

"I should go do my turn with Bram."

"Can I come with?"

Of course, Peter is allowed to come with. When Jemmy visited a while ago, he helped Dad set up a television in Bram's room and the kid's learned to use the basic functions of it. He's sitting up in the hospital bed with his affected arm on a pillow and the remote in his left hand, watching a speech therapy video – a woman saying simple sentences with the words and corresponding pictographs underneath.

"The dog jumps over the fence."

"Put the glass on the table."

Theoretically, Bram will learn some stock phrases by hearing them repeatedly. He may never be able to speak per se, but he might be able to produce parrot phrases or understand and respond with yes/no or some gesture.

"Bram, is this what you want to watch?" Trust Peter to ask. Bram frowns, then mutes the TV. I didn't know he knew how to do that. Peter repeats himself.

Bram shakes his head, does this weird gesture where he seems to grab something from the screen, try to insert it into his head where it explodes and then he tosses it in the corner.

"Bram, can I?" Peter indicates the controller. Bram hands it to him. Peter navigates to Netflix.

"That's going to be too much for him."

"Just wait."

Peter finds a nature show that is mostly animals playing and a bit of narration. He turns on the subtitles. Bram smiles. I mean, he lights up. Peter hands him the controller again.

"To go back." He pantomimes. Bram nods. "This button." Peter points to it. Bram nods, turning his head as if to bring the button into focus. Then he nods again.

"How'd you know that would work?"

"He's been doing some form of therapy all day. Why would he want to do more? And then I like to watch videos like that to zone out so I figured it was low-language enough that he might be able to follow it. I could have been wrong though."

"But you weren't. You really are amazing at this. Maybe you should be a speech therapist."

Peter smiles and for just a second there's a glimmer like he might actually be contemplating it. He touches my lips with one of his fingers.

"Let's get back to the party. There should be cake pretty soon and then presents."

"What did you get Ben?"

"Sheepskin car seat covers."

Expensive and not really Peter.

"I had the perfect gift–I mailed it from England last year and Tilly says it came in when I was all bruised up last summer, but it's not where she said she put it, so – unfortunately, I didn't have time to do anything better. But he's wanted them for a long time. He has synthetic ones, but the real ones are a lot better."

"I see." I don't. Car accessories really aren't a thing I get. We go outside just in time to sing Happy

Lela Markham

Birthday. The cake is delicious. Peter asks Ben if he'd like to join us viewing the regatta from his boat next week, but Ben's working. The subject shifts to skiing come winter.

"Now that I have wheels again, maybe I could drive up and we could go snowboarding a few weekends."

Ben nods. He's not unenthusiastic, but I know Peter senses his reserve. It must hurt.

"Maybe you could come down some time and I'll show you the Manhattan scene." Trevor winks at Peter.

"If it involves getting drunk, I think I need not to do that anymore. But I'd love to see one of your performances. If we can figure out some nonalcohol fun, I'm all for it."

Ben visibly relaxes. Trevor grins.

"Yeah, of course. It's going to take some getting used to."

"For me too. I also promised Alyse that I'd come home on more weekends since I can now drive."

"That'll be good for her. Hey, Ben, did you hear Finn's plan for this fall."

"Bible School. Yeah. Whatever works for him, man."

"That's what he said." Trevor jerks his thumb at Peter. "You two are no fun." He's joking.

"It's called growing up." Kristen grins at Trevor and then at Peter and Ben.

"Ick, no thank you." Trevor pulls a little-kid-eating-spinach face that sets us all to laughing. I think about Bram's half-expressions. More and more, spontaneous expressions appear on the right side, but any sort of deliberate expression is always only on the left. I wonder if someone like Trevor could teach Bram to use both sides again. The therapists don't seem to think it's important, but if Bram is never really going to talk again, wouldn't expressions help him communicate?

Ben likes Peter's gift. I gave him a poem on a card and that makes him smile. I had a good thought about mountain biking before I wrote it. He passes it to Peter and Peter laughs and gives me a thumb's up.

The exhaustion I saw earlier in Peter's eyes returns and he is actually one of the first to leave the party. I walk him to his car.

"I'll come over tomorrow to work on chess again. I'm bringing Wes, who plays, so he can help on Bram's side."

"That's great. Do you really think he can learn chess?"

"I think it doesn't matter so long as he's using his brain." Peter yawns, covering his wide open mouth with his hand. "I need to get home before I fall asleep at the wheel." He unlocks his door. "Thank you."

"For?"

"Just helping Ben and I bridge the gap. Now, I gotta get to bed before I can't think anymore."

I watch his taillights as he drives away. A shiver runs down my back. Feels like rain.

Grandpa Jack

Peter

I feel weird slipping into the fellowship hall of Ben's church at noon on a Saturday. Usually the crowd at a noon meeting is sparse – either old retired people or people coming from work and in a hurry. The low numbers make me feel more onstage, but today there are enough people I don't feel like I stand out like a sore thumb. I still wear a baseball cap and keep the bill pulled down low so I'm not as identifiable. Dad's fishbowl makes anonymity impossible.

Meetings have a rhythm. A leader gets up and rambles on a subject for a while and then opens it to group discussions. I've only been to a few noon meetings, but they're usually tighter than the evening ones – the leader knows people are on their lunch hour. The oldsters maybe hang around to socialize afterward, but I've never stuck around for that.

Ben's grandpa Jack is the leader of the meeting and he has chosen the subject of sponsorship – how to find a sponsor and how to use one. I found Rick by accident — we're suitemates — were suitemates. I probably need it to be that way this coming year, but Rick might prefer a little less closeness. That occurs to me during the discussion.

"What do you do when a sponsoree just plays at recovery?"

My body flushes with heat. I don't mean to play, but I know I do. The woman's question is answered by several people.

"It's painful but you aren't doing them any good if you let them play."

"Often they need an ultimatum." I think about Rick's increasingly sharp suggestion that I go to rehab.

"They may need to go to rehab." I am going, tomorrow, right after Ben's party. I'm taking Lily home in time for her curfew and I'm going to bed so I can get up to go tomorrow. I am.

"Rock bottom hurts, but nobody gets better until sobriety is their only option."

The meeting ends and I pop up to get out of there, but Jack must have been a sprinter in a former life because he meets me at the door.

"Hey."

"Hi." We talked around AA last night. It can violate anonymity if we talk about it around outsiders. Am I an insider? I doubt it.

"How you doing? Feeling better than you were last night?"

"Yeah. I slept."

"That's good. You need someone to talk to?"

"I have a sponsor."

"You kids today – long distance on your phone, right?"

"Uh, yeah. He picks up when I need him to."

"And that's good. Sometimes it helps to have someone who can look you in the eye and call nonsense when you're lying to yourself."

I can't meet his eye. This old man who has known me half my life sees right through me. I don't really know him. He took us to ice cream a few times. I hadn't talked to him in three or four years before last night. But he *knows* me somehow and I feel it deep in my soul.

"He can't see you right now, for example."

"I'm not drinking." I can meet his eye on that. I haven't had a drink in two days.

"Not today." He smiles, his crags moving up and outward. I shift my gaze. "That's not uncommon, Pete. Relapse happens, at least until you decide they won't anymore. And, you heard in the meeting, most people don't get sober until they hit rock-bottom, but that's simplistic. Rock-bottom can be whenever you're just sick and tired of doing this to yourself. Because my grandson cares about you, I know you've been through some stuff and I think maybe you're there."

"I've been trying since last August. I was sober for four months and then I've been on-and-off since December."

"Your sponsor knows that?"

Mostly, yeah, Rick knows that.

"Has he suggested maybe you need rehab?"

Most of the oldsters I've heard at AA are anti-rehab, so my eyebrows go up. Jack laughs.

"If you've been trying for almost a year, kid, AA alone is not working for you. It could work later, but it isn't working now. You living in an unsafe environment?"

"No! You know who my dad is."

"I'm not talking about living in substandard housing, kid. There's alcohol in your house and it's easily available, right?"

"Yeah. That was part of the problem at school too. I couldn't stay away from it because it was always around."

"But you made four months."

I nod.

"You have withdrawal symptoms?"

"Yeah. The first three days is usually bad – not if it's just one time, though."

"You looked like you were detoxing yesterday."

"Two days before that I drank a whole bottle." I can't believe I'm saying that aloud.

"You're 18?" I nod. "You need rehab, kid. No wonder you can't quit long term. There's some great ones here on Long Island. I'll drive you to one if you need me to."

"I'm going tomorrow."

"Your folks taking you?"

"No. I just – I decided when I woke up the other morning."

"So why aren't you already there?"

"I just have a couple of things to do before I go."

"Kid, if you're going to keep making excuses, you're never going to go. What's your cell number?"

"Why?"

"So, I can send you mine and you can call if you need to. I'm serious. Anytime, night or day. I'm retired. I got work to do, but no schedules, so you can call me, and I'll do what your sponsor can't because he's your age and in another state."

I give him my number and a minute later my phone dings with a text.

"Thank you."

He pats me on the shoulder. I don't agree that he can sponsor me, and I don't tell him I'm going to a party tonight. I won't drink. Lily will be with me and I'll be good. I'll get up in the morning and go to rehab. It'll be fine. I'll be fine.

Misdirections

Alyse

I'm packing my overnight bag when Tilly knocks on my door.

"You're spending the night where again?"

"Kristen Cavanaugh's. Daddy knows her father. He'd be fine with it."

"I probably should talk to her mother."

"Her mother is dead. Her older brother Hil is at the house. I know you know Hillary. He's a couple of years older than Peter. They used to play tennis together."

"I don't think I ever met him. He was just one of the older boys on the team. Can I have his phone number?"

I sigh and try not to roll my eyes as I send the number to her. Hil is onboard with the whole thing and will say the right things.

"We're going out on the yacht in the early evening, so we might not have coverage."

"Yacht. Is that the one with the yellow sail?"

"No. I don't know. I've never sailed with them before."

"I'm teasing you. You and I really need to talk about your attitude sometime."

"You're not my mother. You're paid to put up with my attitude."

"Is that what you think? I guess your dad needs to explain some things to you."

"What does that mean?"

She sighs.

"it's not my place to tell you. But I will remind you of the rules he's set up. You have to tell me where you're going and who you're going to be with."

"Why is he doing this? He never did it with Peter."

"And look how well that is working out. Your brother is having a rough time and we don't want that for you. We're trying to protect you from some of the stupid mistakes Peter has made. So, follow the rules because your dad wants you to."

I sigh, but it's all show. I've already got Tilly completely in the dark. Even Peter is clueless and tonight, I'm going to prove it. With Kristen and Hil's help, I'll spend the night with Trevor and get rid of a lot of Peter's complications as well. The party will go off as planned and so will my plans for Peter.

Party of the Year

Peter

Mel Grey owns a media empire and could afford an estate every bit as big as my grandparents' in Old Field, but he chooses to live in a middling mansion with some age on it. It's a great Art Deco Craftsman, a testament to the rich being willing to make do. I think there might have been a great yard out back once, but now there's a pool and a couple of back houses encompassing it. Trevor moved to the pool house when he turned sixteen. Grey has the same philosophy of child-rearing as my father – a light touch, trust your kid, wait for things to blow up, put out the fires. There are *no* adults in evidence anywhere.

It's not worked well. I am who I am and Trevor – okay, he's not lit when we get there. I knew the whole sobriety thing wouldn't last long, but he's scaled back over where he's been earlier in the summer. He has irises. His sister Kristen joins Alyse as the party runners. I made Alyse promise not to use substances tonight and she knows I'm watching.

Maybe that's why she keeps suggesting I have "just one beer". She knows I'll pay less attention if I'm drunk.

I don't want to drink. I'm having fun with Lily, who is a good dancer, even though she's never taken a lesson. Unlike a lot of modern girls, she's familiar with partner dancing because her parents do ballroom and so her dad has taught her how to follow. Trevor's signature music playlist means we dance a lot.

Trevor catered some good food and I'm starting to appreciate the ability to distract myself with canapes. I don't remember food tasting so good when I drank. I'm going to need those dance sessions if I keep eating like this.

I'm not really surprised to see Macaria at the party. The girl likes to have a good time, even sober.

"I wanted to thank you for the other night," Lily says.

"No problem. I would have liked it if someone treated my little sister so well when she got herself into a situation like that. Hey, Peter."

"Where's Finn?"

"Probably still at his dad's place." I lift an eyebrow. "We're not dating. I just gave him a ride back from Sag Harbor and offered to stay because the party freaked him out. Your first sober party is crazy-making. Anyway, everything else happened, so...."

She shrugs. Her dark hair has grown out since last summer, now hangs in an unstructured bob below her shoulders. I think it's probably the first time I've seen her sober since...we went to an assembly together in junior high. Was she sober that day? I just remember how much I hated the taste of her cigarettes when we kissed.

"What happened to you and Trevor anyways?"

"No drama, if that's what you mean. He went to Joffrey and I decided to give sobriety a chance. It'll be one year August 25."

"Nice."

"He showed up at DTPM when he got back, and I told him no thank you. I guess that's when he turned his sights on Alyse. Sorry about that."

"You didn't do it, although you could have texted me and let me know it the score."

"Yeah? That didn't occur to me." She winces, then laughs.

"Do you know what happened with him at Joffrey?"

"What do you think happened to him at Joffrey?" Drugs and alcohol, I think.

Lily's moving her shoulders to a Latin song. I sweep her up in my arms and we leave Mac behind. Lily gets a little self-conscious. It's not a style of dance she's used to.

"Mind if I put my hands on your hips?" Her eyes widen, but she nods. Most guys my age could not put their hands on a girl's gyrating hips and keep it platonic, but I'm a dancer and she's my student. I can do this. "Listen to the music. It's a little syncopated." She nods. "Now watch my feet and do what I do."

Soon she's got the rhythm, but the song changes to something else. I'm starting to feel warm from the proximity and so I step back.

"I need something to drink." I mean water. "I'll get you one too." I turn to where the bottled water is on ice, but Andy Harmon comes by and puts a Solo cup in my hand, flitting off before I can hand it back to him.

The foamy head of the beer tantalizes me, and I freeze for a few seconds as a deeply familiar craving stabs through me. My throat goes instantly dry as I battle my inner man. I need to get rid of it and I need to do it now. It's like everybody in the party is now looking at me to see what I'm going to do, but nobody's offering to take this cup of poison from me. I can't think straight until I get rid of this beer, so I squeeze through the thousands of people at the party to get to the kitchen sink in the pool house. I upend the cup into the sink and realize I haven't breathed in a minute or two. I turn around to toss the cup in the trash and find Ben staring at me. *Shit!*

Is He or Isn't He?

Ben

I don't see Pete and Lily arrive because everybody and his sister wants to wish me a happy birthday. I finally manage to break free so I can get some ice in the pool house, only to see Pete rush to the sink with a Solo cup and dump it down the drain. He just poured a great cup of hoppy goodness into the sewer system. He turns, gaze scanning for a trash can and then blinks at me like he's been caught with his hand in the cookie jar.

"I didn't drink it." Yeah, I can tell. His eyes are clear, I can smell his breath and I can smell the beer as it lingers in the sink. "Sorry, I'm so weak, but I had to get rid of it or I would have."

"That doesn't really look weak." He's not comforted by that. "Seems like it's pretty strong to pour out something you really want." I'm saying that, but I'm still questioning. How'd he end up with the beer in the first place? Did he draw it and then think he didn't want to get caught drinking here? Or did someone give it to him? Why would he take it if he didn't want it?

"I do want it. I know I can't, but--. Happy birthday."

"You said that on my actual birthday."

"Just trying to change the topic. I need to get back to Lily." He grabs two water bottles from a bucket of ice and turns back toward the pool. "Where's Pam?"

"We're not dating any longer. We're still friends, but I didn't invite her. She hates parties like this, and I figured there's no law that I have to bring a date to my birthday party."

"That's true." Across the way someone is screaming loudly for beer. The crowd parts and I see Lily standing with Macaria Berber who is drinking from a water bottle similar to the ones Pete is conveying. He hands one to Lily.

"Well, hello, Ben." Macaria smiles at me, her nicotine gum scenting the air. Someone jumps into the pool with all their clothes on. "So, grown up." She's not wrong, though a year ago it might have been her doing that. "See you found our long-tailed cat at the rocking chair convention."

She's right. Pete is nervous beyond what is normal. But what do I know about what's normal for alcoholics? It seems like maybe he should avoid parties like this. I remember what Mac said about the interval between maintenance drinks. Pete's hands are shaking. Yes, I saw him dump out a great cup of beer and that's a sign that he's trying to stay sober, but I really don't know what he's been up to earlier in the day. I suddenly don't like the idea that he probably drove Lily here.

"Remember that time Trevor hosted a party for Finn's birthday?" Pete's watching the guy in the pool.

"Was that the time you, Brian Hansen and Andy ended up in the pool?"

"I didn't. It was Brian, Andy and Trevor. I took pictures, so it couldn't have been me." He doesn't remember and that scares me for him.

"God, does anyone think that's a cool thing to do at a party?" Mac's shaking her head.

"After several shots of tequila, a lot of things seem cool." Pete's watching as the guy's friends pull him out of the water.

"They do. I seem to remember jumping in with them."

"Oh, yeah. I have the photographic evidence."

"You kept those?"

"I figure you never know when blackmail might be in order."

They laugh and Lily looks at me as if wondering what is so funny.

"What was I doing during that time?" I kind of remember the incident, but it's vague. So maybe I shouldn't get on my high horse about Pete's lack of memory.

"Probably organizing the designated drivers. I wonder who is in charge of that tonight."

"Trevor?" Lily looks thoughtful.

"Not trustworthy." Trevor's promise that he'd stay sober for this party had already been blown away by the time I arrived. He's not falling-down-drunk, but he's definitely not sober either. I'm concerned about Alyse. "Where's your sister?"

"She's fine." This comes from Mac. I raise an eyebrow at her. "I saw her fifteen minutes ago sober. Maybe she learned her lesson from last time. It only took once for my little sister."

Peter looks doubtful, but he takes Lily's hand and whispers in her ear. They start dancing again. I drain my water bottle.

"So, what are you up to these days?" Seems like I should make conversation with Mac at least.

"Working for my dad and trying to decide what I'm going to do this winter."

"Go to college?"

"No. There's a fiber consortium over in Long Island City and they're looking for quilters."

I just stare at her. It sounds like a waste of effort, but what do I know?

"And, what are you doing?"

"Working the loading dock at a manufacturer."

"Good money?"

"Since I'm a returnee, yeah. It'll pay about a quarter of my tuition."

"Dartmouth, right?" I nod. "Seems like they have a very high opinion of their degrees." They do have a good reputation. "I'm not spending thousands of dollars a year to get a fine arts degree. It makes no sense."

That's true. Fine arts will never pay enough to make up for what it costs to get a degree in it from one of the IVs. But it's a prestigious degree for engineering. Peter's probably making some great connections for business or architecture during his time at Yale.

"Do you want to dance, Mr. Anderson?"

I'm not really a dancer, but Macaria can make any two-left-footed guy look halfway decent, so I take her hand and we mingle on the deck beside the pool that is the unofficial dance floor.

Be Careful Where You Stand

Peter

I need to pee – like *bad*. There are three bathrooms – the pool house, the billiard room, and one off the sunroom in the main house. You can't go any further into the house because Mel Grey is not stupid. He doesn't allow Trevor's guests full range. I decide to avoid the pool house because that's where the kegs are. There's an incredible line out the billiard room. The sunroom line is also longer than is comfortable, but it's shorter than the other one, so I get in it. The relative distance from the kegs makes it a little more tolerable than the pool house would have been. I kind of wish Lily had joined me in the line, but Alyse swept her up and transported her somewhere. So, I'm standing in this long line surrounded by people who have cups of beer, but at least I can breathe fresh air.

"Hey, there you are. What do you think?" Trevor looks very dapper in skinny-fit khakis, a grey t-shirt and a maroon suit jacket. "I told you I could do this."

"Kristen and Alyse are doing a terrific job. How lit are you?"

"I'm good." He's got a Solo cup in his hand. I can smell the beer. "Seriously, this is my third one of the night. I'm being social."

I'm beginning to understand that if you need to defend your "social" drinking, you're probably no longer a social drinker. Behind him, I see Andy and Hillary Cavanaugh setting a case of vodka and another of rum on a table at the end of the room.

"Things get sketchy when the hard liquor comes out."

"You always have hard liquor at your parties."

"So, I would know, right? Don't get more drunk than you already are, man, because you can't keep control of it without your wits about you."

"I'm not drunk."

"You're not sloppy...yet." His eyes glitter briefly. I'm pushing my luck here, so I let it go. "It's a great party, man. Kristen and Alyse did a great job and you're keeping things mostly under control. I'm just warning that the hard liquor is harder to control."

"Not if you're not drinking it." He pats me on the shoulder and heads off somewhere else. I'm next for the bathroom. Andy unloads the vodka, Hil sets up plastic shot glasses and Solo cups, and Regina puts Coke and soda water on ice. I don't like vodka or rum, but my tongue clings to the roof of my mouth and it feels like electricity courses through my body.

I'm so full by the time I get into the bathroom that it takes a few minutes to get my bladder to release. I taste bourbon the whole time. I haven't seen any since I got here and it's not a common drink among my friends. It's a real drinking man's drink, not something most 18-year-olds develop a taste for. I scoop water into my mouth from the sink and wash my face.

I can do this.

The long wait time irritates the guy in line after me. He seems to think I took too long to use the facilities. I'm headed out to the pool again when Andy Harmon comes up to me.

"You are incredible!"

"Excuse me?"

"I caught you rescuing Alyse at Finn's the other night."

"You were there?" Of course, half of our graduating class attended that party and Andy loves to party as much as I do.

"What was up with that?"

"She's been experimenting lately."

"I saw that. It's like she's subbing in for Macaria."

"Hey." The comparison pisses me off for Alyse, but it's on the tip of my tongue to admire Mac's recent choices. I get how hard it is to choose not to drink and I think Mac's problems aren't so singular. Hil slides up beside Andy and puts a shot glass in my hand.

"Relax, man." No! Alarm bells jangle through my brain. "You looked together the other night. And you should care that your little sister is another notch on Trevor's belt. I keep wondering when you're going to kick his ass."

"I'm, uh, it's started before I got back from school, so I wasn't here to warn him off."

My arm has a life of its own, headed up toward my mouth even as I tell myself to hand the shot back. I. Don't. Like. Vodka. The shot is down my throat before I can win that argument. Damn! Vodka still tastes like paint thinner, but that familiar warmth spreading across my chest bathes the room in mellow tones.

"What are you up to these days, Hil?"

"Kristen and I hopped the Pond for a couple of weeks."

"Really?" I remember that Trevor and Hil are stepbrothers. I think their parents were married a long time ago, but for some reason, the step kids are still visiting the ex-stepparents. I can hardly keep the two point five parents and three siblings I have straight. I couldn't manage multiple series of stepparents. Trevor seems to keep it all in hand, though. "Where'd you visit?"

"Paris this time."

I didn't really like Paris. I spent my whole time in Paris drunk and not feeling good. Collin dragged me around to the club scene and I didn't get to see much of the city.

"Enjoy it?"

"Yeah. We did the tourist bit – the artist tourist bit. She's really into photography."

"Nice."

Somehow, we're next to the table where the booze is set up. One shot is not going to make me drunk. I'm no light-weight and my liver is back to normal. Pretty sure anyway. I pour myself one more shot of vodka, reminding myself that it's the last one, and pour it down my throat.

"Is there any bourbon?" Andy laughs and shakes his head.

"Sorry, Trevor said not to get any. You want a flask?" I down a third shot and nod. I'll just take a sip now and then so I'm not drunk, but the crowd won't feel so oppressive.

I slide the plastic pint into the inside pocket of my jacket and head back toward where I'd last seen Lily and Alyse. I pause at the door, warm air washing my face, looking around. I scan the crowd which no longer feels so encroaching. The bodies part and I see Lily's bright blue dress as she dances with Ben.

A Change

Lily

Alyse isn't angry with me anymore, but I somehow end up with Macaria again. She's a nice girl – more middle-class than many of the other girls here. We're talking about how the rich kids here often don't realize how they come off when Ben comes by and asks me where Peter is.

"The bathroom."

"How long ago since you saw him?"

"It's been a while, but there's the line." I point it out to him.

"Poor guy. The line in the pool house is shorter."

"He's avoiding the kegs." Ben frowns at Macaria, who sounds knowledgeable. "You can't blame him. If he's trying to quit, he needs to do that."

"But you don't?"

"Oh, I do. I couldn't stand in a line for long near them. It's like – I don't know – demons start talking to you and pretty soon downing a fifth sounds perfectly sensible."

She reaches out an arm to a passing boy and asks him if he'd like to dance. They move off together. She is an *amazing* dancer.

"He was fine the last I saw him." Ben gives me an apologetic smile. "I should have insisted we go camping."

"I think he would have gone with you. Does Trevor really need a reason to have a party?"

"Trevor is the life of every party, so no. You want to dance?"

We start moving to the up-tempo song. It's a great night. The sky is sprayed with stars and the outdoor location means it's comfortable. A slow song starts. Ben holds me at a comfortable distance as we move to it. He's not as good a dancer as Peter, but he makes conversation while we dance, so we don't feel awkward together.

"I need to get some food. You want anything?"

"No, I'm good. Thanks."

Ben walks away. I turn to look toward the pool and Peter steps into my vision.

"Hey, having fun?" His voice is too loud, and his eyes are narrowed like – like – it's not an emotion I've seen from him before. Anger? Another salsa number starts, and he sweeps me into his embrace without even asking me this time. "Keep the beat, girl. Cha-cha-CHA." That's kind of mean and unlike his earlier encouragement. "What were you and Ben talking about?"

He's jealous? Of Ben? I feel my face getting hot.

"You. He was saying he'd have preferred to go camping with you instead of having this party."

"Uh-huh. He sure looked like he enjoyed dancing with you."

"We were just killing time until you got back. That must have been some line."

"Impressive, for sure."

The music switches to a modern swing song and Peter spins me into a twirl. I really do feel graceful and attractive with him. He's an incredible dancer. At the end of the song, he deposits me near Macaria, who seems to like this spot near the dance floor.

"I'm thirsty. You ladies want something?"

"Water," Mac says.

"Soda."

He winks at us and heads toward the beverage tables. Macaria watches him go.

"Sorry." I lift an eyebrow. "He's a saint when he's sober – an absolute prince – but get a few shots into him and he becomes the devil."

"Shots? I didn't smell anything."

"That's the point of vodka. My parents are recovering alcoholics, but I kept a drinking habit secret from them for years because of vodka."

"How do you know he's drinking?"

"His change of behavior. Bigger gestures, more comfortable with people staring at him. I'll bet he's switched to orange juice too, so he can drink his beverage without giving himself away. And I'm really sorry for how the rest of your night is going to go. Peter will be sorry in the morning."

Peter comes back to us with two Solo cups and hands me the one with the cola in it. He then hands Mac her water. She's right. He's drinking orange juice. He's said before that he doesn't really like sugar. Macaria's prediction is uncanny, but it makes total sense.

"What have you been up to this summer, Peter? Seems like I haven't seen you around at all."

"Yeah, it's been kind of a weird summer for me. I had to take some correspondence courses and my driver's license was suspended until just last week, so I couldn't get around."

"Unfortunate, what happened to you and Cheyenne."

Peter nods, sipping from his cup. He's not listening to her. It's the first time I've heard anyone include Peter in the injured of that accident. Even he seems to forget he got hurt too. He looks sad for a moment and then takes a long suck on his cup. We're chatting about nothing when someone from the dance floor bumps into him. Peter manages to spill the orange juice on the deck rather than his shirt or me.

"Fuck, man! What the hell?" He turns on the guy, angry. The guy apologizes, but Peter's standing over him, aggressive.

Macaria gives me another apologetic smile.

"Oh, look, they've replenished the food."

She wanders away. I briefly see Peter through the crowd. Alyse slides up beside me.

"Where's my brother?"

"He went that way." I point to the far end of the pool. I haven't seen Alyse looking so clear-eyed and clean-faced since the start of the summer. "I think he's drinking."

"Yeah. That was inevitable at a party. He can't help himself. Do you want to go to the Oyster Bay Fireworks Display tomorrow night?"

Huh? She switched that subject quickly. I struggle to keep up.

"Sure. It'll make up for missing the fireworks at Long Sands this year." The crowd parts on the far side of the pool and I see Peter talking to a girl. He's sipping from the Solo cup still.

"Just a warning – Peter is a slut when he's drinking." Alyse touches me on the shoulder, her sympathy apparent. A tall blond girl signals her from near the pool house. It's Kristen with her hair pulled up. "Sorry, I have to go check on some stuff. Make sure he knows that he's ruining your evening. He'll do it again if you don't."

I sigh. There's no one near me that I know. I guess now is a perfect time to use the bathroom. I head toward the pool house. Ben is in my path.

"I keep running into you."

"That's deliberate." I frown at him, perplexed. "I'm worried about you, so I'm keeping an eye on you. He's drinking. You know that, don't you?"

"I'm kind of guessing. He's been doing so well. He shouldn't have come tonight."

"He shouldn't have, but he should know that, right? It's a damn shame that he can't seem to figure it out, but I've been watching it happen for a couple of years now. Whatever you do, you're not letting him drive you home."

I am nodding when suddenly Ben stumbles into me, shoved from behind by Peter whose face looks like a thunder cloud. I imagine Zeus looked like that when he started throwing lightning bolts. Ben turns to face him.

"Get the fuck away from her," Peter screams. He shoves Ben again. This time, Ben doesn't stumble, but pushes back.

"Go cool off. Drink some water. Stop doctoring your drinks."

They wrestle and Ben shoves hard enough Peter loses his footing. He sprawls on the ground. A plastic pint bottle slides out of his jacket onto the slate. He tries to get up, but he's sloppy and fails to stand. Ben breathes heavily.

"You're screwing up, buddy. With me and with her. I don't know whether you're lying all the time now or if this is a slip, but you'd better get your head screwed on straight before everybody who cares about you gives up."

Tears roll down my cheeks as Peter twists to the side to hurl. He heaves several times. Everybody is staring at us now.

"Can you take me home?" I ask Ben.

"Of course."

Peter is up off his butt in a heartbeat, but as Ben and I angle away from him, Trevor confronts him.

"I called you a ride. You're leaving."

"He's got no right to interfere."

"What the hell is wrong with you? Really, Peter, this is not like you."

Ben steers me down the side of the house and into the street. I'm still crying as he unlocks the door and hands me in. He comes around to the other side and settles behind the wheel. We don't say anything as we drive away.

Well-Laid Plans

Alyse

I tell Vic that under no circumstances should he take Peter anywhere other than home, then I turn back to the party. Kristen looked bereft when she thought I might leave to deal with Peter. It really is too much for one person and Trevor is only good at the entertainment part of things.

Things couldn't have gone any better if I'd planned it – and I did. Andy and Regina played their parts and Peter caved like I expected he would. When the beer didn't work, Andy massaged Peter's ego and he drank the shot. Regina met Peter on his way to getting food that probably would have kept him from getting so drunk. Of course, he paused to talk with her and sent a wrong impression to Lily. Andy has always hated Ben and considered him an obstacle to a friendship with Peter, who I think Andy might fancy now that I think about it. Regina has always wanted to date Peter. They don't care if Peter's trying to stay sober. They rushed to cooperate, almost as they aren't his friends.

I couldn't control the wild card Ben. I know he has a thing for Lily, so I suggested he should keep an eye on her because of Peter's history of driving drunk. Peter didn't bring his car, but Ben didn't know that. He's a knight in shining armor and Lily needed him. I get to keep my friend without having to watch her and Peter kissing and blocking me out. He probably won't want to see her for a while, but he'll be off to school soon enough.

I pass through the party, smiling at everybody I see. I haven't felt so good in months.

Truth-Telling

Ben

The summer evening envelops the car. It's peaceful here in my driveway. The windows are down and the Rose Tree of Sharon bushes across the street are just starting to scent the air. Lily stopped crying and now texts.

"You okay?" She sets the phone in her lap.

"Yeah. I just texted Peter to tell him we should break up. We weren't really dating, but I don't want to have to deal with him later."

"I wish I could do that." Macaria's warning about maintenance drinks echoes through my mind. "I know it sucks."

"It'll be okay. Alyse already texted me and said she's on my side."

"Really? That's weird. She *always* takes Pete's side."

"I don't know. I'm going to fireworks with her tomorrow. I told her I don't want to see Peter and she promises me he'll be too hung over to do anything tomorrow."

"Probably." I wonder if that's a sign that his liver isn't working right anymore. Pete used to be really good at avoiding hangovers. "She'll pick you up, anyway, right?"

"You're right." Lily giggles. She's way too young for me, but she's handling this with incredible maturity. "Thank you for getting me out of there."

"No problem. I didn't really think you should be with him anyway."

"Because he's so much older than me?"

"Naw. My parents are about the same age difference as you and me. I didn't like it because he can't handle his booze and he won't or can't leave it alone."

"It just makes me so sad for him. And for you. It must be tough to watch your best friend just destroy himself like that."

"Maybe. I think maybe it's more about being jealous."

"Of?"

"You and him." I sigh. My heart is not in the wisest place right now, but I know I should be honest with her. A part of what's wrong with Pete is the inability to be honest. "I started this thinking I needed to protect you, but in reality, some of it might be because I really like you and I didn't want to see you get hurt because of that."

She's blushing. The relationship with Pete was still so new that she's not devastated by what just happened. Good for her.

"I think I just liked the excitement and hanging out with him, and Alyse – Alyse means well, but – well, I couldn't afford Fire Island and Peter understood that."

"He can be a good friend when he's sober."

"He mainly just wanted to entertain me. He's kissed me exactly once. We were going to do the regatta next week. I guess I'll be doing that by myself, from the beach rather than his boat."

"Oh, the view from the harbor is not to be missed. Um, Russell does a regatta cruise. I'm crewing for him. You want to come and serve canapes?"

"Really? Don't you need to ask him?"

"I will, but I'm pretty sure it's okay. It's a date then?"

She blushes.

"A date?"

"Well, not a date date, but yeah. A hang out. Watch the fireworks. Make some money."

"Not talk about Peter."

"Oh, yeah."

"I hope you can salvage your friendship with him. He was a jerk tonight because he can't control his drinking, but I know he really regrets he damaged the friendship. Promise me you'll try to fix it."

"I will, but – it takes two and he keeps screwing it up."

"Maybe this will be his wakeup."

"My grandfather says he needs to hit rock-bottom, feel like everything in his life is about to go over a cliff. Maybe this is it. I don't know, but yeah, I'll let him stew for a few days and then actually try to be a good friend, so long as he stays away from you."

She nods.

"Thank you for being there tonight and thank you for warning me, all those months ago."

"I'm a little worried he's driving drunk right now."

"He isn't. Vic dropped us. Peter said the parking would suck, but maybe he decided not to drive because he knows he can't trust himself at a party."

"Maybe he did learn something from Cheyenne and the classes they made him take. Anyway, I've seen the curtains twitch twice. What are you going to tell them?"

"That Peter flirted with another girl, so I asked you to give me a ride home. And I'm over it"

"You're going to lie?" That seemed so unlike her.

"It's not a lie. It's just not the whole truth."

"Parents usually can't handle the whole truth when you're 15."

"Can they when you're 19?"

"Mine can. Not sure about anyone else's. Anyway, this – sitting in a car with you – not a good idea right now."

"Oh? Oh! Yeah. Okay. Thanks again."

She lets herself out of the car and I watch her walk up the driveway. Would she be worth ending my already fractured friendship with Pete? Oh, yeah! Maybe. I take my thoughts in control and head into the house.

Consequences

Peter

The next few days suck. Of course, the first day sucks. Hangovers always suck and hangovers like mine suck more than most. Mostly I sleep and puke.

It's the second day before I even feel up to calling Lily. I have a good excuse – a flu bug. Alyse keeps telling me it won't work, but I'm stubborn that way. I pull up Lily's last message to me and reply.

> PETER – Look, I'm sorry. I warned you about me and parties. I. Can't. Be. Trusted. But I didn't mean to ruin the evening and I won't do it again. I'm incredibly embarrassed. I've never been that angry before. I think I need a few days to get my body back under control, but then I can work with Bram and – I really just don't want to lose another friend. Please!"

I hit SEND and stare in shock at the return message saying her phone rejects my message. I dial her number and get a message that she's not accepting calls from my number.

"I told you," Alyse says, leaning comfortably on my headboard. "When you screw up, you screw up spectacularly."

"Yeah, I'm an overachiever." My stomach threatens to heave as heat washes up and down my back and leaves me covered in cold sweat. "Can you leave me alone, please?"

Alyse looks reluctant, but she leaves my room and I sit in the darkness, my arms across my knees. I liked Lily from the minute I met her, but I'm shocked to discover her importance to me. God, she's important to me. What the hell is wrong with me that I treated her...? Hell, I don't half-remember the party, but I remember the look on her face as she walked away with Ben. God, Ben–I just got him back as a friend.

> PETER – I shouldn't have gone to the party. I'm sorry you saw me like that. I didn't mean whatever I said or did. Please don't shut me out this time. Relapses happen and I'm going to figure out how to stop having them. Please!

I'm sitting in the dark, bawling, when my phone lights up.

> BEN – You need to decide to save yourself, Pete. I'll help you with that if you tell me what you need, but you have to stop lying to me. If you can't do that, we're done.

I roll onto my side, hugging the phone like a life preserver, and cry myself to sleep.

Interference

Alyse

I feel sorry for Peter. I hate to see him miserable. Well, unless I'm putting the hurt on him. He does owe me for making our mother leave. He thinks I don't know about that, but Laren told me all about it once when she came to visit – about how Peter made up a story of finding her and Sam in a spare bedroom having sex. She admits they were having an affair and that Peter must have found out somehow, but he never saw anything. He maybe thought he could break Sam and her up, but Daddy got so angry he demanded a divorce.

So, he does owe me for that and so does Daddy for always treating her like she's somehow toxic to me, so I can't even be alone with her. I'm supposed to love that she left, and I got Tilly in her place, who acts like nothing is going on with my father, but I know differently. How Peter never sees that is beyond me.

When I decided to break him and Lily up, I didn't realize Peter felt so deeply for her. He's really depressed, sleeping all the time. He's not drinking because the bar's locked but sleeping all the time makes him even more unavailable than when he's drunk. I thought Lily would be good for him, but I made a mistake, which is why I set it up for Peter to damage the relationship beyond repair. But I didn't foresee Peter would sink into the darkness when he lost her.

Apparently, he didn't destroy his friendship with Ben entirely. He gets a text from him and calls him one afternoon. I walk up behind him while he is eating something just after he wakes up on the fourth day. It's the first he's stirred from his room since that night.

"No, I was an ass. I get it. I'm sorry." He listened to Ben. His shoulders hunch and his head dips. Then comes a relieved sigh. "Thank you for accepting my apology. No, she's not talking to me. I'm going to let it go. I'll miss working with Bram, but I shouldn't – not for now. Is Wes doing okay there? Great. No, really. I just want what's best for him – and her. I'm not going to be around anyway. I just – there's something I need to do." He takes a deep breath. "I'm driving out to a rehab this afternoon."

What? No way! Peter lets Ben talk for a moment.

"I'm serious. I just can't keep doing this to myself anymore. But it's still hard and I figure if I tell someone, I'll actually do it. So, if you don't hear from me for a month, that's why. No, I can still make the fall semester at Yale – barely."

He's going to ruin the rest of the summer and miss my birthday for the second year in a row. No!

"I don't know why I got so jealous. Alcohol. I know there's nothing going on between you two. She's too young for you." Peter snorts. "Yeah, well, guys like Trevor and I are immature. Thanks for listening. I promise – promise I'm going to do better."

He and Ben talk a moment longer and then he hangs up. He sits with his head lowered over his coffee cup. I pretend I'm just dashing down the hall and sit down across from him.

"Hey." He doesn't sound enthusiastic to see me. His hair is still wet from a shower and there are dark circles under his eyes.

"You okay?" I've got to figure out a way to keep him from doing this stupid unnecessary thing.

"No. I feel like shit. Lily's phone is still rejecting my calls. Have you talked to her?"

"We went to fireworks the other night. She doesn't want to hear from you."

He nods, staring at his hands around his coffee cup.

"So, let's make plans for the regatta."

He stirs and stares at me like he's struggling to bring me into focus.

433

"Um, no. I don't feel up to it."

"It's tomorrow night. Trevor suggested we picnic and then go. His – uh, well, I think she's his step-sister – Bethany – is in town and he'll bring her with, so you don't even need to worry about a date."

"Aly, I can't. I'm – uh, I decided I'm taking myself to rehab today. Right after I get some coffee and carbs down, so I don't pass out while driving."

"Really? But why?"

"Because I need help, Aly." His eyes look like deep wells of torture. "I can't keep doing this to myself. I don't want to." He wipes away a tear. I put a hand on his.

"Wow, you're really depressed."

He nods. I touch the coffee cup with my free hand.

"That's cold. Let me get you some warm."

He relinquishes the mug, sits staring at nothing while I take it to the counter. I slide the Altoids box from my pocket, careful that my body blocks his view and drop two Clozapine in the hot liquid and then a fair amount of sugar to cover the taste. I pour myself a cup of coffee too and sit down across from him. He sips, grimaces.

"Kind of overdid the sugar."

"Sorry. Figured it would help with the hangover."

"This isn't hangover. This is withdrawal. And I hope this is the last time I feel it."

We finish our cups of coffee and as the
conversation goes along, he becomes fuzzier, not
sure of what he's saying. Is that how I look to other
people when I'm high? Maybe I have another reason
not to use those pills any longer. Good thing I didn't
toss them though because I had another use for
them

He stands up when his cup is empty and nearly
falls over. I catch his arm and guide him up the
stairs. He dissolves into giggles on the landing, but
then sobers.

"I need to go—go--."

"You need to sleep. You can go later."

I tuck him into bed and on my way out of his
bedroom, I snag his car keys. I find Tilly vacuuming
the carpet in the den.

"Is the bar still locked?"

"Yes. Why?"

"No reason. Peter's just really depressed."

"I noticed. According to the Internet that
happens with alcoholics when they fall off the
wagon. He'll feel better in a few days."

I nod.

"Can you take me to dance intensive tonight?"

"Of course."

"And – could you stay? I used to like it when
you'd watch." I've pleased her just as I planned.

"Really? Sure. I'll meet you in the garage at
4:30."

"Great."

That takes care of the transportation issue. Vic's gone to visit his kids and Tilly won't be available to provide Peter a ride – not that I think Peter will admit what he has planned to the housekeeper. This is coming together so well. Operation Rescue Peter from Eternal Boringness is well underway.

Detours

Peter

My keys are still missing, Vic decided to stay an extra day with his kids, and my window for rehab is closing rapidly. I'm a legacy. I could check myself into rehab, call Dad and ask him to fix Yale for me. Or take the semester off. It's not that big of a deal. I know I need to do this and I'm going to do it. Where the hell are my keys?

I've torn my room apart three times looking for them. I've never lost them before, not even when I've been blackout drunk, but I can't find them. Finally, I call Ben, hoping Rick is right about him.

"Hey." There's that hesitancy. My damage precedes me into every room. "What's up?"

"Hoping you can help me. I need a ride somewhere this afternoon and I can't find my keys."

"Oh. Well, I can't. I'm just carrying boxes onto *The Mimi* for the cruise tonight."

"Oh, yeah, right. Sorry. Forgot you'd be doing that." I'm missing a day, I think.

"You forgot about the regatta?"

"Yeah, I don't really want to go this year. I'm trying to get myself to rehab, but it's like the universe is conspiring against me."

"Wow, I'd help you with that if I weren't already working. I can't really call off now that I'm here. I could take you tonight afterward."

"No, I get it. It's my problem anyway. Thanks for answering."

"Sure. Maybe – Vic – or Tilly ...."

"Yeah. You're right. She'd do it. I'll call you in a couple of weeks."

I hang up the phone. Maybe the keys somehow got left somewhere in the house. I head downstairs to look.

There's not a lot of clutter in the house, so it shouldn't be hard to find them. Tilly went shopping, I think. I'm going to need to call her soon to ask for help.

I hear Trevor, Alyse and another girl talking in the courtyard. It had better not be Lily. I can't take seeing Lily right now, even though I owe her a heart-felt apology. I steel my spine and head that way. I'll say I'm sorry, that I know we need to break up and then I'll ask Trevor for a ride to rehab. It's twenty minutes away. He could drop me and get back to his life in less than an hour.

"...tiny little backseat."

Bethany is golden-red and absolutely gorgeous. She's not my type, but her beauty is intoxicating. It slices right through detox. She's clearly a rich girl, her clothes impeccably casual, showing a tan that just won't quit. With that hair, it's probably fake, but you really can't tell.

"Hey," Trevor calls. "There you are. You want to help a guy out?"

"With?"

"I got three passengers and a car that only really seats two."

"Who's your fourth?"

"You are, man."

"I can't, Trev. I've got somewhere to be, and I can't find my car keys."

"You check your room?"

I want to scream at him as my already-taut nerves stretch tighter than a drumhead. Alyse comes from the back of the house with a tray of four lemonade glasses. I'm impressed with her dexterity while giving Bethany and Trevor their glasses and then handing me one as well.

"How'd you know I'd be out here?"

"I heard your voice, silly."

My body is freaking out from withdrawal. The lemonade tastes weird, but I'm so thirsty, I don't care, so I drink it all in about three gulps. It helps, but not as much as getting on the road to Briarcliff would. While I'm gulping, Trevor wanders into the garage. There's a bathroom there, so maybe that's not so weird. He comes back out with my car keys.

"Ignition." No way! I've never done that before, and I haven't driven since the night of his party. I wasn't drinking the last time I drove. I *know* I wasn't.

"Weird." I don't know what else to say. It is weird, but not as weird as losing my memory yesterday. I remember talking with Ben on the phone and then – yeah, I have no idea what I did that afternoon. I woke this morning feeling like I'd not moved all night and that might be exactly what happened.

No wonder Ben expressed reluctance to help me this afternoon. I technically lied to him yesterday...but I didn't mean to. What happened? I fully intended to go to rehab, but somehow, I ended up sleeping the night away. I'm staring at my car keys when Trevor puts a hand on my shoulder.

"Something up, buddy?"

So far, everybody has fallen down on the job of helping me. I don't think Trevor will be any different, but his dark blue eyes are clear, and I don't smell rum on his breath.

"I'm trying to check myself into Briarcliff."

A wave of disorientation washes over me and I blink while he replies to me.

"Drug rehab?" I nod. What the hell is wrong with me? My hands go inexplicably numb. "Dad threatened me with that place after Finn's party. It's why I'm being so careful before heading to the City.

You got like five weeks before school and it's only 28 days. How about this? Let's go watch the regatta and then you can go to Briarcliff tonight. They're a 24-hour facility."

That sounds reasonable. Trevor's brow furrows.

"Seriously, man, you look wiped. Hey, Alyse, get your brother some coffee and a big glass of ice water."

He steers me into the backyard and makes me sit down at one of the patio tables. I prop my head up on my hand as he keeps talking to me. A cup of coffee and the ice water clears the cobwebs. The coffee still tastes weird. Bethany is from Connecticut. Her mother is Grey's current wife. She's 17 and getting ready to go to Brown. I start the conversation struggling to follow, but by the time I've finished the coffee, I'm feeling oddly awake – keyed up and antsy, actually. My heart feels like I've been mountain biking. I don't need to go to Briarcliff tonight. There's always tomorrow.

"So, yeah, the picnic and then regatta sounds like fun." I say I'm going to grab my jacket from upstairs. The window is open. I figure I better close it in case it rains.

"What the hell, Alyse?" Trevor mutters. I can't hear anything more that he says because he drags her over toward the roses, but he looks pissed at her. I head back downstairs, my keys firmly in my hand.

"We ready to go?" I look among the three of them and they all laugh. Did I mistake what I saw from the window. Trevor catches my arm on the way to the car.

"Do you really want to go to Briarcliff?"

"I really want to stop screwing up." Is that the same thing? Maybe. His gaze flickers over me. I've scared him, I think. "But what's one more fun evening before I do it, right?"

Trevor smiles, but he's still looking at me like he's trying to read my mind. He nods and smiles.

"I hear a lot of people do one last time before they go. And, I promise you, I'll drag you there myself tomorrow morning if you can't do it for yourself."

"Yeah. I need to go. And, I don't really want to drink tonight."

"More rum for me."

"Sounds good."

I've said this before and I know I can't trust myself, but it's the regatta and I'm not feeling so depressed anymore. And Trevor will make sure I get to Briarcliff tomorrow.

What could go wrong?

Road Show

Alyse

I can't believe Trevor is mad at me for keeping Peter from doing something stupid with his life. As soon as Peter walks away to get his jacket, Trevor rounds on me, eyes stormy.

"What the hell, Alyse?" Bethany looks interested in our conversation and he drags me toward the rose bushes. "There are limits to how much someone can take of that stuff. Yeah, he's bigger than you, but he's not used to it and you can't just make decisions like that for him. Cut it out!"

"I'm just trying to keep him from doing something stupid and you just did something without his permission."

"Yeah, I know what I'm doing, and our weight isn't that much different. And you gave him enough he would have fallen asleep. And, here's the thing – if he wants to go to rehab, you shouldn't try to stop him. Maybe he's right that he needs to go. The other night at the party, he couldn't control it, just like last year. And he's been trying not to drink all summer. Maybe he's sick and tired of being sick and tired."

"What does that mean?"

"It's something Macaria explained to me. That when addicts are tired of being addicts, they often struggle for a while to get over it and then they decide they're done. Maybe he's done. And, if that's true, you trying to sabotage him is a shit move. Like putting his keys in the ignition of his car. That's so unlike Peter. That's why you did it, because you knew he wouldn't look there for a really long time."

"I'm just trying to help him."

"Well, you're not. Seriously, if you do this again, I'll drive him to Briarcliff myself."

He's joking...isn't he? Trevor loves to party more than Peter. Surely, he isn't serious, but he might be a mind-reader.

"I am serious, Lyse. I like to party as much as the next guy, but I'm not a pusher. If he wants to stop, I'm not going to get in his way."

Peter comes out of the house. He's washed his face. You can tell by how his hair starts to curl.

"Go get in the car and we'll meet you in a minute." Trevor catches Peter's arm and they huddle. It only takes a minute and they join us at the car. He's probably making sure that Peter is safe to drive.

We're going to a park for the picnic, which Trevor has in a cooler in his trunk, so he makes the transfer. Peter makes a joke with Bethany. She's only here for a week, so I don't have to worry about him falling in love. Maybe they'll have sex, but it'll be a one-night-stand like the girls at college that he says he barely remembers.

We pull out of the driveway. Peter asks Trevor to drive, saying he feels a little weird. He sits in the front with Trevor because of the leg room. Bethany asks me If I like schnapps. She pulls out a flask. Oh, this is going to be a fun evening!

Falling by Degrees

Peter

I don't have to drink. Yeah, Trevor is drinking and somehow the schnapps I hate tastes very good on Bethany's lips. I start out not wanting to kiss her. It feels too soon after Lily even though she and I weren't really dating. But she keeps kissing me and I keep letting her. But I get halfway through the picnic sober. And, then Alyse pulls out the bottle of bourbon.

"I don't want that." I mean it. It's against the law and we're in a public place and I just got my license back. Besides, I mean to go to rehab tomorrow morning. It'll be hard to do if I'm hung over. "Put that away before a cop sees it."

"Oh, relax, Peter. There are advantages to your father being the governor."

There are no advantages to our father being the governor. Everybody knows who we are, and I've already got one DUI on my record. I'm not going for more. I promised Ben I'd do better. But God, I'm thirsty! Alyse puts the bottle back in her bag, but I know it's there now. We're in a kind of secluded spot, near the Old Mill Pond and there's really no one to see us. I resist it for nearly an hour before I pull it out of the bag. By now, Trevor and Alyse are dancing to music on his phone and the thrill of kissing Bethany is wearing off. I crack the seal and take a deep, deep swallow. I'm halfway down the bottle, enjoying pulls off it between make-out sessions with Bethany when Trevor announced we'd better get a move on if we want to see the regatta. I stare at him, struggling to bring him into focus.

"You okay, man?"

"I don't think I should drive." I pull out my keys and push them at him. "Seriously, I'm wasted."

Trevor frowns.

"Where'd you get the booze, man?" He looks over his shoulder. "Alyse, did you give him that?"

I'm having trouble focusing on them. I take another pull on the bottle, which doesn't help the fuzziness. I don't understand what Trevor is yelling at Alyse about – something about dosing and alcohol. I'm completely confused.

"I'll drive." I giggle at Trevor's announcement since he already has my keys. I sit down in the passenger seat, trying to remember what I meant to do after this. It felt important – vital, but I'm too fuzzy to remember what I planned. I think I doze off on the way to the marina. I don't remember the ride anyway and Alyse has to shake me vigorously to wake me up.

"Where are the boat keys?" I stare at her as she holds out a demanding hand. She doesn't know how to operate the boat. What's her problem?

"Russell's."

"What?! How did you expect to use the boat if you don't have the keys?"

"I can get them."

"Man, you cannot go in there drunk. He's not going to give you the keys." Trevor is the voice of wisdom here.

"Russell's is already closed." Alyse huffs in annoyance. "We can't get the keys."

"Not true." I'm starting to wake up. "I know a way in."

A few years ago, Ben accidentally showed me how to get into Russell's by a side window that can't be locked. It just happens to be the window next to the hooks where he keeps the keys. I'm rubbing my eyes while working to get the window open enough to push it all the way up, but I'm waking up because Bethany has her hand on my junk.

"You need to take one of these." She holds out an orange pill.

"I don't do pills." I take another pull off the bottle and ease the window all the way up. Turns out the key hooks are further from the window than I think, so I pull myself all the way through and stare around by the light from the window. I think I left my phone in the car. Or maybe the park. Shit. I'm screwed up. The bottle is nearly empty. How'd that happen and I'm still on my feet? I find the keys. Mine has a distinctive cruciform cross key tag, a souvenir I picked up in England. I slide the window back down.

Laughing, we run down the pier. My blue-and-white Malibu awaits us. Dad let me use it last weekend, though I had to turn the keys back in, so it's all gassed up and ready to go for my date with Lily. Damn, that sucks. A wave of depression surged through me and I take another pull on the bottle.

A figure moves on the boat, causing me to flinch and Trevor to rip off a bunch of swear words. The specter resolves into Ben's little brother.

"Hey, Wes, what are you doing here?"

"Recording the regatta for Bram."

"That's a good idea." I'm slurring and having trouble keeping him in focus. "You can't see anything from my boat. You should go up on the yacht. You've got a good view from the stern."

"You're drunk." He sounds more angry than shocked. I don't want him to tell Ben.

"Yeah, listen --."

"No, I don't want to listen. Alyse, he's going to hurt himself – or you or someone else. Trevor, don't' let him drive."

"I'm not." I hold up the boat keys, try to hand them to Trevor, but Wes snatches them from my hand like something out of a ninja movie.

"You *can't* drive the boat, Pete. You'll hurt someone."

"Who is this child?" Bethany tries to put her hand down my pants, but I push her off.

"Wes, I won't drive it. Give the keys to Trevor. He's a lot less wasted than I am."

Trevor nears Wes, talks to him in low reasonable tones. I kiss Bethany again, but I push her hand away from my crotch. Wes is 11, maybe 12. She needs to cool it around the kids. My bottle is empty.

"You need a lemonade." Alyse hands me the bottle, cap already off. I swallow some of it. It's a hard lemonade, but what I want is more bourbon. A vein in the back of my head starts to throb. Trevor assures Wes he'll drive. Bethany and I get into the boat. She holds up one of those orange pills again.

"This will make a mere mortal into a beast in bed."

There's no bed here, but she puts it on my tongue anyway. I hate pills. I finish the lemonade in two gulps. The world takes on this lurid, neon cast.

"Alyse, what did you do?" Trevor demands. "Girl, are you trying to OD him? Stop dosing him."

Dosing who with what? I'm feeling great.

"We don't want him to fall asleep. I only used half."

"He could have a stroke. Stop it. And what the hell did you give him, Bethany?"

I don't hear her answer because I'm digging in one of the gear boxes, pleased to find a half-bottle of bourbon buried under a bunch of other things. I take a deep draw off it. It tastes a little weird from being in an unstable environment for months on end, but it's still got some kick.

"Let's go," I bellow. They're all three laughing as Trevor eases the boat out of the slip. Bethany shoves me down in the seat to kiss me and I feel her unbutton my jeans as the sky turns an iridescent green.

Boredom

Alyse

Trevor is an old lady. He drives the boat like we're hauling eggs. I can't believe how utterly boring this night has become. Bethany monopolizes Peter and Trevor is tied up with operating the boat. I want some action.

"Hey, Peter, show this man how to drive a boat."

"I'm wasted, Alyse. I can't drive the boat." He also apparently can't get an erection, which is majorly disappointing Bethany who I've decided to hate. Really, stupid blondes make my teeth grind. With everything else Peter has consumed tonight, did she really think MDMA would be a good idea? That's what sent me into orbit the night of the Hampton's party.

We're out on the harbor and there's a lot of sailboats and other watercraft around us. The land behind us is starting to glow with that late-afternoon almost-sunset sheen it gets. Peter is alternating between laughing at things that aren't there and crying about how crappy his life is.

"Just show him how it's done. God, this is so boring!"

Bethany undoes the buttons of her blouse and flashes her lace-embraced breasts at Peter.

"You can have these after you show him how to drive this boat, Mister."

Peter pushes himself up off the seat to join Trevor at the pilot's station. Suddenly I must sit down because the boat leaps into action. Peter swings wide for open water, showing Trevor how to work the throttle, swiveling the steering wheel, which makes water spray from the stern. I think we sprayed a sailboat. I hear someone shout. Peter clears the field of sailing boats and then stares out across the harbor at a blue fishing boat, its rigging covered in Christmas tree lighting that's just barely visible against the Techno Color sunset.

I scramble up to stand beside him.

"You know she's with Ben, don't you?"

"What? Who?"

"Lily. She's on Russell's boat."

Peter stares at me. I'm not used to him not having pupils. Maybe Trevor's right and Peter is a light-weight when it comes to medications.

He takes a long draw off the bottle of bourbon. It seems like he should have finished it a long time ago. He drops the empty bottle on the deck and revs up the engine. The boat bounds from wave to wave, headed right for the blue boat.

I laugh with the thrill of it. Behind us, Trevor bellows encouragement. The boat grows closer and closer, filling our sights until Peter twists the wheel to spray Ben and Lily where they stand staring from the deck.

Impact

Ben

Lily and I pause in our duties to look out across the water filled with graceful sailboats. There are a few powerboats on the waves too, mostly just sitting quietly. Captain Russell's *Mimi* is the largest of them – a converted fishing boat – but he has a cabin cruiser in his fleet of three tour boats and it's just a little way off our bow.

"It's gorgeous." Lily has Christmas in her eyes as she gazes upon hundreds of sailboats working the winds against one of the most beautiful sunsets I've ever seen. Merrick Winter's red-and-white sail draws my attention. He's a master of visually beautiful sailing.

"What is that guy doing?" A woman to my left points at a speedboat skimming the water too fast for the confines of the bay. Her husband grabs her back from the railing. It looks like the boater is going to ram us full speed ahead. Lily freezes. I wrap her in my arms and run as I hear the speed boat change trajectory and throw the throttle forward. Classic spraying, except the boater has failed to judge the distance properly.

A tremor runs through *The Mimi* at the moment of impact as I shield Lily from the inevitable collision. I glance over my shoulder to see a body hit the railing, arms flailing. She tumbles across the deck, coming to rest on her back, hands grasping the air. We all stare at Alyse as she chokes on her own blood and then Pete is there, clamoring over the railing, sliding on his knees beside her.

"No, don't!" His wild eyes take her in as he gathers her in his arms. He's bending over her, breathing life into her. I hear Captain Russell shouting, but I don't know what he's saying. All my attention focuses on my best friend trying to breathe life into the sister he has just killed. She stares up at Peter in terror as blood runs down his chin. He dips his head again to try to push life into her. Her hands shake as a quiver runs through her and then she stops moving. Her eyes grow cloudy and Peter screams a visceral growl of pure grief. "Don't go!"

A man in yachting clothes says he's a doctor and tries to examine her, but Pete pushes him away, huddled over her body like he's defending her. There's more shouting, something about a body in the water, but I just stand there watching Pete fight to change the unchangeable. Dr. Lundquist finally stabs Pete in the shoulder with a hypodermic needle. Pete doesn't let go of Alyse, but his screaming slows, quiets and stops. There's sirens and more people board the boat. Lily weeps into my shirt, inconsolable. We're pushed to the back of the crowd, so we don't see what happens to Pete and Alyse. Russell doesn't ask me to help with taking the boat back to shore and I don't offer. I feel like I'll never be able to talk again. I hold Lily and pray I'll awaken from this nightmare and discover it's all a fever-dream.

###
The End

STEPS

My name is Peter. I'm an alcoholic.

Briercliff-Hope

Alyse is dead!
My life is over!
Nothing left to lose

Step 1—"We admitted we were powerless over alcohol and that our lives had become unmanageable."

Step 2—"Came to believe that a Power greater than ourselves could restore us to sanity."

Murderer, liar, reckless. Sex w Mom! Sex w Alyse?

Step 3 = "Made a decision to turn our will and our lives over the care of God as we understood him."

Step 4—"Made a searching and fearless moral inventory of ourselves"

I don't believe in you. Help!

Step 5—"Admit to God, to ourselves, and to another human being the exact nature of our wrong."

Step 6—"We became willing to ask God to help us remove our defects of character."

Long list of people I'll never see again.

Step 7—"Humbly ask Him to remove your shortcomings."

Step 8—"Made a list of all persons we had harmed, and be came willing to make amends to them all."

Write letters since you're not going any- where.

Step 9—"Made direct amends to such people wherever possi- ble, except when to do so would injure them or others."

Step 10—"Continued to take personal inventory and when we were wrong promptly admitted it."

25 to Life?
5-25?

Step 11 -"Sought through prayer and meditation to improve our conscious contact with God as we understood Him, pray- ing only for knowledge of His will for us and the power to car- ry that out."

1 day at a time

Step 12 -"Having had a spiritual awakening as the result of these steps, we tried to carry this message to alcoholics and to practice these principles in all our affairs."

Is there any hope?

Can't make amends to Alyse.

Trevor? Ben? Dad? Tilly? Lucy? Mike? Rick? Helen & John? Lily? Her parents? Russell? Everybody on the boat? Grandpa Jack? I can. It's just not going to be easy.

Nothing will ever be easy again!

A Word from Lela Markham

I didn't have a classic white-picket-fence upbringing. I grew up in the frontier town of Fairbanks, Alaska, and my parents were not Ward and June Cleaver. One of my mom's best friends was a retired madam. My brother was a bad boy. I knew boys who might have been Peter in my childhood and adolescence.

But for the grace of God go I.

I just destroyed Peter's life. I hope you'll stick around for the redemption. Trust me. Peter has a future. It just won't be an easy one. He's going to have a lot of reason to wonder "If I'd done this or that differently, this might not have happened", but ultimately "What If ... Wasn't" so how will he choose to live through the dumpster fire his life has become?

Faith has always been a quiet understated background in this series. You know Ben and Lily used to be Sunday School kids and that Peter walked an aisle at summer camp. Do any of them have what Francis Schaeffer would have called real-real faith? A crisis like what the group will face in "Pocketful of Rocks" has a way of making your faith real as well as realistic.

Non-Christian readers, don't worry. I promise not to get preachy. I think I've proven I'm not a buckle-of-the-Bible-belt kind of writer.

I didn't set out to write a Christian genre book. This is a work of fiction that can be enjoyed by teens of every faith group, or

461

none, and "Pocketful of Rocks" aims for an older audience –
New Adult. So, readers encounter swearing, sex, alcohol and
drug abuse in these pages. If that upsets some readers, I don't
intend to apologize. I sought to portray American young
people as realistically as I could in a work of fiction and
American society today swears, drinks, hooks up, and tattoos
itself. Their best friends from high school are sometimes gay
and their college dormmate wanders into their room naked. I
touch on all of it, but I don't dwell because while those
experiences exist, I also don't think they need be the center of
the universe. They are the world we are in, but not of and we
have to stop expecting the people who are "of this world" as if
they aren't.

While we might hope our Christian teens don't do these
things, we know many of them do and we certainly should
know unchurched Christian kids do. Pretending it doesn't
happen doesn't mean it won't happen. And by not pretending,
we open the door to discussing it and maybe avoiding it. Or
not. Maybe it'll still happen, but we won't see it as the end of
the world, but as something we must practice forgiveness and
redemption to overcome. As someone who accepted Christ
after I experienced something of the world, I surely hope
Christians refocus on redemption sometime soon.

If you'd like to discuss it, feel free to drop me an email at
lelamarkham@gmail.com or visit my Facebook page
LelaMarkham7. You can come for the morality discussion and
stay for the liberty conversations.

A Taste of
"Pocketful of Rocks"

Alan

I go back to where Peter is staring into space.

"Come on. Let's get you home."

Peter doesn't react, so I grasp his blood-stained arm and he follows me meekly. I've already checked him out, so I simply lead him past the ER staff and out to where the car is waiting. Vic has done a masterful job of finding a door that isn't in the public eye and Peter offers no resistance. It's right on the cusp of dawn, just the barest lightening of the sky. I sit beside Peter, but it's like sitting next to a statue. He doesn't move. His eyes are blank, unseeing and nothing moves behind them. I wipe my hands with a wet wipe and try to decide what I should do first – call the lawyer or the rehab.

The sun breaches the horizon, casting Peter's face in planes and angles that seem almost skeletal. He looks up and out of the car, staring at the gray and flat world with the pastel shades of dawn behind it. His eyes start to twitter and then he looks down at his shirt and jeans and starts rubbing his hands together, keening.

Vic looks at me in the rearview mirror and pulls the car over. He wisely chose to take the Post Road so to avoid most possibility of news coverage. Peter scrabbles for the door and stumbles out into the weeds. On his hands and knees, he heaves a dozen times, puking three or four. Vic stands beside him, watching over him or just pitying him, I'm not sure. I can't bring myself to get out of the car. I watch as tears drip from his nose into the slime pile. I should care that he's going through this, but I don't.

"You done?" Vic's voice is cold and flat as a morgue table. Peter flicks a nervous gaze up to him and stands, nearly falling. Vic makes no attempt to catch him and I can't raise interest in rebuking him for that. Peter gets back in the car.

"Dad?"

"Don't talk. Whatever you say right now is only going to make it worse. Just shut the fuck up."

Peter tucks his hands into his underarms and sits there shaking and crying all the way to the house. I get out of the car as soon as we're stopped. Peter doesn't move.

"I can't." Vic nods like he expected that, and I walk away.

If you enjoyed this book, leave a review.

Watch for Book 3 sometime in 2021

Breakwater Harbor Books

Moscow, 2138. With the world only beginning to recover from the complete societal collapse of the late 21st Century, Zoya scrapes by prepping corpses for funerals and dreams of saving enough money to have a child. When her brother forces her to bring him a mysterious package, she witnesses his murder and finds herself on the run from ruthless mobsters. Frantically trying to stay alive and save her loved ones, Zoya opens the package and discovers two unusual data cards, one that allows her to fight back against the mafia and another which may hold the key to everlasting life.

www.breakwaterharborbooks.com

Other Lela Markham Books

Fantasy

Daermad Cycle

The Willow Branch

Mirklin Wood

Fount of Wraiths

(pending)

Anthologies

Echoes of Liberty

Unbound

Encountering Jesus

Gateways

Fairytale Riot

Faith and Fire

Apocalyptic

Transformation Project

Life As We Knew It

Objects In View

A Threatening Fragility

Day's End

Gathering In

Winter's Reckoning

A Death in Jericho

(Pending)

Satire

Hullaballoo on Main Street

Young Adult/New Adult

What If...Wasn't

Red Kryptonite Curve

Dumpster Fire

Pocketful of Rocks

(Pending)

Meet Lela Markham

Hi. I was raised in a house made of books in Alaska and told tales from the time I could talk. A teacher eventually made me write one of them down. I hated the exercise, but it was the spark that ignited a fire that has never gone out.

My daring husband, two fearless offspring and I live the adventure of a lifetime here on the Last Frontier where the midnight sun encourages wandering the wilderness and the long dark winters favor reading, writing and staring at the northern lights ... hence the moniker Aurorawatcher.

It's all about the aurora watching!

www.ingramcontent.com/pod-product-compliance
Lightning Source LLC
Chambersburg PA
CBHW030533260626
47157CB00006B/2015